the Nation We Knew

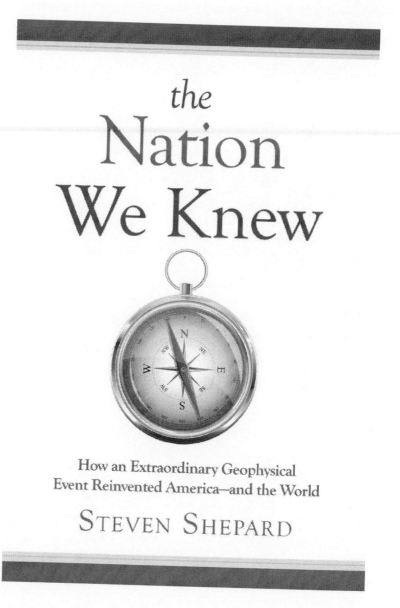

How an Extraordinary Geophysical
Event Reinvented America—and the World

STEVEN SHEPARD

The Nation We Knew: How an Extraordinary Geophysical Event Reinvented America—and the World

Dr. Steven Shepard

Copyright © 2021 by Dr. Steven Shepard

Published in March 2021

978-0-9892492-9-4

Shepard, Steven, 1954—

The Nation We Knew: How an Extraordinary Geophysical Event Reinvented America—and the World/

Dr. Steven Shepard

978-0-9892492-9-4

1. fiction. 2. polar reversal. 3. politics. 4. education. 5. science. 6. leadership. 7. technology.

For Ayla, Maya, and Jaxon.

Described in this book is the world I'd love to leave behind for you.

Tell me to what you pay attention, and I will tell you who you are.

José Ortega y Gasset

Acknowledgments

I've never written a book like this before, which means that to do so I had to step waaaaaaaaay outside of my realm of comfort. I'm not a politician (thankfully), and I have no official training in politics other than a Political Science course I had to take as an undergraduate at Berkeley to satisfy a breadth requirement. As a writer, that lack of experience, knowledge and insight into the world of politics and a host of related fields that were well outside of my knowledge purview translated into three things as I set about to write this book: far more research about unfamiliar topics than I normally have to do; far more learning than I ever thought possible; and far more reliance on people whose expertise about the various themes discussed in this book far exceeds what I could ever know. I am immensely grateful to all of them.

Specifically, I thank:

Dennis McCooey and Pete Mulvihill, both old friends going back to our mutual SCUBA diving days, who lent their names as the mythical scientists who first detected the event detailed in the book.

I want to give a major shout-out to Pete, for whom I have created and assigned the title of 'Editorial Engineer.' Pete is a professional Fire Protection Engineer whose career began with a major consultancy and ended when he retired as the Fire Marshal for the State of Nevada. He looks upon manuscript editing as an engineering challenge. His observations about my writing shortfalls are always frustratingly, exquisitely on-target, and my books are much better for it. He also served as the consulting engineer for the many projects described in the book that needed that sort of expertise. Basically, he kept me from burning the planet down. Thanks, Pete.

Phil Asmundson, former Deloitte luminary and now, with his wife Kim, a very successful, technology-dependent vineyard operator and winemaker (sorry, Phil, I still have a hard time calling you a 'farmer'); your experiences with technology enablement at Deep Sky Vineyard helped me envision what could be with regard to smart agriculture in Africa;

Joe Candido, for teaching me so much and helping me navigate some of the ideas in this book;

Rob Bender, musician, writer, film director, and now, editorial consultant;

Mike Rowe and his 'The Way I Heard It' Podcast, for lending his name and philosophies, not to mention inspirational values, to the flow of the book. Folks, if you're not familiar with his Work Ethics scholarship program, or the Mike Rowe Works Foundation, you need to be. Please check it out at MikeRoweWorks.org;

Kenn Sato, a name well-known to my readers and Podcast listeners, for being my sanity-checker and editor par excellence;

Deb Shannon, collaborator, reader, leader, and sanity checker;

Mary Slaughter, for providing much of the inspiration about common sense and the power of a learning organization that hopefully comes through in the story, and for the many years we spent professionally, following each other around far-flung corners of the planet;

Doug Standley, who also lent his name for use in the book, and for being a thoughtful, active contributor of ideas and technology insights to the book's flow and story;

Cristina, Joe, Steve, Mallory, Ayla, Maya, and Jaxon, for making me so unbelievably proud and happy as Dad and Papaw;

And as always, my wife Sabine, for everything—and I mean *everything*.

Finally, to my readers, who are willing to take a step back every now and again to think about what could be, rather than what is. Maybe some of the things described in this story can come to pass; whatever the case, we owe it to our children and to their children to leave the world better than it is today.

Thank you, all.

Preface

Dear Reader,

First, thank you for picking up this book and considering it as something to add to your reading stack. In today's busy world, that's a major commitment on your part, and I appreciate your consideration.

Let me tell you why I wrote it.

I've spent my entire life traveling. I've had the good fortune to live in and visit more than 80 countries in my lifetime, many of them more than once. Each of them presented me with numerous gifts: A window into a previously unknown culture, exposure to different foods, immersion in the deeps of incomprehensible languages where hand signals and smiles create fluency, and the opportunity to compare another country with my own. But the most important thing I came to understand from all that travel is that people are people, no matter what. Mark Twain said it well in *The Innocents Abroad:*

> Travel is fatal to bigotry, prejudice, and narrow-mindedness, and most of our people need it sorely on all three counts.

Truer words, as they say, were never spoken. As I moved from nation to nation over the course of my life and career, exploring the elements that made each one so different and unique, a realization struck: at the most important level, at the level where people live their lives, each place was identical to my own country, in all the ways that matter. Everyone, I realized, whether they lived on a palatial estate, or in a dirt-floored hovel in a Brazilian favela or South African township, or a small apartment in a high-rise, or a suburban neighborhood, wanted the same things: to live a good, fulfilling life; to take care of those they love; to live mostly free of want; and to love and be loved. Whether it was Pavel from Moscow, who told me that Americans are identical to Russians, or Richard in Botswana, who wanted to know if the cowboys and Indians still got into dust-ups in Texas, or Tony from Croatia, who couldn't understand why there were so many brands, grinds and flavors of coffee at the grocery store in California and was annoyed that *they* didn't just *pick the best one for us* and put it on the shelf, or the little guy in Guatemala who sold me a pebble so that he and his wife could eat and he wouldn't have to beg (I still carry it in my computer bag), all of these people wanted the same things from life that I and most Americans want.

Some of you have read my email signature line, which is a quote from biologist EO Wilson:

May I now humbly ask, just where do we think we are going—really? I believe the great majority of people on Earth would agree with the following goals: an indefinitely long and healthy life for all, abundant sustainable resources, personal freedom, adventure both virtual and real on demand, status, dignity, membership in one or more respectable groups, obedience to wise rulers and laws, and lots of sex with or without reproduction. There is a problem, however. These are also the goals of your family dog.

In other words, these things we want from life are pretty straight-forward. They're species-specific, not nation based. If my dog wants them as badly as I do, they can't be bad. I know my dog.

Over the last few years, we've faced some serious challenges, not just in the US, but across the world: A global pandemic. The rise of global nationalism. Economic uncertainty. Fear of unbridled technology. Climate change. The realization that we haven't exactly been the best neighbors on this planet, and the fact that the landlord is beginning to notice.

But rather than coming together to face off against these challenges and actively doing something about them, we've chosen instead to point fingers at each other as a way to discharge blame.

Meanwhile, social media sucked us in and, while it gave us access to family photos and people we hadn't seen in years, and helped us create communities of interest so that we could find and bond with like-minded individuals, it also served to isolate us in those communities, creating an artificial tribal effect that turned us against one another by pointing out (wrongly, I might add) that we are far more different than we are alike, and that 'different' is something to fear rather than a quality we should find intriguing and attractive.

As a result, some have begun to realize that *social* media is actually *antisocial* media. It provides an effective platform for the expansion of confirmation bias and serves as an influence conduit for bad actors to have their way with us, including Russia, China, QAnon, Antifa, and others. In essence, it serves as a megaphone and echo chamber, providing an amplification effect for ideas and points-of-view that are nowhere near as widespread as their relative loudness would seem to indicate. But because they appear bigger than they actually are, they create fear, further dividing us as a cohesive society.

Before social media came along, rest assured, all of these voices existed. Whether anti-government conspiracy theorists, flat-earthers, white supremacists, anti-vaxxers, the Christian right, or the ultra-socialist left, all had their adherents. But in keeping with the bell curve that defines any statistically large group, including a society, and, therefore, most countries (with a few rare exceptions), these voices are fringe elements that have always existed at the periphery of civilized society, a place where they are free to rant as loudly as they like, without causing harm to the vast numbers of people under the bulk of the bell who don't adhere to their beliefs.

Today, however, those fringe voices enjoy an advantage that only comes through the influence of social media's unlimited geography: They can be both distant from the controversial conversation that they spawn, which is the ultimate hallmark of cowardice (it's akin to tossing a firecracker into a crowd from the top of a building), while at the same time enjoying the artificial, echoing loudness that social media and the Internet make possible, turning low-volume noise into hurtful rhetoric that spawns fear and distrust. They are like the Mighty Oz: A loud, commanding voice on the surface, but when we pull back the curtain, we find a timid little bully of a man with a megaphone—and no real message to share. Things are not always as they seem.

It's interesting that we speak routinely about the political polarization that has taken place in the nation, and the paralyzing effect that this separation brings about. I say 'interesting' because the theme of polarization plays a key role in this novel, as you'll see—but not in the political sense. I wrote this book because of the fatigue that plagues the country today—not COVID-related fatigue, although that is serious stuff, but fatigue associated with the loud, meaningless, drone of noise emanating from many of our elected officials, going all the way to the top, that serves to divide rather than unite us—at a time when we need the power of national unity more than we have at any time in the recent past. In the United States, two phrases are well-known to everyone: 'We, the People,' and 'e Pluribus Unum.' From the many, one. When did the one become many, so polarized that coming together is like trying to get the south poles of two strong magnets to touch?

In my work as a consulting analyst to the greater technology industry, I often run executive teams through an intensive, multi-day workshop called Reverse-Engineering the Future. If an organization and its leadership are wrestling with a significant, often existential moment in their business, those executives often find themselves in a state of 'analysis paralysis.' They know they have to march ever-forward, but they don't really know where they're headed, because they find it hard to disconnect from the reality of the present to think effectively about the qualities of the future they desire. So, what happens? Their inaction reinforces and institutionalizes the status quo. 'If it ain't broke, don't fix it' is an oft-heard aphorism about this scenario. What this inaction leads to is complacency, which is the deadliest disease an organization can contract, and is more often than not fatal. It creeps up on leadership, it creeps up on their employees, and it permeates entire companies, encasing them in a web of fossilized dogma that is paralyzing, but highly seductive. Reverse-Engineering the Future tears away the web of complacency by forcing executives to consider what could be, rather than what is, and then shows them how to share their vision of a better status quo, along with a methodology to make it real for all concerned. The most critical part of the process, the most tenuous, the hardest, is getting participants to let go of their current reality, just for a little while, and to consider the possibility of an alternative reality, a fantasy, if you will, that's better than the one they know today. Backsliding is normal, because of the phrase, 'Yeah, but that's not how we do things here.' But, as you'll see in the book, as the main character uses the technique to chart a better future for the country, there are ways to deal with those institutional speed bumps.

People tend to roll their eyes and mutter under their breath whenever the word 'fantasy' is applied to companies. 'We don't have time for games—this is serious business.' Really? Do companies ever engage in scenario planning? Do militaries engage in war games? Do companies have office football pools? How many of their employees watch their favorite dramas on TV (other than reality-based David Attenborough programs, although given today's crumbling commitment to the environment, even those may be fantasies), or go to the movies to watch Hobbits and wizards and Jedi Knights do what Hobbits and wizards and Jedi Knights do? How many of them read novels? How many of them play fantasy football or hockey or baseball?

By the way, the word *fantasy* comes from an old Greek word that means *imagination*. Do you ever imagine a better life, a better job, a better career, a better company, a better country? It's one of the things that makes us human, and sentient—the ability to imagine. There are few things more powerful than that skill.

Here's what I ask. For the next few hours, as you enter the fantasy I have created between the covers of this book, leave your blue donkeys and red elephants outside to tear up the lawn. Take off your political hat, put on your human citizen hat, and sit back, read, and enjoy. Allow yourself to pretend (it means to stretch your thinking, by the way)—that most human of all things—and immerse yourself in a warm, relaxing story of what could be—*if* we could just agree to fill that great dividing chasm that threatens so much of what we stand for as a nation.

For the next few hours, please join me for a game of fantasy United States of America. I hope you enjoy the read.

Steven Shepard

Williston, Vermont, USA

March 2021

Introduction

Monday, January 20, 2041

"Meadows!"

My editor's voice came rumbling over the plexiglass walls separating the desks in the newsroom, a pressure wave of sound that heralded a summons to his office. Rising, I saw him standing in his doorway, waving me over. I grabbed a pad of paper and made sure I had a pen in my pocket before navigating the cubicle maze.

"Better you than me," one of my colleagues mumbled as I passed. I snorted.

"Close the door," he said, as I entered the office. I was always mildly surprised that in this day of all-digital all-the-time, his office always smelled vaguely of slightly moldy paper. It was a smell I loved, but my sensory reverie was broken as he got straight to the point.

"I need a retrospective," he began.

Uh-oh. "On what?" I asked. Already, my spidey senses were starting to fire— 'retrospective' was not a term that most journalists responded favorably to. It was right up there with covering the bridge club championships and floral displays at the annual irritable bowel syndrome national fundraiser. In other words, run.

"I've got a pretty full plate, Van," I said, "and I don't—"

"Shut up and sit," he snapped, leaving no room for the retort I was already formulating. "This is an important story, and I want you to write it. It's gonna need a lot of research, something you're good at, and more than that, you like doing it.

"Here's the deal: Ten years ago next month, Fadhili-Mason finished her term and left the White House. We need a piece on her—quick coverage of what she got done while in office, the influence of the flux thing, what she's been doing since. Make it good and I'll put you on the front page. It'll probably be below the fold, but so it goes.

"Let me be clear: I'm not looking for dirt, here. She was an important player—maybe the most important president we've had in 50 years. And the things she did while she was in office are still in play for the most part, and they're pretty damn good. So, don't go all National Enquirer on me. I want a solid piece of reporting that will remind people what can happen when somebody fucks with the system for all the right reasons."

"Do I have a budget for travel?" I asked. In for a penny, in for a pound, I thought...

"Don't push your luck, asshole," he smiled at me. His smile was more of a gas pain grimace. "I'll pay for T&L because you're going to want to go to her presidential library in Detroit. I'll give you three days—after that, you're on your own."

"Deadline?" I asked.

"Two weeks," came the reply. "Keep me in the loop on this one, Michael. It's an important story and I want it to glow in the dark. It's been ten years since she worked her magic—and the planet went all cockeyed. So, dig in and give me something worthy of the front page."

"OK, Van, I'm on it. I'll start in the morgue and dig up whatever stories I can for background, and I'll plan to head over to Detroit on Monday."

"You're welcome," he snorted, as I left the office.

Chapter 1: The Project

The morgue, of course, was the room in the basement of a newspaper building where old newspapers go to die. Luckily, they were also available online in digital form, so my search didn't require a visit to allergen central.

Van was right about one thing: research was where I was at my best. I was a decent writer, an equally decent editor, but when it came to ferreting out the invisible details of a story, nobody had mastered the dark art like I had. Google? Amateur hour.

So, I dug in. Writing a story about a president's time in office, even a front-page story, is like trying to write the Idiot's Guide to String Theory, or The Heisenberg Uncertainty Principle for Dummies. Way too much information. But that was where my superpower came into play. If there was one thing I excelled at, it was doing research, separating the important wheat from the meaningless chaff, and building a story from what was left.

I'd had this job as a staff writer at the Times for just about five years, my first and only 'real' job since graduating from Columbia Journalism in 2037. To be clear, I did my undergrad at NYU in political science, and then enrolled in the part-time, two-and-a-half-year program at Columbia. But I was only 16 when Fadhili-Mason took office, so I was too busy discovering girls and getting regular visits from the hormone fairy to pay much attention. I did well in school, could have done better, but I had a lot of fun. And somewhere along the way, I discovered that I love to write. Strangely, the story meant less to me than the craft. I took enormous pleasure in the process of assembling words into sentences, sentences into stories, stories into concepts with impact. Which is why I ended up at Columbia. Call me

whatever you want, but I love stories with soul. And I knew that, somewhere deep inside, there was one buried in my gut. I just hadn't found it yet. Woodward and Bernstein, Murrow and Rather, Pelley and Stahl, Cronkite and Huntley and Brinkley and Amanpour and Bradlee and Friedman and Graham and Cooper were my sources of inspiration. Journalists as heroes—who knew that was a thing.

The first couple of years at the Times were like walking over a lava field in flip-flops, but I finally adjusted to the pace of the job and managed to eke out a few pretty good stories. Van had been my editor from day-one, and even though he worked hard to project the personality of a wolverine on crack, his passion for the news and what it represented shined through like a supernova. Turn in a sub-par story and you'd feel as if your flesh had been flayed with a bread knife.

So, with Van's bread knife sawing away at my psyche, I began to assemble information about the woman who had served as the nation's 47th president back when I was a teenager. I started with the most obvious basics: Cabinet members; advisors; family; scandals (I know, I know…no National Enquirer stuff…but you have to look); political adversaries; controversial actions; major legal decisions; initiatives and outcomes; the economy and jobs; military spending—like I said, the usual stuff. I printed piles of paper so that I could highlight and mark up each article. I had long ago reached the conclusion that the idea of a modern, paperless business was laughable—it was about as likely as a paperless bathroom. Not in my lifetime, especially in the newsPAPER business.

Before I could write anything resembling an article, I had to know who I was writing about. Armed with pen, pencil and highlighter, I attacked the paper piles, a separate stack for each major topic. I read everything, highlighted important sections, filled the margins with notes, made separate lists of secondary sources to interview. Slowly, a structure emerged, an outline, a framework, but there were pieces missing. I still had questions, so I made arrangements to travel to Detroit. The answers I needed were surely to be found in the Ahadi Fadhili-Mason Presidential Library.

Chapter 2: What Have I Gotten Myself Into?

"What the hell have I gotten myself into, Ahadi wondered, as she looked at the towering piles of folders that covered the table in the meeting room adjacent to the Oval Office. They were vetted personnel folders—potential options for cabinet members and key positions in the administration, most of them suggested by members of Congress or party advisors. And, most of them not at all what she wanted to help her chart the nation's path for the next few years. The majority were Washington insiders or longtime politicians, people who undoubtedly would bring wisdom and experience, but they'd bring it from a perspective of 'more of the same,' which neither she nor the nation really wanted—or needed.

"Did you say something, Madame President?"

She jumped—it was Al Gordon, the head of her security detail. "Al, you scared the crap out of me. I thought I was alone in here—does the Secret Service have some kind of transporter beam I don't know about?"

"Sorry to startle you, Madame President," he replied, without a hint of a smile. "Your next interview is here. I'll escort you whenever you're ready."

"Give me five minutes if you would—I just need to get my thoughts together."

"Yes, Ma'am," he nodded, reaching for the door. I'll wait outside."

"OK—Al, hang on a minute."

"Yes, Madame President?" His hand fell away from the door as he turned and faced her.

"OK, Al, look. If we're going to be joined at the hip for the whole term, this 'Madame President' stuff has got to go. My name's Ahadi—I'd prefer you call me that. I'm going to have enough formality in my life for the foreseeable future without having to deal with it in private. OK?"

A hint of a glimmer of a smile. "Yes, Madame President. I'll be outside."

Well, at least I got a smile out of the guy. That's something. Turning her attention back to the table, she located the thick folder that held the dissected life of her next candidate. She took two minutes to scan the contents, going over the questions she had written in the margins. Opening the door, she smiled at Al, who turned without a word and walked with her to the meeting room.

"Polestar is moving," Al spoke into his sleeve mic, notifying other detail members of her whereabouts. Another agent stood at the door of the meeting room. Nodding at Al, he departed as Al and the President arrived to meet with the person who waited inside. Al opened the door, looking inside before allowing her to enter. He stepped back and ushered her in, before entering behind her and closing the door, taking up a discrete ready stance, his back to the door.

Al was what many would call an old school cop with a new school way of thinking. His father was a police sergeant in Savannah; his mother taught fourth and fifth grade science.

After graduating from Emory with a degree in computer science and a minor in cybersecurity, he worked for an IT firm for two years before deciding it wasn't for him. He left and entered the Georgia State Police Academy, where he graduated with honors. After a year on patrol, he was called on to work as part of a cybersecurity task force, where he distinguished himself as a serious investigator who ended up playing a major role in apprehending a group of right-wing nutcases who were launching cyberattacks on maritime assets in Savannah and Brunswick, disrupting trade and in some cases causing serious damage. No one died, but the cost to the target organizations was on the high end of six figures— and that doesn't account for the reputational damage they suffered.

Al's role in untangling the maritime cyber-hairball caught the attention of Treasury, and he soon found himself part of a multi-jurisdictional task force targeting bad actors in Bulgaria and Serbia that were probing critical infrastructure in the West for vulnerabilities—multimodal ports, power grids, telecom networks, GPS systems, hospitals, that kind of thing. The task force ended up dismantling several criminal hacking organizations and seizing sizeable assets along the way, and at one point it was suggested that Al consider the Secret Service as a career direction. He thought about it and decided to apply. He was accepted, initially as a Treasury Investigator, working on cybercrime and cyberfraud as a field agent with a discrete understanding of both the way bad actors think and the technology that underlies their ability to do what they do. His peers began to jokingly call him 'The Bit Whisperer' because of his innate ability to tease the faintest clue out of a data stream.

But the event that changed the path of his career was a case he inherited from another agent who died in the line of duty. The agent was someone Al considered a friend, and when he was killed, Al asked for and was given a position on the investigative team.

The case was as ugly as they got. It began as a local domestic abuse case that had nothing to do with Treasury—multiple calls to 911, it's all a big misunderstanding, more calls from the wife, move to a women's shelter, it isn't his fault—he's really trying. Then he hit one of the kids, this time in front of a neighbor. Enter Child Protective Services who move the wife to a safe location and put the kids into foster care. The wife feels guilty, calls the husband, one thing leads to another and she leaves the shelter. He violates the order of protection and beats her bloody. Then he grabs the kids at school and leaves the state, which, of course, makes it Federal. What also made it Federal was the fact that when they looked into the guy, whose name was Darryl Loames, it turned out that he was wanted for failure to pay taxes for the last eight years. So not only did that make it Federal, it made it a Treasury case.

They located him at a motel in downstate Virginia thanks to a license plate grab, but when they went to serve the arrest warrant late that evening, Loames fired a pistol through the door, killing the agent at the door—Al's friend. The remaining agents tried to shoulder their way into the room, but Loames had moved furniture in front of the door, making it impossible to open. In the confusion following the shooting, Loames crawled out the bathroom window and disappeared into the woods behind the motel. By the time they managed to get into the room he was long gone—and there was no evidence that the kids were ever in the room, which meant that he had either stashed them elsewhere or done something that the agents didn't want to contemplate. Bottom line, Loames and the kids were gone, and the mother was in a coma, fighting for her life.

The trail went cold, but Al kept at it. He went down

countless cyber trails, each a disappointing dead-end. But he could feel the guy: he was out there, and he may have thought he was invisible. But Al knew better. There may have been no physical trail to follow, but sooner or later, he'd show himself, a cyber-shadow.

Months passed. Al worked other cases, but he kept this one going, a hobby project in the background. The break came on a Thursday morning. Hoping that the kids were still alive and that they might find a way to communicate their whereabouts, Al had placed digital trackers on their social media accounts and on the accounts of as many of their friends as they could find. He also had triggers on all of the suspect's credit cards. If any of their identities popped up, if any of the cards were used, they'd trigger. Al knew that the suspect probably wasn't that stupid—anybody who watched TV would know better—but stranger things have happened. As it happened, both kids were very much alive, and a whole lot more cyber-savvy than their father. The boy managed to take a credit card from his father's wallet. That Thursday morning, he accompanied Laomes into a convenience store in extreme western Virginia where they were hiding out in a remote cabin. The boy didn't buy anything, but as they were leaving the store, he inserted the card into the reader at the counter. It was enough to generate an activity record. Agents, led by Al, discretely converged on the town, and the store owner confirmed that the man had been there—most recently with an 11-year-old boy. So, they hid in the shadows, and they waited.

It didn't take long. Two days later, a battered, mud-covered VW Jetta parked across the street, and Loames emerged and headed into the store. The agents held their ground; when he emerged with a shopping bag and drove away, an agent in a battered, equally mud-covered pickup followed him at a discrete distance. Twenty minutes out of town, he launched a drone from the bed of the pickup, and it gave the other agents a birds-eye view of the suspect. When Loames turned off the main road, the agent following him continued down the road, but the drone remained above, tracking the suspect's movements. Meanwhile, the HRT team moved in. They pulled off on a dirt road a mile from the suspect's turnoff and drove deep enough into the woods that they could not be seen from the road.

The vehicle continued deep into the forest, following what was most likely a logging road. 15 minutes later, it pulled up to what looked like a rustic cabin—perhaps a hunting camp. When Loames emerged from the vehicle and went inside, the agents recalled the drone and began to plan their takedown of the suspect and the rescue of the two kids.

Ultimately, they decided on a fairly standard strategy. They would approach the cabin on foot through the woods, no vehicles. One team would approach from the west, the other from the southeast. They would converge on the cabin and plan their entry for 3 AM. "By the book," admonished the team leader. "Job one is to get the kids out of there; then we get the suspect. No heroics—just do your jobs. Are we good?"

All members of the team nodded. "Kit up. It'll take two hours to reach the cabin, and I don't even want the owls to know you're in the forest. Full stealth until we get there— then we go loud."

As the HRT began to do weapons checks and lay out arms and armor, the team leader called Al over. "What else do we know about this guy?" he asked.

"Not much more than you already have," Al told him. "Your basic scumbag cop-killer and spouse-abuser, who also kidnapped his kids. He may also be a steroid tweaker, so I'm worried about state of mind here. He could snap, and with the kids in there—"

"Gotcha," the team leader replied. His name was Ridell. "We'll get close enough for thermal imaging, so we'll be able to tell who's in the cabin and where they are. It'll be cold enough that we should be able to tell what's going on in there. I'll have overwatch somewhere on high ground looking in a window; if the guy even twitches at the wrong time, we go ugly early and paint his brains on the wall."

"That works for me," Al replied.

At just after midnight, the team divided into two groups and headed into the woods, converging on the cabin as planned. By 2 AM they were in position.

"Radio check," the team leader whispered into his throat mic. A series of eight brief double-bursts of static came through, confirming that all were online. "Give me thermal."

The thermal imager was a lifesaver in the truest sense of the word. It could sense the tiniest differences in heat in an enclosed space, and with its built-in AI engine could tell whether a heat source was a rodent, a recently removed shoe or a slowly-cooling lightbulb. Large objects, like people, were a piece of cake, especially on a cold night like this one.

A whisper came over the earpiece. "I have three heat sources, two small, one larger," the disembodied voice said. "Kids are in corner orange; adult is in corner yellow. No movement that I can see." The colors referred to the code used by the team to identify locations inside the takedown space. Red was to the left of the door, with each adjacent corner labeled according to the colors of the visible spectrum—ROY G BIV for red, orange, yellow, green, blue, indigo and violet. This meant that the kids and their father were in the back left and right corners of the cabin, most likely asleep.

"Overwatch—report," ordered Ridell.

"Overwatch. I'm slightly to your left, 100 feet out. I'm dialed in on a window with a view toward orange and yellow. I can make out heat signatures, but it's too dark for serious detail. Good to go."

Ridell clicked his transmit key to signal that he had heard. "We go in three," he ordered.

Dressed in full body armor and kitted out in black, the HRT members moved through the woods on their bellies like wraiths. Taking their assigned positions around the cabin, they signaled ready, then waited for the go signal.

"On my count—prepare to breach: three—two—one— "

"Hold breach!" The words hissed into their earpieces. It was the voice of the overwatch sniper. They froze as one.

"What the hell, Overwatch!" Ridell snapped.

"I have movement at orange," he whispered in response. "Hold one."

The team held steady, frozen in position, waiting for the go command. Seconds ticked by.

"Overwatch, report." Ridell's voice.

"Hang on...something..." a pause. "Not kids."

"Overwatch, say again?" Ridell was clearly agitated. "What the hell?"

"It's not kids. I can see movement, and I've got two forms. But they're not kids. They're big fucking dogs, and I think they know you're there."

Sure enough, the breach team could now hear the low growl of an animal inside the cabin, soon joined by another.

"No sign of the kids but I've got movement at yellow," the sniper whispered. 'I think the suspect is waking up. I've got him painted, so if you're going to go, go now."

"Roger that," hissed Ridell. "Breach, breach, breach!"

The shattering of glass indicated that a window in the one-room cabin had been broken. It was followed by a thump in the cabin, and the sound of movement. The team members instinctively turned away from the cabin, just as the flash bang grenade detonated, slamming the cabin with a 170-decibel burst of sound and a blinding seven-million-candlepower flash of light, designed to disorient and temporarily disable whoever is nearby. Immediately thereafter, the breach team blew the front door and stormed into the cabin. Loames wasn't moving; none too gently they zip tied him and dragged him outside, followed by the Rhodesian ridgebacks, trussed like Christmas turkeys and muzzled with plastic zip ties.

Al stood in the center of the cabin and did a 360. Where were the kids? He walked outside, where the team's medic was holding an ammonia snap under the suspect's nose. He groaned and snapped his head back and forth to get away from the odor. His eyes opened halfway, unfocused. Al stood over him and squatted down.

"Where are the kids?" he asked.

The man's gaze slowly came into focus; blood leaked from his right ear and nose as he stared back at Al.

"I asked you a question, asshole," Al snapped. "The kids—where are the kids?"

"How's my wife?" Loames asked, staring at Al.

"She's recovering from the beating you gave her," he responded. "She'll be well enough to testify against you. Now, where did you stash the kids?"

Loames smiled faintly at Al, then turned his head away. He uttered one word. "Lawyer."

Al Gordon didn't remember what happened next, but it became part of HRT lore, and paid for more than a few beers that night. According to Ridell, Loames repeated his demand for a lawyer, followed by, "Did you get that?" Al slowly smiled, leaned close, and slammed his knee hard and deep into Loames' crotch. "Did you get that?" he asked, with no sign of a smile at all. Loames screamed and tried to roll away, but Al had him trapped. "I didn't make that out, Darryl," said Al. "Let me move closer so I can hear you." He leaned closer and again rammed his knee into the man's balls. Loames' eyes rolled back in his head and he expelled a long wheezing scream, like a boiling teakettle. Al picked up the discarded ammonia snap and held it under the man's nose. "I can do this all day, Darryl, and I will, until I have an answer. Now where did you stash the kids?"

They weren't far away. 100 feet behind the cabin were the remains of an old icehouse. It was basically a cellar hole lined with decaying hay bales, covered with a roof. The kids were inside with sleeping bags, and the door was padlocked to prevent them from escaping. They were traumatized, but physically fine.

Al and Ridell were at the hospital a week later when the kids were reunited with their mom. She wasn't completely back yet, but her prognosis was good, although she'd be doing physical therapy for some time to come. *This is what this job is all about,* Al thought. *This is why I do it.* They explained to Loames' wife that he was in custody and would be staying there. They strongly recommended that she press charges against her husband, then start a new life with her children somewhere far away. She readily agreed. "He can't hurt you again," Al told her.

"You might also want to tell her that he now walks funny," Ridell told Al, once they had gotten to the parking lot. "He wears his balls up around his armpits now."

Al looked at him with a question on his face. Ridell smiled. "Sure wish I had seen how you got Loames to talk," he smirked. "We were all loading gear when he decided to open up to you. Pretty high voice for a kidnapper."

"I can be very convincing," Al replied.

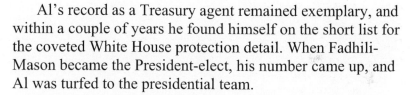

Al's record as a Treasury agent remained exemplary, and within a couple of years he found himself on the short list for the coveted White House protection detail. When Fadhili-Mason became the President-elect, his number came up, and Al was turfed to the presidential team.

He had a hard time getting his head around whatever the hell it was that was happening in the country. Politically, the place was a chaotic mess; neither the Republican nor Democratic parties were recognizable anymore; they still claimed the name, what Al thought of as their brand, but that was as far as either got to representing the values that they each supposedly stood for. Each person who had spent time in the Oval Office for the last two terms had yammered loudly about their goals and values, but little had changed; the ideological deadlock, untempered by reasonable thinking, was unyielding, and social media didn't help, giving an amplified voice to every nutcase brigade in the country and making them look a lot bigger and more powerful than they actually were. On the one hand, they scared people because they were loud and threatened the social order. On the other hand, their volume made them visible, which made it easier for law enforcement to locate and keep an eye on them. They weren't exactly members of the national brain trust.

And now, the new President. Al didn't know what to think about her. She leaned left on some things, right on others; she was compassionate as hell about whatever she took on; and she seemed to understand the idea of building a team based on capability rather than party line. She picked her opponent in the election as her Vice-president, for God's sake. She had even asked Al a few questions about what *he* would do to give the police what they need to do their jobs more safely and effectively. Al had begged off with a half-assed answer, but that was just weird. He was protection detail, not her spiritual advisor.

Ahadi Fadhili-Mason walked around the table to welcome her visitor, who rose to greet her firm handshake with his own. He was smiling, but also looked puzzled. So was Al: He couldn't figure out why she was meeting with the guy, but he'd know soon enough.

"Thanks for agreeing to meet with me, Mr. Rowe," she smiled, gesturing for him to sit. He did, and she took the seat next to him.

"Thank you, Ma'am," he responded. "I'm not in the habit of getting calls from the White House; I have to admit that I thought it was a joke at first. But I'm very happy to meet you."

She smiled. "There are times I think this whole thing is a joke, Mr. Rowe—a bad one. But there has to be a punch line in there somewhere, and I figure I have four years to find it, and I'm hoping you might be able to help me."

He laughed at that. "Your people were very persuasive on the phone, Mrs.—I mean, Madame President, but you'll have to forgive me—I still don't exactly know why I'm here."

"Mr. Rowe, I'll get right to the point," she began. "Every president that wins an election sweeps into office with grand plans for greatness—and equally grand plans to win reelection. But here's the deal: I have no interest in reelection after my four years. Call me naïve if you like, but I want one kick at the can to make a difference here, after which I'll turn things over to whoever comes next. And I'll tell you why. In my opinion—and this is the naïve part of me, so don't laugh—every first-term President spends the second two years of the four-year term campaigning for the second term. In other words, they don't really focus on the job they were hired to do, and I have a problem with that. The people have hired me for four years, so I intend to give them four uninterrupted years of my best effort. Which means that if I screw it up, I don't have to spend time unscrewing it in my second term.

"So: Since I have no plans for a second act, I can do some things a bit differently than my predecessors have done. And that's where you come in.

"I don't need to tell you that there's a whole lot wrong in this country, Mr. Rowe, and a lot of it comes down to a few simple things. Education is broken, the whole jobs thing is broken, and frankly common sense has gone out the window. So, I'm going to spend the next four years doing my damndest to fix as many of them as I possibly can."

He nodded, scooted his chair back, and turned it toward the President, placing his arms on his knees as he leaned over. "I agree completely, Ma'am, and you're preaching to the choir. But I still don't understand why I'm here."

"Well," she smiled, scooting her own chair back and

leaning toward her guest. "I'm not the sharpest knife in the drawer—I'll be the first to admit that. But I'm also not an idiot, because I'm pretty good at finding the sharpest knives. I can't do the things I want to do by myself—nobody can. And here's a little secret in case you haven't already figured this out: politicians will *never* fix things. Frankly, I'm surprised that most of them can manage to get themselves dressed in the morning, based on what I've seen.

"I have to put together a Cabinet, Mr. Rowe. The intent of assembling a Cabinet is to build a drawer full of sharp knives that advise the President. In one pretty important area, you're sharper than most. I'd like you to consider becoming a member."

He showed no emotion, but Al Gordon, who had heard the entire conversation, was stunned. *She wants this guy on her Cabinet? What the hell!?!*

Rowe was equally stunned. "Madame President, I don't know what to say. I mean, first of all, thank you—I'm honored that you'd even consider me. Frankly, I'm wondering if you have me confused with somebody else. This table knows more about politics than I do."

She laughed. "That's precisely the point, Mr. Rowe. An old friend of mine always says that if you want something different, you have to do something different. Well, if I build a Cabinet that's made up of Washington insiders, all I'm doing is recreating what's already been done before. I'd rather not do that. I want to shake things up, and that's going to take different people with different ideas about how to do things. So, what do you say? Are you in?"

"I—I—well, I—may I ask, what would I be doing?" He hadn't been this flummoxed since the first time he sang on stage.

"You've got credibility, skill, and people respect you," she replied. "You stand for the kinds of things that this country needs right now. I'm all about dependencies, Mr. Rowe. We need major infrastructure work—roads, bridges, water systems, and that's just to start. But we can't do those things without people who have the skills and knowledge to do the work. So, I'm creating a new Cabinet position: I need a Chief National Infrastructure Officer, and you're it, if you want it. Oh, and I'm also eliminating a Cabinet post. There's no more Secretary of Education. I'm lumping it all under you. I can't imagine a world where job creation and education aren't joined at the hip."

Al Gordon was speechless. He didn't show it—at least, he hoped he didn't—but he sure as hell didn't expect this. He was already envisioning the rabid response from Washington old-timers. *Holy shit, this is going to be fun,* he thought. A fleeting smile crossed his face.

"So, what do you say, Mr. Rowe. Can I count on you?"

He looked at her, and for the first time, realized that she was serious. "Ma'am, I don't believe for a minute that you aren't going to wake up tomorrow and wonder what the hell you were thinking—please forgive my language. But if I can bring some kind of value to what you're trying to do, then it would be my honor to serve. Just one thing, though. Mr. Rowe is my Dad. My name is Mike."

Yep, thought Al. A month from now, if this is any indication, the Washington silverbacks are going to feel like they've been through a blender. I don't know if what she's doing will work, but I was wrong about one thing. She's no snowflake: she's more like a hailstone. The kind that kills cows.

Chapter 3: The Ahadi Fadhili-Mason Presidential Library

I booked a room at a Hampton Inn a few blocks from the Library, an easy walk along the Detroit River. I had called ahead to determine what I needed to do as a researcher to gain access to the archives; they vetted my credentials, spoke with Van, and confirmed that I would be allowed to enter the archives for the research I intended to conduct.

At 9 AM I entered the Library and checked in at reception. I was issued a pass and was required to place all pens and highlighters in a locked box before entering the actual archives. In exchange, I was handed a box of sharpened Yellow Dixon Ticonderoga number three pencils.

As I filled out the visitor form, I heard a voice behind me calling my name. Turning, I saw a strikingly beautiful woman approach, her hand extended. "Mr. Meadows? Sylvia Antonino," she said, introducing herself with a smile. "I'm the Chief Archivist with the library; welcome."

I shook her hand, returned the greeting, and finished the form. Wow, I thought. Sylvia was hot. This may turn into a longer assignment than I planned. Sexy librarians—who knew?

"Sorry about the formalities," she apologized. "Like any archive, we do everything we can to protect the original documents that are entrusted to us."

"No need to explain," I smiled. "I did a piece on 14th-century manuscripts a few years ago, and I had to go through similar protocols at the museums I visited. I have to assume that most of what you have has been digitized, right?"

She sighed. "Actually, not as much as you'd think," she told me. "We may be living in a digital world, but government still runs on pomp and circumstance—which means lots of paper. Even today, you can't hold a bill signing event using Adobe EchoSign. They want pens, fancy paper, wax stamps, the whole works. So yeah—a lot of what we have is digital, but I suspect that more than half of what we archive is still physical. The conversion takes time, people, and therefore money—and, as you can imagine, we pretty much run on donations. So be prepared to breathe a lot of paper dust."

"Hence the pencils."

"Hence the pencils. Your creds give you unlimited access, and we'll set you up in a research carrel. It's not what you think—it's not one of those little desks that you remember from college. We'll put you in a room with a table that you can spread stuff out on, and we'll give you a temporary lock code for the room so that you can come and go as you please. And, we'll assign you a circulating nurse— I hope you understand."

"Circulating nurse?"

She chuckled. "Sorry, a term I stole, but it works. My brother's a nurse in Baltimore. Whenever they do surgery on somebody, one of the people in the OR is a circulating nurse like my brother. They do lots of things, but one of the most important is to count sponges. If 13 sponges go into the patient's body during the procedure, 13 should come out before they close. Simple math, but somebody's responsible to count. So, we'll assign a person to you to ensure that whatever you check out is the same as what you check back in. Sorry, but it has to be that way—I'm sure you understand."

"Absolutely—I'd expect no less," I responded. I'd heard

stories of manuscripts disappearing from less carefully curated institutions, or worse, pages removed and secreted out in the false bottom of a briefcase or hidden in plain sight in a stack of papers. I wanted no part of that.

Sylvia led me through the public spaces of the Library, a mini tour of sorts. Interestingly, they also had an area devoted to the flux reversal that had occurred during Fadhili-Mason's presidency. A weird thing to be part of a presidential library, but given the circumstances and timing, entirely appropriate.

We came to a door marked 'PRIVATE,' which she opened with her card key.

"Your card will also open this door," she told me, "and you're welcome to work as late as you like. There's also a separate entrance around the side for researchers and staff; that might be more convenient for you to use while you're here so that you don't have to deal with the lobby and crowds and such. If you do stay late, just be aware that everything will be locked up and you won't have access to anything other than what you have in your study area, so make sure that you have everything you need before 5 PM when the staff goes home. After that, you'll have to wait until morning to get access to anything—I mean, physical documents. Digital stuff is available all the time, obviously.

"One more thing—no food or drink is allowed in the archive area, for obvious reasons, even in spill-proof cups. There's a cafeteria in the basement that's actually pretty good."

I nodded as we entered the archive proper. I inhaled deeply; it smelled of age, and paper, and library dust, the smells I had come to associate with knowledge—and Van's office. We walked down the long library stacks, past researchers and archivists who smiled and nodded as we passed.

"Your room is right up here on the left," Sylvia said, pointing. We came to the end of the rolling stacks and turned left toward a door with a cypher lock. "The door code is printed on the back of your badge."

I lifted the badge, found the number, and pressed the silver buttons in the correct combination. The doorknob turned, and we entered a small, brightly lit room with a six-foot-by-six-foot table, and two chairs—nothing else, other than a zippered clear plastic case on the table.

"The bag on the table contains a package of cotton archival gloves—please use them at all times when handling documents. It also contains more pencils, an eraser, a few pads of paper in case you need them, a small LED flashlight to help with faded print, a magnifier, and a dust brush. If you need to sharpen your pencils, please do it over at the circulating desk that we passed on the way in.

"If you need anything copied, please let whoever's at the desk know, and they'll take care of it for you. Pretty much anything is fair game, although there are a few that, for one reason or another, we're not allowed to copy. Copies are two cents a page, and you'll get an invoice at the end of your work here. And don't worry—I already told your editor that he'll be getting a bill." She smiled and winked.

Damn, I thought. She's cute—and I think she may be flirting with me.

"That's it, Michael; we're glad to have you here, and I hope you find what you're looking for. If you need help, ask any of the archivists; they know this place and what it contains better than anybody. Here's my card" she said, extending her hand. "I'm in and out but call or text if I can help in any way."

She shook my hand, waved, and closed the door behind her. I turned, put my bag on the table, and got to work.

Chapter 4: Policing the Police

"Al, got a minute?"

Al Gordon heard the President calling him from inside the Oval just as her schedule coordinator was exiting. The woman winked at him and smiled as she passed him. "She's on a roll—eat your Wheaties," she whispered loudly.

"I heard that," the President called from the Resolute Desk.

Al entered and closed the door. "How can I help you, Ma'am?" he asked, taking his usual position at the door.

She motioned for him to join her in the seating area, where six comfortable armchairs formed a circle with a table in the middle, like a campfire. She poured him a mug of coffee and handed it to him without asking, before pouring one for herself. "Madame President—"

"Shut up and drink, Al," she told him. He drank. "I need your advice on something."

Damn this place had good coffee, he thought. "Yes, ma'am. How can I help?"

"Tell me about your background, Al. How did you come to be in the Secret Service, and what brought you to the White House? Humor me—there's a reason I'm asking."

So, Al told her about his cyber studies, how the corporate world didn't work out, and how he chose to enroll in the Georgia State Police Academy and become a cop like his father. He told her about the task force work he did with Treasury, and how a couple of high-profile cases—he didn't share details—had gotten the attention of higher-ups in Treasury, and that they had suggested he apply for the Secret

Service.

"Thanks for that," she smiled. "Al, is it safe to say that you were a cop long enough to get a sense of what that the job is really like? I mean, I know that this position is sort of like being a cop, but not really. Do you understand the things that cops go through every day that makes their job good, bad, whatever the word is?"

He nodded, not sure where this was going. "Yes, Madame President, I think so," he responded.

"Good. I need to have a conversation with somebody who understands the job, because I don't, but I need to. Here's the deal. Remember back in the day when George Floyd died, and the phrase du jour was 'defund the police?' Well, that was bullshit then and it's bullshit now. And it's the gift that keeps on giving—it won't go away. The answer isn't to de-fund the police; the answer is to re-fund the police. I would no more take money away from the police than I'd take it away from firefighters or ambulance services. That's ludicrous. But here's what I need help with, and I need you to call bullshit if I cross a line. Okay? Brutal honesty, Al."

"No problem, Ma'am," he replied. *Where the hell was this going?*

"Okay, good," she responded. "Here's what I believe to be true, so listen carefully and stop me at any time to course correct. I believe that police are generally underpaid and underappreciated. I believe that we ask them to do far more than they should be doing in terms of situations and scenarios. I believe—"

"Sorry to interrupt, Madame President. Can you say more about that last statement? I want to make sure I understand what you mean by that."

"Absolutely, Al. I've never read a real police log or

whatever they call the list of things that a cop deals with on a single shift. Everything I know about being a cop comes from *Blue Bloods* and *Law and Order* and Harry Bosch novels—great books, by the way. But if half of what I believe is true, we're asking them to do a lot of things that should be done by somebody else. For example, having to deal with a homeless guy because he makes a neighbor nervous isn't a police matter. Dealing with a domestic dispute shouldn't be handled by the cops, unless it's gone violent; it should be handled by a counselor, somebody who's been trained specifically to handle that kind of situation. And a homeless guy who's legitimately hungry isn't a threat that the police should have to deal with; there should be somebody with public health, or mental health, or some kind of sociological training to deal with that.

"But here's the thing. I know that it isn't that simple, that things are a hell of a lot more complicated than that. A homeless guy with a drug problem can turn violent, or he may be a scam artist. A domestic dispute situation can get dangerous, and when that happens, or when there are kids in the household, cops have to be there to provide protection and eliminate threats. But my question is this: Do they get the training they need to handle those kinds of things? Are they really paid to be counselors and such? Every cop likes to say that their primary job is to de-escalate, yet they go into every situation wearing a gun, a stick, pepper spray, a TASER, and handcuffs. I mean, instead of partners being two cops, should they be a cop who's also trained in the social sciences or whatever, and a social worker or psychologist or whatever who also graduated from the Police Academy?

"De-funding the police is asinine, Al. I want to *re*-fund the police—and I don't mean that as in 'refund.' I mean that I think we need to take a long, hard look at the job of being a cop and re-think how we fund it, how we train cops, how we counsel them, how we staff departments, and a hundred other things."

Well, this isn't what I expected, Al thought. "Madame President, being a cop isn't a job," he began, "It's a calling. When I was a police officer in Georgia, my little brother made more money than I did while he was going to college, and he was a Barista at Starbucks. My Dad used to say that cops become cops to become cops. Are some of them dirty? Sure, and some Baristas steal from the till. But most people who join a police force do so because they truly do want to make a difference in their community.

"I think there are a few things at play that need attention. First, it's impossible to un-see a lot of what cops see doing the job. The line's been used in every police show and movie ever made, so it's become kind of a stereotype, but cops really do see things the rest of the world shouldn't have to see. They get called in when people are acting badly in the worst possible way, and they're expected to do something about it in a socially acceptable manner. They show up on a call and they see a kid who's been beaten by her drunk father or starved half-to-death by her strung-out mother, and they aren't allowed to react. They have to get in between a drunk couple who are threatening each other with kitchen knives, and when one of them gets hurt, it's the cop's fault. They have to manage a crowd that wants to throw things at them, and often do, but of course, they're not allowed to respond. They pull over vehicles all the time, knowing that at any time they could get shot because they stopped a guy who's desperate enough to do something stupid.

"And here's the real problem: they do this every day, day in and day out, with little in the way of support and a public who are either oblivious or hateful—the reward they get for wanting to make a difference. 'Cops become cops to become cops' is not something the public understands, and if they do, they have a pretty—*unappreciative* way of showing it. So yes, Ma'am—they need some consideration."

She looked at him with steel in her eyes. "Then let's make sure they get it, Al."

Al escorted the President back to the Oval Office. She thanked him for his insights, then went inside and closed the door so that she could prepare for her next meeting. *Who woulda thunk it?* he mused, taking his position outside the door. She never failed to surprise him. She may go down in flames for taking on so much, but it'll be a hell of a bonfire.

Chapter 5: The Presidency

Day three.

Few projects had sucked me in like this one had. Part of it was the very real prospect of a looming deadline; part of it was the promise of a front-page story; but most of it was the subject matter. Fadhili-Mason was a very different beast, as presidents go.

The previous evening, over a sumptuous feast of Buffalo chicken tenders and French fries at TGI Friday's, I had thought about the project and its primary subject. Interesting woman, and an even more interesting president. The results of her time in office are still being felt and would for a long time to come—they were that powerful and far-reaching. But the person behind those actions? Grabbing smoke. Sure, there was all the typical public information out there about her, her background, her strong devotion to family and to keeping them out of the public spotlight, David, her husband of several decades, now deceased, her love of dachshunds, her often salty tongue. But it was becoming increasingly clear to me that there was more to this story, and to its main subject, than I was finding.

As part of my undergrad in political science at NYU, I had studied *The Presidency*—meaning the concept, the role, the ideal—in some detail. One of the most telling analyses I read for one of my classes was a book by James David Barber called *The Presidential Character*. I've gone back over the years and referred to it many times since—it's one of the few university textbooks I still have—and its teachings remain eerily accurate.

Barber looks at three indicators of a president's effectiveness in office. The first is character, and he measures that like a Gartner Magic Quadrant—positive-negative on one axis, active-passive on the other. The most effective presidents are typically active-positive; the worst are passive-negative. Active-positive presidents tend to have a bias for action, are optimistic, and genuinely like the job they've been thrust into. JFK and Gerald Ford and Barack Obama are good examples.

Passive-positive presidents, on the other hand, tend to be less effective in the role because they want to make everybody happy. They tend to suffer from low self-esteem, and therefore rarely get much done that has lasting impact. Ronald Reagan comes to mind.

Active-negative presidents are typically set in their ways, driven to accumulate power, aggressive, and quick to place blame on others. Richard Nixon and Donald Trump—great examples.

Finally, the dregs of the presidential barrel—passive-negative. Low self-esteem, a tendency to abdicate power, and not willing to play the political game—hardcore negotiation—all of these are elements of this character type. Think Calvin Coolidge.

Barber also looks at presidential style, which stems from three activities: engagement with the public and the press; engagement with other politicians; and the reading and writing and introspection necessary for critical thinking. Presidents that engage actively with the media and their constituents—meaning, they communicate regularly and well—tend to be seen as effective. And those that are willing to engage in the smarmy, greasy, nasty business of dealing with other politicians, willing to get their hands dirty, tend to get more in the way of bipartisan-acceptable results on thorny issues. And finally, those who go through the navel-gazing necessary to understand their role relative to the big game, well, they tend to survive with minimal scars.

Finally, Barber looks at the person's world view, which he sees as being less about geography and geopolitics and more about global morality—about stepping away from the short-term and ever-changing pressure of political expediency to consider what's right on a human, transnational scale. Presidents are somewhere on a sliding scale of awareness relative to the rest of the world, in my mind. Nixon gets good marks because he opened China. Reagan engaged with Gorbachev to bring down the Berlin Wall and usher in Perestroika. Meanwhile, Trump couldn't find New Mexico on a map with a GPS and a flashlight. Pathetic. Of course, one could argue that New Mexico didn't *want* to be found by Donald Trump. Reminds me of that famous Saul Steinberg cartoon from the New Yorker, showing the view of the rest of the world from Manhattan[i]. Once you got past the Hudson River, there was pretty much nothing. Wasteland. Corn. Rocks. A big red bridge somewhere out there on the horizon.

Which brings me back to this moment, three days into my visit to Detroit. Who the hell was this person?

My research had given me far more than I had come looking to find, which was both terrible and great. It was terrible because it meant I had a boatload of information to sift through, and the clock was ticking. I still needed to write the damn article. But it was also great, because a tiny little flame was burning deep in my soul, a flame that had been missing for a long time. It was excitement—and maybe, dare I say it? Passion. I hadn't felt this way about a story in years.

My first inclination was to try to classify Fadhili-Mason according to Barber's framework. Part of it was easy. She played the press like a fiddle, meeting with them regularly and feeding them so much information that there was nowhere to go to sniff out scandal or controversy—not that there ever was any. She was a lot like Obama in that regard. She conducted virtual town hall meetings every week that were open to anybody willing to ask a civil, curiosity-based question. She also did a weekly Podcast to share her thoughts about things. It was weird, but it worked. Some people likened it to FDR's Fireside Chats that he did over the radio in the 1930s and 40s. People loved her for the level of engagement she brought to the office.

And, her global view was—well, global. I found an article in which somebody compared her to Copernicus because of her tendency to tell people that the world did not revolve around the United States. And yet, she came across as the finest kind of patriot.

But it was the active-passive/positive-negative thing that kept me up late at the presidential library. Active? Holy crap, did she get things done like nobody else. As I read about the things she went after, I couldn't help but remember a time when I was flying somewhere, and a few rows up, there was a guy reading a book that had a really funny but culturally insensitive name: *Sacred Cows Make the Best Burgers*. I looked it up when I got to wherever I was going and ended up buying and reading it. It was about the fact that most businesses don't seek out and eliminate business practices that no longer work, because they've become blind to them. Well, Fadhili-Mason made it her mission to gore an awful lot of sacred cows during her six years in office. And that was another thing—six years! How the hell did she do that?!? So, on the scale between passive and active, she was somewhere out there beyond active—like, beyond Alpha-Centauri active.

And when it came to the positive-negative thing, positive all the way. I mean, how could she not be? *She fixed freaking everything that was broken about the country.* OK, not everything, but more than anybody else ever managed to do.

Now granted, she had help; first of all, she chose the weirdest, most non-traditional, and most effective cabinet in the history of the presidency. And why not? There's nothing in the Constitution that requires a president to have a cabinet[ii]; all it says is that presidents may occasionally consult the heads of each department of government. In fact, it wasn't until 1907 that the Cabinet was even officially recognized as a thing, and that was only because Congress voted them a pay raise[iii]. And the people she chose! Greta Thunberg as senior advisor to the head of the EPA? Tom Friedman as Secretary of State? Hey, why not. It worked.

Now, granted, she had help—of the weirdest, most wonderful kind. Nobody could have accomplished a fraction of what she did without it. And, nobody could have predicted the reversal. Actually, I guess that's not true; scientists had been predicting it for years; what they couldn't predict was when it would actually happen—or what its effect would be when it did. Well, Ahadi Fadhili-Mason figured it out, and man, did she put it to good use.

What I found to be strange—and that's vastly understating it—was that no one, to date, had written a book about *how* she did all the things that she did while in office. Sure, a handful of books had been written about *what* she did, and they all had colorful names: *Promise and Kindness: Hope for a Nation; From One Reversal to Another: The Changing Face of American Politics;* and my favorite, *Flipping Burgers at the Sacred Cow Café: A Recipe for Change.* Each one of these books offered a laundry list of her accomplishments, punctuated by colorful stories of political game-playing and atypical diplomacy. But as I dug into the piles of information on the table in my reading room, another story began to emerge. It wasn't just the reversal that made Ahadi Fadhili-Mason successful; it was how she thought about and approached the job. It was her personal, academic, and professional background. It was the extraordinarily atypical slate of people she surrounded herself with when she took office. It was her willingness to reach across the aisle, grab people by the hand, drag them *into* the aisle, and beat them into submission with energy, respect, hope, and infuriatingly undeniable logic. It was her recognition and acceptance of the fact that she wasn't an expert on any aspect of the job of being president, but she knew who was. It was her willingness to fail, knowing that the next time she wouldn't. And it was her willingness to give her *people* permission to fail, knowing that if she didn't, she also didn't give them permission to try.

By the time I got to the end of my time in Detroit, I had an article. Okay, it wasn't written yet, but it was in my head. I flew back to New York and knocked out the finished piece in two long days. As promised, Van placed it on the front page of the Times, ten years to the day after Ahadi Fadhili-Mason left office. And, as he also promised, it was below the fold, but whatever.

The next day, I left. In spite of his protests, I talked Van into a one-year leave-of absence, vague though his promises of a job waiting for me were. I didn't care.

I had a book to write.

Part Two: Transition

Chapter 6: Transition

"Polestar is at the door."

Al Gordon spoke into his sleeve mic as the president approached, accompanied by a small entourage—her husband David, and most of her Cabinet. Al's head was on the proverbial swivel. Everybody loved her, and she was leaving office, but there was always a knucklehead out there.

"Good morning, Al," the president said, as she approached, placing a hand on his shoulder. "Looks like we'll be seeing a lot of each other after today."

"So I've been told, Madame President." He extended his arm to gently block her. "Please wait for the car to arrive, Ma'am. It will be here any second."

She looked at him with something between a smirk and a grin on her face. "So, is this how it's going to be after today, Al? You going to block me from going to the fridge because there may be a dangerous squash in it?"

He gave her the faintest hint of a smile. "If that's what it takes, Madame President. Squash can be nasty." As the caravan of vehicles pulled into the drive, her detail formed up around her for the short walk to the car.

"Loosen up, Agent Gordon," she said, as she punched him in the bicep.

"Better listen to her, Al," said her husband, chuckling. "Trust me, this is not a battle you're going to win. She's tougher than both of us put together. And, meaner."

"Don't I know it, Mr. First Gentleman, don't I know it," he replied, looking everywhere and nowhere.

"Polestar is moving," said Al Gordon, the head of Ahadi Fadhili-Mason's Secret Service detail, as he gave the go-ahead to exit the building. They walked quickly to the Beast, the heavily armored Cadillac limousine that would transport the President, her husband, and Agent Gordon to Andrews Air Force Base, where they would board Air Force One for her final official flight as President. The car still awed her; variously referred to as Cadillac One, Stagecoach, and the First Car, during the six years that she had spent being ferried around inside the thing, she learned that it weighed about 20,000 pounds, was hermetically sealed with its own environmental system in case of a gas or liquid attack, had run-flat tires, night vision, and the ability to lay down an oil slick or smoke screen, should they be needed during an evasive maneuver. Each door weighed as much as the doors on a Boeing 757, which was understandable, considering that the walls of the Beast were eight inches thick with heavy armor and the projectile-proof windows were five inches thick. And while no one had ever confirmed it, there was a rumor that the door handles—hell, maybe the whole body— could be electrified to repel attackers. She wondered if it had rotating license plates and machine guns behind the headlights, like James Bond's Austin-Martin. Do we have our own Q? she had asked Al, early in her presidency. He didn't reply. She took that as a yes. Hell, we probably have an army of Qs.

She had written the letter for her successor and left it on the Resolute desk; she had bid a fond farewell to the White House staff; and she had taken a final walk-through of the property with her kids and grandkids. Her term had come to a satisfying close, and now she was flying home to begin the next phase of her life. She and David had chosen to retire on the property they owned in Tennessee, and Al Gordon would lead the small protection detail that all Presidents enjoy after leaving office.

They made their way to Shared Base Andrews without incident; people lined the route, waving at her, holding flags and cheering. The entourage sped through the heavily guarded base gate and stopped in the looming shadow of Air Force One. As she left the vehicle with her husband on one side and Al on the other, a receiving line of military officers in full dress saluted her smartly as she approached the plane. She stopped and thanked each of them in turn for their service, for keeping her, and the nation, safe. She climbed the air stairs for the last time, turned, and waved. The door closed, and the trappings of Washington were on their way to becoming memories.

Halfway through the flight, Al Gordon and the other Secret Service agents on-board approached and asked if they could have a moment. "Of course, Al," she smiled, "you don't have to ask."

He turned to the group behind him, and nodded at the junior Agent in the detail, Andrés Ávila. Ávila approached, and extended a small, wrapped box.

"Madame President, it's been an honor to have worked with you, and we want to thank you. We know that Presidents aren't supposed to accept gifts, but we hope you'll make an exception in this case. We can always say it's for Sam and Taylor," referring to her grandkids.

"Why, thank you, Andrés—thank you all," she smiled with delight, unwrapping the package. It was a long square wooden box, and when she opened it, she found inside an exquisite brass spyglass, about nine inches long, twice that when extended, lying in green velvet. She immediately pulled it open and looked out the window of the jet.

"As you know, we codenamed you Polestar, so we

thought, what better gift than to give you a telescope you can use to find your own polestar?" explained Ávila.

She smiled and rose from the leather couch. "Gentlemen," hugging each one in turn, "I love each and every one of you. Thank you for the sacrifices you've made over the last six years. And don't tell me you haven't—I know better. I don't know who came up with this idea for a gift, but it's perfect, and I'll treasure it. I can also use it to keep an eye on David when he's out wandering the grounds, pretending he's working."

They all had a good laugh at that, even David. "It might come in handy with Al as well, Madame President," laughed Ávila.

Chapter 7: Library

My apartment in Detroit was in a part of town that was called 'up and coming' by realtors. In English, this meant that you wouldn't want to live there if you could help it. But I couldn't help it. The apartment was close to the University of Detroit Mercy campus, but not close enough: the college dorms were palaces compared to this place. But it was an easy 15-minute drive to the Library, the food was plentiful and cheap, and the neighborhood had a great energy and vibe. Most of my neighbors were students, which was kind of weird, being the old guy in the building, but I didn't mind.

I'd managed to save quite a bit before leaving the Times, so between my savings, a small inheritance from my Grandmother, and regular freelance jobs, some of them from Van, I had enough money to live comfortably.

I had two residences—sort of. One was my apartment, where I slept; the other was the study room that I had been graciously allowed to keep at the Fadhili-Mason Presidential Library, where I did everything else. Sylvia Antonino, the Library's Chief Archivist, had adopted me; she knew I was living like an ascetic monk, and several times a week showed up with some ridiculously delicious sandwich, or pasta, or dessert that she had made. Every time, she claimed that she had made too much and that these were leftovers, but I knew better. Thank goodness.

We had spent a lot of time together in the weeks that I had been there. Sylvia graduated from Stanford, where she double majored in library science and political science. I kidded her about basically creating a major that uniquely qualified her to work at a presidential library. That wasn't her plan; originally, she had wanted to work in Washington as a lobbyist and researcher, but after interning for a beltway bandit lobby firm in DC for two consecutive summers, she changed her mind. A friend in Detroit told her about the Library that was nearing completion, and she applied for a researcher job. Instead, she was offered the position of Chief Archivist, which paid more. She also had the opportunity to meet the former President several times and realized that she was a serious force to be reckoned with. She was also able to answer questions about who Fadhili-Mason was as a person, based on her encounters with the former President.

"Mix passion, intensity, focus, and humor into one package—you get Ahadi Fadhili-Mason," she told me. "You need to meet her, Michael. Get deeper into the research and come up with your approach, and I'll help you make the connection. I think she'd be willing to meet you."

So, I kept at it. The book was starting to take shape; I didn't really have a story arc yet, but I had identified what I considered to be the major pieces of the book, which I would ultimately stitch together. But I wasn't there yet. I was still struggling with balance. On the one hand, it was clear to me that Ahadi Fadhili-Mason had been a gifted, driven-to-succeed, visionary President. She had accomplished most of what she set out to do, and she had also managed to cobble together cooperation from both sides of the political divide. She had turned the staid, conservative, decorum-driven job of the presidency on its head, somehow maintaining decorum, pomp and circumstance while changing just about every aspect of the job—and she did it without pissing people off too badly.

And here's where the balance comes in. The Library had a very large room dedicated to the polar reversal and its impact on Fadhili-Mason's presidency. On the one hand, there's no question that it was a contributing factor in her success. But more and more, I was coming to believe that while it helped, the majority of her successes came from her unique approach to empowering people, enabling dreams, and communicating as transparently as she possibly could at all times. I was getting close to what I believed was a central thesis for the book: that while the flux reversal contributed to the radical shifts that took place during her presidency, it was precisely that—a factor.

"Hey, pencil-boy! How about dinner?" It was Sylvia. I looked at my watch and groaned; it was 7 PM, and I hadn't even had lunch.

"Absolutely," I replied. "My treat, and we're going someplace nice. What do you like? Italian?"

She shot a scornful look my way, tempered by a smile and crossed arms. "Seriously? My last name is Antonino, so you naturally assume I like Italian. Gee, you must be a researcher. Yes, pencil-boy, I do like Italian, but tonight we're going to Texas Roadhouse because they have the best catfish on the planet and I want catfish. So, pack up—you've got five minutes and we're outta here."

I gathered my things and met her in the lobby. Sylvia drove; I had opted not to rent a car, because taking an Uber back and forth from my up-and-coming apartment every day was cheaper. Sooner or later, I'd have to buy a car; living in New York, I'd never needed one.

"Where did you grow up, Michael? Are you originally from New York?" She asked, as we pulled out of the parking lot and headed toward downtown.

"Nope, not even close," I replied. "My Dad worked for IBM, selling cloud services to big companies. I was born in Germany; my parents got transferred to Frankfurt two years before I was born and stayed there until I was six. IBM has a big development center in Germany, and my Dad was attached to that. We eventually got transferred back to the States, and I started first grade in California. My parents still live in San Jose, but I wanted to get away from California, so I went to school at NYU and then did journalism at Columbia. My heroes are journalists: they tell stories that matter, which is what I want to do. It's what I've always wanted to do. And what about you? You a long-time Detroit person? Big Eminem fan?"

"Sorry to disappoint you," she laughed, "but I'm afraid my tastes run more to Spirogyra and Kenny Burrell. My Dad was an English professor who also played sax in a jazz band, and my Mom was an architect. I grew up in Columbus, Ohio, and ended up getting a scholarship to study at Stanford. Getting out of the Midwest was always part of my plan, so when the offer came, I jumped at it. I loved Stanford, but I was amazed to realize that after four years, I missed home. So, when this job became available, I took it. Mom and Dad are three hours away, so I go visit them once a month or so."

We arrived at the restaurant, and Sylvia parked out at the edge of the parking lot and we walked inside, her arm in mine. *I could get used to this,* I thought.

"Sylvia!" the hostess called. "Good to see you! And who is this?" The host looked me up and down before giving Sylvia a hug and then introducing herself to me. "I'm Anne," she smiled. "Professional PhD candidate in evolutionary biology, working here to support my addiction to academics," she laughed. "Sylvia takes pity on me and eats here a lot to make sure I don't starve."

"Actually," said Sylvia, "I eat here because of the catfish and the beer. Oh, and the rolls and honey butter. You're a distant second reason," she laughed.

Anne laughed back. "I'm deeply, deeply hurt," she sighed. "All these years and I thought I was the attraction.

That's what I get for falling for a political geek. Oh well, so it goes. Table for two, madame?"

She sat them at a small corner table, as far away as possible from the raucous center of the restaurant—line dancing, loud laughter in the bar, and the unceasing noise from the kitchen. True to form, Sylvia ordered the catfish; on her recommendation, I ordered something called roadkill, which turned out to be chopped sirloin steak with mushrooms and onions piled on top and a couple of side dishes. We each ordered a Fat Tire.

"So, Sylvia," I asked, "I have a question for you. You've pretty much been with the Library since it opened, right?"

She took a long draught of her beer. "I actually started the week before they opened," she replied. "It was a blank slate—tabula rasa. All the shelves were in place, all the tools, so my job for the first year was to basically turn a fancy warehouse into a library. For the first six months I was basically a one-woman moving company, hauling boxes of documents, organizing them, filing them on shelves, that kind of thing. I also had to hire IT staff to create and set up curation of what would become the online holdings. It was a beast of a job, but I enjoyed it."

"And I assume that Fadhili-Mason was directly involved?"

"If you're asking whether she helped me file papers, nope. She was apparently much more involved at the beginning because she wanted to make sure that the place would serve the vision she had for it."

"Which was what, exactly?" I asked.

"The first time I actually met her was about six months into my time here, and she showed up unannounced to show some people around and see how things were going. She actually sought me out and asked me to have lunch, because she wanted to pick my brain. Did you hear that? She wanted to pick *MY* brain. So, we went down to the cafeteria, and once we sat down and started eating, she asked me if I was familiar with Percy Bysshe Shelley's poem, 'Ozymandias.' I told her that I had read it in college but admitted that I didn't really remember it. She smiled and told me that she remembered it—in fact, had committed it to memory—because it haunted her. She said, 'It goes like this—listen carefully,' and then recited it.

I met a traveller from an antique land,
Who said— "Two vast and trunkless legs of stone
Stand in the desert . . . . Near them, on the sand,
Half sunk a shattered visage lies, whose frown,
And wrinkled lip, and sneer of cold command,
Tell that its sculptor well those passions read
Which yet survive, stamped on these lifeless things,
The hand that mocked them, and the heart that fed;
And on the pedestal, these words appear:
My name is Ozymandias, King of Kings;
Look on my Works, ye Mighty, and despair!
Nothing beside remains. Round the decay
Of that colossal Wreck, boundless and bare
The lone and level sands stretch far away."

"You may have noticed, Michael, that it's engraved on the wall behind the welcome desk in the main lobby. Anyway, she told me that she didn't want this library to be another 'colossal Wreck,' as Shelley wrote. The last thing she wanted to create with her library was a monument to herself. She told me that as I set about the business of turning the building into part of her legacy, I should keep in mind that it was really a monument to everything the American people were able to accomplish during the time she was

President. She wanted the library to celebrate their will and skill and promise, not so much her own role. So, what she told me was that she wanted her library to be a place where anybody could come to learn about their own potential. She wanted it to be a place that inspired people, that made them want to be more and do more than they thought they could. She loves the word catalyst; that's how she sees herself."

At that point, our server arrived with dinner, and we ordered a second beer. We started to eat—the roadkill was great—so we small-talked for a bit before diving back into the conversation.

"Okay," I began. "Fadhili-Mason sees herself as a catalyst. And, based on what I've learned about her so far, she was—and the flux reversal sure didn't hurt. But I have to ask: is she really as selfless as you make her out to be? I mean, I can't imagine—and maybe this is just a failing on my part—but I can't imagine being president, wanting to be president, without a healthy dose of ego somewhere in the mix. I mean, this isn't a job you stumble into because nobody else wants it; you have to fight to get it, and then you have to believe you can do it. I mean, being President isn't like managing a Home Depot."

Sylvia held up her index finger, signaling a pause, while she finished chewing and swallowing a mouthful of catfish. "No," she replied, "you're right. She has plenty of ego. But here's the thing. She doesn't wear it, like so many politicians; she wields it."

"OK," I responded, "you're gonna have to explain that."

She nodded. "I'll try. Way too many politicians—and frankly, other people in positions of power and influence—seem to believe that 'because I am in this position, and am therefore powerful, you are obligated to respect me.' Fadhili-Mason isn't like that. She's more like, 'I've worked hard on

75

your behalf to do the things you hired me into this job to do. If I've done them well enough to meet or exceed your expectations, then I hope I've also earned your respect.' For her, respect isn't an expectation—it's something you have to demonstrate you deserve, every day.

"My Mom was in sales for a lot of her career, trying to get people to buy off on architectural projects. She used to tell me that when you meet with clients, you earn their trust 30 seconds at a time. You don't earn it all at once. I think Fadhili-Mason kind of worked that way, too. Just because she made people happy on Wednesday didn't meant that she could assume the same for Thursday or Friday."

"So, what did that mean for you as the Chief Archivist?" I asked.

She laughed and drank, and in the process spilled beer down the front of her shirt. "Drinking and laughing—bad combination."

I grabbed a clean napkin from an adjacent table and handed it to her.

"Thanks," she acknowledged, taking the napkin and wiping the front of her shirt. "What, no offer to help?" She smiled.

"I suspect that you know the terrain better than I do," I laughed. "But please call on me anytime. I'm always willing to learn."

"I'll bet you are," she replied. "So, to get to the question you asked before I decided to take a Fat Tire bath. Her way of looking at the world was challenging. Before I accepted the position, I spent a lot of time—a *lot* of time—studying presidential libraries all over the country, trying to get a sense of their purpose. What I found was that most of them are monuments to the person they're named for and designed to be places where political science scholars can do research. They're basically document repositories."

"That makes sense," I replied. "The volume of records produced during a presidency is stupendous. Just managing them and making them available has to be several people's worth of full-time work—I've gotten a sense of that just in the short time I've been here. So how is your place any different?"

"Well, in a lot of ways, it isn't. It's still a document repository, it's still a physical testament to the woman's presidency, and it's still a place where people come to do research—like you. Most days, in case you haven't noticed, the place is crawling with professors and researchers and journalists from all over the place. But there's a difference. Just about every initiative she drove while she was President—jobs creation, education, healthcare, changes in constitutional law, prison reform, infrastructure—they all have what we call advocacy and advancement centers at the library. Just about everything she did—not everything, but just about everything—had far-reaching impact because of the way she approached them and, let's face it, the way the polar reversal messed with people. She didn't make incremental changes; she completely reinvented those functions in ways that were so radical that in some cases they aren't even recognizable as the same agencies. And for the most part, once she and her people reinvented them and the country saw how well her changes worked, they kept them that way.

"So yeah—Ahadi Fadhili-Mason sees herself as a catalyst. She didn't necessarily create the changes that happened during her time in office, but she gave them runway and resources and velocity. That makes her different than a lot of her predecessors, in my book, anyway."

I nodded. My mind kept wandering back to Ozymandias. All empires crumble, and with them, the monuments they build to honor themselves. It was the story of the ages, the tale of self-worship and hubris that had defined humanity from its beginnings. Whether we're talking about Mexico City's central Zócalo, or Ceausescu's palace in Bucharest, or the massive monuments created by Franco in Spain, or Tiananmen Square—or Washington DC, for that matter—they were all temporary. The only thing that endures is the positive impact we have as a species on the planet.

Sylvia interrupted my musings. "Can I ask you a kind of personal question?"

"Of course," I replied.

"I'm just kind of curious. You graduated in Journalism and got a job at the Times in New York. It seems to me that that's like the Holy Grail for journalists. Why did you leave? I mean, I know you want to write this book, but what's the draw?"

I nodded and sipped the dregs of my beer. "Good question," I responded, "and I'll try to answer. You're not the first person to ask; in fact, I think my parents were the first on the list. And honestly, I don't know that I've ever had a good answer.

"I loved my work in New York; I had a great editor, worked with a super team of people, and did some really good work—at least, I think it was good. One thing I learned during my time there was that while I'm a decent writer, I'm a really good researcher. My editor used to call it my superpower. I don't have any special skills; I just have a knack for uncovering stuff that no one else can seem to find.

"When he gave me the assignment to write about Fadhili-Mason, I wasn't all that thrilled, because it was just another article and I honestly think I was burned out. But once I got into the material and started digging in, I realized that it wasn't an ordinary assignment. I mean, the *assignment* was just an assignment, but there was so much more to talk about than I could possibly get into an article. I think I kind of rediscovered what it means to be a writer."

"How so?" she asked.

"When you write for a paper, or probably a magazine as well, you live in the world of deadlines, which teaches you to be super-focused on each project. You don't get much time to be creative; it's about getting the story out there by deadline, without frills or local color. You learn to be disciplined, but you don't really learn how to be creative. The writers I admire are the people who don't just give you the facts, but who also tell you a story that they wrap around the facts. The story makes them real and relevant. So, people like Walter Isaacson, John McPhee, William Least Heat-Moon —"

"Bill Bryson?"

"Bill Bryson, absolutely. These people are storytellers first, writers second. Somewhere along the way, I realized that that's where I tend to lean as well. Part of the reason I'm good at research—and the reason you've seen me in the library late at night—is that I keep running across these little hints of story, and I follow them down a rabbit hole in search of something much more interesting than just the 'she did this, then she did this' process that too many writers use. I always want to know the back story, because that's the interesting part. That's where you leave the 'what' behind and focus on the 'why' instead." But you can't do that if you're afraid to get the knees of your pants muddy by crawling down rabbit holes. That's where I do my best work."

Sylvia was smiling at me. "What?" I asked.

"Nothing," she laughed. "I just don't often get to see somebody who's so excited about their work. You're an interesting man, Michael Meadows."

"You're pretty interesting yourself, Sylvia Antonino. But let's see how interesting you *really* are. How do you feel about dessert?"

"Fried ice cream. Two spoons. It's as big as an astronaut's helmet."

"Done."

Chapter 8: Raccoon Holler

"Whoa," David exclaimed, as they reached the top of the driveway. "This place is going to need a lot of work. Stop here for a second, would you mind, Al?"

Al slowed the car to a stop, and as he did, David Mason opened his door and stepped out. Ahadi did the same. Al put the car in park and emerged as well, looking around, always vigilant.

Al scanned the property from where he stood. The roof of the house looked like a moss farm; the grasses on either side of the road were as tall as he was; and the hills behind the house were covered with scrub that had encroached all the way to the circular driveway that surrounded the big oak tree in the center. It alone looked happy and healthy; everything else had seen better days.

"A labor of love, David," chuckled Ahadi.

"Yeah—emphasis on the 'labor' part," he snorted in response.

"What are you complaining about, mister?" she responded. "You're gonna be lawyering your ass off while Al and I run an army of contractors. Somebody's gotta pay for all the renovations I have planned."

"Yeah, yeah...Al, help me out here," he pleaded.

"Sorry, sir," Al smiled. "You're on your own. I'll stop a bullet, but arguing with your wife? Scares me to death, sir."

"Sigh...me too, Al. Me too."

Ahadi and David walked down the driveway while Al parked the car. No one had lived continuously on the property for years, and while a crew of maintenance people kept it from being completely overtaken by the lush plant life of the region, it still had the look of a lost city in the jungle. They walked around the sprawling oak tree that dominated the circular entryway, ending up at the front door of the old house. Ahadi unlocked the front door, and they entered.

Inside, it was dark and slightly musty. Ahadi wasted no time, turning on lights and moving from room-to-room, opening windows to air things out. When she reached the kitchen, she stopped in the doorway. So many memories: her grandmother standing in front of the sink, peeling potatoes and carrots and cutting them into pieces before dropping them in the pot while she hummed to herself. The two of them, sitting at the kitchen table, playing pickup sticks. Her grandfather had died when she was very young, and she had no memory of the man—although her grandmother had regaled her with stories of his life.

"You okay?" It was David. He put his arms around her and kissed the top of her head. "Starting to worry about the work you've cut out for yourself?" he teased.

She turned and hugged him. "Just thinking about my Nana—and the memories that we're going to create here with our own grandkids," she said softly.

"Well, then, we should get started," he replied, looking into her eyes. He kissed her softly. "House to home."

"Yes, indeed," she echoed. "House to home."

They walked through every room in the house, opening windows, making mental notes of things that needed work, creating a sense of priority along the way. The roof would have to be task one; it was over 30 years old and looked every day of it. The outside needed to be pressure washed, and the whole house was in dire need of paint—not to mention carpet in the bedrooms and an overall refresh of the décor. They realized before long that the renovations required to make the house livable were drastic enough that they couldn't be in it while they were underway, so they considered options. On the one hand, they could rent another place, but neither of them was in favor of that idea. Ultimately, they decided that, given that they had plenty of land, they would buy a small prefab house and have it constructed on the property. They would live there during the renovations, and then it could become a guest house when the main house was ready for occupancy.

They both intended to dedicate themselves to the work required to make the house livable, but they also had to face reality. David had a law practice to return to, and Ahadi had an arm-long list of post-presidential tasks that she had to initiate—starting with the planning for her presidential library, fundraising for which was already well underway. And, there was the matter of her memoirs: that seemed to be something that presidents did, but she was in no hurry.

"Hey Haddie—check this out! Hurry!" David was calling her from the front of the house. She jogged back toward the front door and saw him standing at the windows that faced the back of the house. As she approached, he signaled her to be quiet as he pointed to the chaos that had once been a flower garden just beyond the windows. There, a family of raccoons—two adults and three kits—were snuffling around the bed, looking for food. The youngsters were too busy playing to take foraging seriously, jumping on each other and rolling around on the ground like playful puppies. Ahadi and David stood and watched, enchanted.

"I love those things," David smiled. She nodded, and as she did, one of the adults stopped and looked at them through the window. The big raccoon froze for a few seconds, then resumed looking for food as if nothing had happened.

They watched the raccoon family for ten minutes or so; they eventually wandered off and disappeared around the corner of the house.

"Raccoon Hollow," said David.

"What's that?" she asked.

"Raccoon Hollow. That's what we should call this place. It needs a name, don't you think?" He looked at her expectantly.

"Okay" she replied, "but with one modification. We are in Tennessee, after all; how about Raccoon Holler? Minor change."

"Raccoon Holler it is," he replied.

And with that, the house became their home.

Chapter 9: Research

My days at the Ahadi Fadhili-Mason Presidential Library turned into weeks, and the weeks became months. Never had a writing project consumed me like this one had; of course, I had never taken on a project as broad as this one either, or with so many moving parts. Not only did I have to research the former president's time in office and compare her accomplishments to those of other officeholders, I also had to dig into the whole polar reversal thing. I was having a hell of a time separating the accomplishments that were owed to her skill as a leader and president from those that were the result of the flux reversal.

"Why does it matter?" Sylvia asked me one day over lunch. "I mean, every president takes advantage of every opportunity that comes their way, don't they? Why should she be any different? Or, let me say it a different way—why should she be assessed differently, as long as she did things morally and legally?"

It was a good question. After all, presidents always take credit for successes that are actually the result of work done by their predecessors and are equally quick to blame bad things on them, as well. In one of his stage routines in the 1980s, Robin Williams famously said, *Blaming the state of the economy on Ronald Reagan is like blaming Ronald McDonald when you get a bad burger. Neither of them actually runs the place.* It was largely true; the presidency is a continuum, not a series of start-stop events that can be assessed individually, like movies. Presidencies flow one into the next, and it's impossible to separate them since presidents deal in tasks that have long and often invisible completion horizons.

"I understand your point," I replied, "and am in agreement with you for the most part. But the Library has a whole wing dedicated to the polar reversal; if it isn't important, why dedicate so much space to it? I mean, I can see doing it at the Air and Space Museum, but here? It kind-of flies in the face of your argument, doesn't it?"

She thought for a moment before responding. "Well, most of the presidential libraries have space that's not related to documents and archives," she began. "And remember— not all presidents have a library. This is only the 20th, and we've had almost 50 presidents. Reagan's library has a mockup of the Oval Office; Kennedy's has an exhibit of Jackie's clothing, since she was such a fashion trendsetter. So, it isn't all that unusual to dedicate space for exhibits that highlight things that happened during that president's time in office, or even to things that characterize their presidency. The Polar Reversal was a very big deal—nothing like it had ever happened before. Everybody agrees that it caused changes that affected Fadhili-Mason's presidency. Even she admitted that she couldn't have done the things she did without it. She's an amazing woman, and even without the flux thing, she would have accomplished a lot. But I agree with her—I don't think she could have done as much as she did without its help. So, when they did the planning for the space, they decided to dedicate a large piece of the building to the Reversal, including space for scientists as well as presidential researchers. We haven't been open all that long, and already a tremendous amount of good work has come out of here."

That afternoon, I walked through the Mulvihill-McCooey Research Center. It was dominated by a model of the planet, a sixteen-foot diameter globe that floated in the air, suspended on a magnetic cushion. I approached it to read the plaque that was set into its base. The plaque described the geophysical event, and suggested I put on a pair of the three-dimensional viewing goggles that were on the table surrounding the globe. I did; instantly, the system detected the movement of the headset and the show began to play in front of me. Flocks of birds and clouds of butterflies migrated as the seasons changed, following the faintly pulsing magnetic lines of force that ran between the north and south poles of the Earth. I watched as satellites as well as terrestrial technologies took cues from them, and I felt comforted as I observed how the planet's strong magnetic field repulsed bursts of deadly radiation from deep space, radiation that would otherwise turn the planet into a lifeless desert.

The show then went on to dissect the Earth in beautiful detail, peeling away the relatively thin crust to reveal the mysterious Mohorovičić discontinuity, beneath which the partially molten mantle was exposed, then the iron and nickel outer core, and finally, the inner core, a molten sphere of 13,000-degree iron. It is the movement of this molten iron, the narrator explained, that creates the planet's magnetic field.

It then showed the flux reversal, documenting its impact, including a science fiction-like dive deep into a human brain to show how it affected human physiology. And then, a series of stories that demonstrated the extraordinary things that resulted from the Mulvihill-McCooey event, including a ten-minute interview with Professors Mulvihill and McCooey about their discovery.

"Wow," I muttered under my breath, as I took off the 3D goggles.

"Kind of cool, huh?" It was Sylvia, standing beside me.

"I'll say—I mean, I've read all about the Reversal, but I never knew much about the science behind it."

She nodded. "I know you're wrestling with balance in the story—accuracy, integrity, all of that. The thing is, it happened, and it gave Fadhili-Mason an advantage, which she took. And why not? If presidents ride into office on a wave of optimism and a strong economy, they use to it to get big, audacious things done, because people feel good about the world. Well, she did big, audacious things, but what's a hell of a lot more important than the fact that she did things is that she did the *right* things. She could have used the Reversal's effects for massive cronyism, or to give herself financial advantages that would kick in after she left office, or to do long-term damage to one party or the other. But she didn't. Instead, she put the country first. She made us the priority. How many politicians can rightly claim to have done that?

"Forgive me for pretending to know what you really want to write here, but I don't think your story is the Polar Reversal, or even Ahadi Fadhili-Mason. I think your book is about a new beginning, and how one person with a vision and a story was able to motivate a country to do a whole bunch of the right things, and in the process, change the world even more than the Polar Reversal did. It seems to me that the balance you're looking for lies in the results she fought for and ultimately got. She used every tool at her disposal to do the job she was hired to do as well as she could possibly do it, which is no different than what I expect from my mechanic when he replaces my fuel pump. So, why are you wrestling with this?"

I stood and stared at her—my mouth opened, then closed; nothing emerged.

"Hello, McFly." She waved her hand in front of my face.

I grabbed her, hugged her, kissed her. Holding her at arm's length, I grinned and shook my head. "You're amazing. Dinner again, tonight, my treat, seven o'clock. Come get me. I've gotta go. "I turned and ran back into the stacks. As the door was closing, I heard her say, "Was it the fried ice cream?"

Sylvia had broken my mental logjam with her mini speech. She was right: My story was not another presidential biography; it was a testament to human physics, not politics or the cult of personality. Ahadi Fadhili-Mason was all about vectors: direction and magnitude. Her direction came from an audacious vision of what could realistically be; magnitude derived from her remarkable ability to enroll smart, committed people to help her convert vision to reality while communicating her intent to the nation and the world with crystalline clarity.

That's what I would write about. My research would continue, but I was now coming to realize that things had shifted. I needed the source: I had to interview Ahadi Fadhili-Mason.

And, I had to kiss Sylvia again. That was rather nice.

Chapter 10: Raccoon Holler

Al Gordon and David Mason walked along the edge of the property, the river on their right, the beginnings of a vineyard on their left. In the distance, workers were putting the finishing touches on a shed that would ultimately house the smart agriculture technology—the computer that would analyze the inputs from sensors all over the garden and vineyard—as well as the mixing manifold for liquid fertilizer and pest control. Ahadi was back at the main house, directing the painters and finish carpenters who were weeks away from completing the remodel—which, of course, had suffered mightily from scope creep. David groused about it, saying that they could have torn the damn thing down and built a small city for what the remodel was costing. But he knew that the house meant much more to Ahadi than it did to him; it was a memory vault, a record of good times, and he wasn't about to take that away from her.

"How you doing, Al?" David asked his companion. Al had been with them since they left Washington, and the three of them had grown close. Ahadi was constantly complaining about the cost to taxpayers of keeping a security detail at her beck and call, but it wasn't her decision to make. Besides, Al and David had become close friends; they played guitar together and were known to do damage to Tennessee's beer stock on occasion. On weekends, Al and any other agents who happened to be on-prem would join Ahadi and Dave for cards.

"Hanging in there, sir," Al replied. A sound in the brush to their right caused Al to step in front of David; it turned out to be an opossum, rummaging in the underbrush for grubs.

"Former First Gentleman dies from killer opossum

attack," David laughed. "Al, you seriously earned your salary today, I'm here to tell you."

"Just taking one for the nation, sir," Al chuckled. There had been no serious security breaches during the time that Ahadi and David had moved to the property; a few curious lookie-loos had tried to get close by walking up the riverbank, but the security systems installed by the Secret Service detected them long before they got anywhere near the actual property. As Al explained the first time it happened, they were 'aggressively discouraged' from doing something like that again.

"And in answer to your question, sir, I'm fine—really. I think about her all the time, but I feel the pain a little less every day. It'll never go away—at least, I hope it doesn't—but I'm managing. Thank you for asking."

"Anything you need, Al, just ask," David replied, one hand on Al's back. "You know we can do without you for a bit if you need a break. Don't get me wrong—we love having you here, you're part of the family—but take care of yourself, okay?"

"Yes, sir, I appreciate that, sir. Actually, working and being with the people I care about is pretty therapeutic. The Service wanted to pull me off the detail, as you know, and I never got the chance to thank you for what you did to keep me on. That means a lot to me, sir."

"Al, one of these days you're going to have to learn that my name is David—or Dave. I don't think the grapevines or the tugboats give a damn if you break protocol."

Al looked over and smiled. "Yes, sir—Dave."

"Much better," said Dave. "Keep working on that."

They continued around the base of the low esker that wound between them and the river. Their path took them back to the main house, where they could smell paint and hear the whine of a chop saw as they approached the front door. The only remaining room to be completed was the great room at the back of the house. It had originally been a small den with two smallish windows that looked out on the back yard. Ahadi had chosen to knock it down and push it out, creating a warm, high-ceiling sunroom with floor-to-ceiling windows that looked out over a gas fire pit and patio, a small lawn, the vineyard and garden beyond, and the river in the distance. They found Ahadi there, in conversation with the two painters who were completing the room.

"How's it going in here?" David asked. Ahadi and the painters looked over as they entered.

"See for yourself, guys. Will and Bill are geniuses. Look at this," she said, pointing to the far corner of the room where the two walls met the ceiling. "No tape—they did this all without any guides and you can't tell. Geniuses!"

The painters beamed. "Lots of practice, Madame President," one of them—Will or Bill—said. "Glad you're happy with it. This is one gorgeous place, and that patio out there is going to be glorious in the evening."

"Well, guys, you're just going to have to come back to help us christen it with a glass of champagne when it's finished," said David.

"He means it, guys," Ahadi smiled. "Expect an invite once we're done and we'll have a big bash. Al makes the best barbecued brisket you have ever tasted in your life. He doesn't know it yet, but he's cooking. Right, Al?"

"Whatever you say, Madame President," Al replied.

Chapter 11: Research

Four months. That's how long I had been researching my book, which I had begun calling 'The Nation We Knew.' That was the working title, anyway. Who knew if it would survive editorial scrutiny? I had also created an outline of the book, which was now somewhere north of 50 pages.

But something else was happening, as well. Like all outlines, mine started out looking like Charlie Brown's anemic little Christmas tree. But, as my research went on and I hung more and more information ornaments on it, the outline began to look more like the General Sherman Sequoia. But there were gaps, and try as I did to fill them from the near-limitless resources at my disposal, I couldn't. I needed more. But what I needed was not to be found in the archives of the Ahadi Fadhili-Mason Presidential Library. I didn't need the 'what;' I needed the 'why.' There was only one source for that information, and it was in western Tennessee.

Opening my laptop, I began to compose a letter.

13 April 2042

Dear Madame President,

I'm a staff writer, currently on sabbatical leave from the Times in New York...

Back at her desk, Sylvia returned to the letter she had begun composing earlier that day.

22 March 2042

Dear Madame President,

As the Chief Archivist at your Library, I am constantly on the lookout for new resources that might add to the value of the holdings that I am responsible to curate. Over the last few months, a researcher has been working in the Library, assembling material for a book he intends to write about your presidency. His name is Michael Meadows, and he is a former journalist who took a leave of absence from his position with the Times in New York to do this research. His approach is different from most. The other books that have been written about your time in office focus on what Mr. Meadows calls 'the what,' that is, the things you accomplished while in office. Mr. Meadows' book takes a different approach. He is more concerned with what he calls 'the why,' which is a focus on the president and her team and the reasons for your, how shall I describe it, 'atypical approach' to serving as the President of the United States.

I suspect a time will come in the relatively near future when he will ask you for an interview. For what it's worth, I would urge you to meet with him. His work is unique and will provide a different view of what drove you to do the things you did as President, a perspective which we both agree is lacking in existing works.

I hope this finds you well and I look forward to seeing you again the next time you find yourself in Detroit. My very best to you and yours.

Respectfully,

Sylvia Antonino

Chief Archivist

Ahadi Fadhili-Mason Presidential Library

Chapter 12: Transition II

"We're never going to be done with this place," groused David, wiping his brow with his sleeve as he tipped his water bottle back for a long drink. They'd lived on the property now for four years, restoring and expanding the house, landscaping the grounds, putting in the requisite security as demanded by Al Gordon, and generally making the place livable.

"Sweetheart, you're missing the important part," she laughed in response. "We haven't made as much progress as we'd like, but we've done it together. And besides, it's not a race—I mean, look over there." She pointed to what was rapidly becoming a respectable vegetable garden and fruit orchard, not to mention the beginnings of a small vineyard—all within walking distance of the house. "None of that was here when we moved in and look at it now. We're eating from our own garden—it doesn't get a whole lot better than that."

"Yeah, but who knew that farming was so much work," he laughed. "Two steps forward, one back—that seems to be the cadence of life these days. Good tomatoes—broken water pump. Enough zucchini to feed Rhode Island—fungus in the watermelon. Nice fruit on the grapevines—"

"OK, OK, I get it," she laughed, exasperated. "The land giveth, and the land taketh away. But I think there's a lot more giving than taking away going on. Besides, remember when you used to complain about not having enough to do? Well…"

"You do have a way of turning a pain in my ass into something slightly less-painful," he laughed. But I still have a lot—" he stopped talking, his gaze faded, and he doubled over in pain as he collapsed to the ground. Ahadi screamed, following him down as he fell. "No—no—no …"

Al Gordon was at her side instantly, gently pushing her away as he simultaneously spoke urgently into his radio and rolled David onto his back. His face was ashen, and he was unresponsive. Al straddled him and began to administer CPR, as another agent ran for the defibrillator that was stashed in the house. But it was too late; by the time they heard the wail of the approaching ambulance, the nation's first First Gentleman was gone, taken by the aortic aneurysm that had been silently, invisibly spreading for most of his adult life.

Part 3: Moving On

Chapter 13: Transition III

After living under the alternate reality bubble of the White House—not to mention a bubble of impregnable security and a daunting schedule that controls every minute of every hour of every day of their lives—the return to 'civilian life' by an ex-president can be a disruptive undertaking. Some retire to a more-or-less normal existence, like Harry Truman, who, when he left office in 1952, had to buy his own railroad ticket home from Washington, and only had a Second Lieutenant's Army pension from WWI. He lived in his mother-in-law's house because he had very little income and no money saved to buy one of his own. Or, George W. Bush, who lives on his ranch in Texas and paints portraits. Others become writers and activists, like Barack Obama. Some, like Jimmy Carter, become more presidential after they leave office—his work alongside his wife Rosalynn with Habitat for Humanity is an inspiration to all.

The presidential salary isn't bad as salaries go, but it also isn't obscenely high—today, presidents are paid an annual salary of $400,000, which doesn't sound like enough, considering the demands of the job. But of course, they also have access to rather luxurious private transportation and a country home, at Camp David. Interestingly, for the majority of the country's existence, presidents were given very little in the way of a reward for time served upon leaving office. In 1958, the Former Presidents Act was passed by Congress, which funded an annual pension of $25,000 for former presidents. Thankfully (if you're a member of the ex-presidents club), that number was raised to $161,000 several years later, thus providing a reasonably livable wage to people who arguably did the world's most difficult job for either four or eight yearsiv. Don't believe it? Look at their before and after portraits. That exercise alone will convince most sane individuals to reconsider their desire to live in the White House. Most ex-presidents, of course, supplement their income with book-writing and traveling on the speaker circuit. They don't tend to miss many meals.

The revised Act also provided a stipend to fund an office and staff for departing presidents for the first four-and-a-half-years after leaving office, ostensibly to provide support for memoir-writing, presidential library consulting, and the exhaustive process of disengagement and decompression from the political boiler room of Washington.

Some former presidents return to politics after leaving office. Andrew Johnson, following his impeachment, became a Tennessee Senator. Twelve years after the completion of his presidency, William Taft was nominated by Warren Harding as the Chief Justice of the Supreme Court. John Tyler, the tenth president of the United States and one of the Presidents that few people have ever heard of, became a member in good standing of the Confederate House of Representatives, a decade after leaving the White House. Ahadi Fadhili-Mason and her husband wanted none of that. They left the fishbowl of Washington behind and settled in the extreme northwestern reaches of Tennessee, not far from Dyersburg. Their property was a throwback to Ahadi's childhood, because long ago it had belonged to her maternal grandparents. When they passed, it stayed in the family and was used as a family retreat for years, but as the older members began to die off, the tradition faltered, and the property was largely abandoned and fell into disrepair. For a fair price, the former first couple bought out the few remaining members of the family, none of whom had interest in the property any longer, and they moved in. They called it Raccoon Holler, because of the family of raccoons that regularly raided the trash cans and which even the extraordinary paramilitary skills of the Secret Service were unable to eliminate.

At first, they lived in a small, manufactured home that they had built on the property (David referred to it as the presidential double-wide). The main house required serious work before it was livable, so for two years they lived in the 'double-wide' while an army of Al Gordon-approved contractors, builders and designers restored the old house where Ahadi had spent so many summers as a child. They replaced the roof, expanded the home's size beyond its original modest footprint, laid brickwork around the sprawling live oak that shaded the front of the house (also bringing in an arborist to ensure that the tree was healthy), and graded the hillsides between the house and the river to accommodate the garden and orchard they wanted to put in and to make the land a bit more friendly for human walkers. 25 months to the day after starting the project, they left the presidential double-wide and moved into their permanent home, sharing it with her grandparents' ghosts.

They allowed the work on the house and surrounding property to consume them as a way to put the immersive world of the presidency—and Washington—behind them. They wandered the property, 33 uneven acres with reasonably good farmland covering a third of it, a half-mile of riverfront, and large swaths of undeveloped forest and grassland. David bought a brush cutter and began to cut walking trails, always under the watchful eye of Al Gordon or another member of the small security detail that provided overwatch for the former President and her husband—and that would be with them for the rest of their lives. At first, they both groused about the ever-present Secret Service agents that prowled the property, but after a while, they became part of the landscape. All members of the team rotated, except for Al, who became a fixture at the residence but who worked hard to be as unobtrusive as possible. But since his job was to be as obvious a presence as possible to those who would harm the former President, his attempt to disappear was less-than-successful. It also didn't help that he was six-foot-six and had to turn slightly to go through a door.

Maintaining a presence in the public eye held no appeal for either of them, especially for Ahadi. David was a highly paid environmental attorney who continued to practice while his wife was in office—to the extent that he could, given the more-than-occasional need for his presence at events of state. By the time Ahadi took office, he had made full partner at the firm, had fought and won some highly visible cases, and as a result, their future financial needs were taken care of. When their time in DC came to a close, so did David's career with the high-power Washington firm. He sold his ownership stake, took the Bar Exam in Tennessee, and hung out a virtual shingle in his new home state as a consulting attorney. "Now I get to be more selective about the headaches I take on," he was fond of saying.

The four years they had together in Tennessee before David's untimely passing were among the fullest and richest of their lives together, and Ahadi missed him terribly. His absence was a physical pain, a hole in her heart that seemed to fade not at all. She knew the pain would eventually ebb but would never entirely disappear. *Love just sucks,* she thought.

David died on a Tuesday and was buried the following Saturday with full honors at Arlington. The press was there in force, but were, for the most part, respectful of the family's privacy. Ahadi felt anaesthetized for most of it. She eulogized her husband as was expected of her, and then returned with family, under the watchful eye of Al Gordon and the rest of her detail, to Raccoon Holler. For weeks, she never left the house. Both of her children and their respective families lived in the Boston area, and they stayed with her as long as they could, but eventually had to return to their own lives. When they left, she went into lockdown. She went into her bedroom and rarely emerged, other than for meals.

It was Al—and her dead grandmother—who brought her around.

Chapter 14: Transition IV

"I'm worried about her, Doc—she hasn't been out of that bedroom in almost three weeks."

Al Gordon was on the phone with the former president's personal physician. He knew he was breaking protocol, and perhaps a professional or personal boundary or two, but he really did care about Polestar. He knew she was grieving, and he knew that it felt like quicksand. Sometimes it wouldn't let you breathe. He knew the feeling well: 22 months earlier, he had lost his wife to ovarian cancer. The pain, which came out of nowhere—the slightest thing could send him reeling—still cut him like the slash of a razor blade.

"Al, everybody in their own time," the doctor told him, her compassion palpable over the phone. "She'll come out of it, but you just have to give her time."

"I get that, but my job—"

"Your job is to protect her from others. You can't protect her from herself; only she can do that. And if you'll forgive me for saying so, you should know that better than most—sorry. Be there for her, talk to her, but whatever you do, don't pity her and don't feel sorry for her. That's what everybody does, and as you know, it's the most isolating feeling in the world."

He knew. But that didn't make it any easier. He was Secret Service, goddamit. He wanted to OODA-Loop his way out of this—Observe, Orient, Decide, Act. He could observe what was happening, he could orient himself to understand, and he could decide what to do when she finally came out of the house. But act? He couldn't do a damn thing, and her pain was his pain.

Shit.

Chapter 15: Transition V

It was the ghost of her grandmother that finally broke the emotional logjam that kept her sequestered in the dark bedroom.

Ahadi, you get your butt out of that bed. We've got things to do.

Ahadi opened her eyes, looked around the room. Nobody, of course. *Just a dream,* she thought. She closed her eyes, pulled the covers back to her chin.

Did you hear me, young lady? Get that skinny little butt out of bed—we've got places to go, things to do!

Hallucinations. Had to be. I can't even remember the last time I ate, she thought. She punched the pillow, rolled over, put her head back down.

Closed her eyes.

I'm not gonna ask you again. My granddaughter will NOT spend the rest of her days feeling sorry for herself. Now get up! Right now!

Yes indeed. I'm hallucinating. She closed her eyes, started to drift off. This time, she heard the voice, insisting she get out of bed and clean herself up. But this time, the bed shook. It's what her grandmother used to do to get her out of bed in the summer to go berry-picking or to fish in the river.

She pulled back the covers and stood up, still not believing, when suddenly there was a hammering fist on the door, followed by Al Gordon's urgent call.

"Madame President, I have to come in. We've had an earthquake and I need to make sure you're safe."

"A what? An earthquake? In Tennessee?" she replied, reaching for her bathrobe. *God, I'm a mess,* she thought. She opened the door. Al barged in, ducking to clear the jamb. He looked her up and down and physically moved her into the doorjamb.

"Stand right there until I can check the room," he told her, tersely. He proceeded to check all four corners of the room for cracks, examined the windows, looked under the bathroom sink for leaks.

"Al, it wasn't much of an earthquake, if that's what it was," she told him.

"Doesn't matter, ma'am—I still have to check. As soon as we know it's safe, you can … go about your business."

"And what business would that be, Mr. Gordon?" she asked him, somewhat sheepishly. "Living in a cave? I'm sorry—I've been a terrible burden on you as—what's the word you use? A protectee? I'm going to take a shower and get dressed. I must look like a Neanderthal, and probably smell like one, too. Will you take a walk with me, please, when I'm presentable?"

"Yes, Ma'am," he confirmed. "But don't do it on my account. If you're not ready to be out and about—"

"I'm ready, Al—I have to get back to the business of living. Nothing's going to bring David back, so I have to accept that and learn to live with his memory. Besides, my Nana just threatened to kick my ass around the block if I don't get up and get with it."

"Yes, Ma'am. I'll be here when you're ready."

"And Al? could you make a pot of coffee? Make enough for both of us. Thank you."

"Happy to oblige, Ma'am."

Her Nana? Thought Al, as he headed for the kitchen. Well, it brought her back to the land of the living. Whatever. Thanks, Nana.

Chapter 16: Acceptance

The river smells like turtles today, she thought. More often than not, the Mississippi had very little smell, but every once in a while, its—*fecundity* rose from the deep silt and gave it a quality that made the river feel as if it were as alive as the creatures that swam in its depths. She liked it.

"Thanks for this, Al," she smiled. He was walking slightly behind and to her left, between her and the riverbank. His position relative to hers always puzzled her, so one day she asked. He went into a detailed explanation of threat horizons and approach profiles and bad actors and threat vectors. When she asked him to explain what he had said, in English this time, he gave the faintest of smiles, and replied, "My job is to make sure that I am, at all times, between you and the direction of the most credible threat."

So apparently, she thought, he's concerned that some giant sturgeon is going to rise up out of the depths and carry me away.

"Who knew that Tennessee was in an active earthquake area?" she said to him, stepping over a large piece of driftwood. We're not in California."

"No Ma'am, but the New Madrid fault isn't far from here, and it turns out that Tennessee has earthquakes all the time. Most of 'em we can't feel, but every once in a while, they get one that registers a three or four—and there have been bigger ones. In fact, back in 1812 they had one that was so powerful it made the Mississippi run backwards for a few hours."

"So, it took an earthquake to shake me out of my funk," she smirked.

"Don't beat yourself up, Ma'am," he replied, with a slight smile. "It took me a long time, too—and I still have bad days. It never goes away, at least it hasn't for me. But it gets better, I can promise you that." A loud splash in the river caused him to step in front of her; a cormorant, diving on a fish.

"I must have a truckload of mail piling up in the office," she sighed.

"Yes Ma'am, and more than a few phone calls. Most are from well-wishers—we've fielded them for you. But a few need your attention when you're up to dealing with them."

"No time like the present, Al. Let's head back. And Al— I—"

"My pleasure, Madame President."

Chapter 17: Decision Point

13 April 2042

Dear Madame President,

I'm a staff writer, currently on sabbatical leave from the
Times in New York. My last assignment with them of any
substance was a retrospective of your presidency on the ten-
year anniversary of your departure from the White House. I'll
be honest—I didn't want the assignment at first, because
retrospective pieces are often assigned to journalists who, in
the minds of their editors, don't have enough to do. So, I took
it on under protest, but once I got into the project, my
feelings about it changed. In fact, I completed and turned in
the article about you and your time in office on a Wednesday,
and on Thursday, the very next day, I asked my editor for a
leave-of-absence. Why? Because after learning as much
about you as I did, I wanted to write a book. By the way, I've
included a copy of the article.

To be honest, Madame President, when my editor handed
me that assignment, I was burned out and thinking about
leaving journalism. But after doing my research, and after
spending time in your library in Detroit, I felt something I
hadn't felt in a long time—excitement. Without sounding
smarmy, it lit a fire; I want to write a book about you and
your presidency.

But let me be clear. As is the case with all former
Presidents, I could fill a shelf with the books that have been
written about you. In fact, I have, and I've read all of them.
Most are pretty good, but they all have the same fault: They

all provide a laundry list of the amazing things you did while in office, but none of them—at least, none that I've found— focus on why you did the things you did, or how. Personally, I think that's a significant element of your time in the White House. In fact, it may be the most important aspect of your presidency. Why? Because, with all due respect to the authors of those books, assembling a list of what you did challenges those who follow to find reasons to tear you down. But detailing why you did what you did, and how, provides inspiration for others to excel. It also provides a reason to explore the impact of your actions—and how others are building on the foundation you created.

I can only imagine how busy you are, and I know you recently lost your husband (I am deeply sorry). I can't think of any other way to say this, so I'll just ask. Is there anything I could do to convince you to give me an interview? I will happily provide questions in advance, submit to whatever security scrutiny is required (I don't hang out with many Presidents), and of course, validate my credentials with the Times. I am also happy to provide you with a folder of clips to give you a sense of my writing style, as well as a proposed outline for the book.

Thank you in advance for considering my request. I attach my business card with all contact information.

I hope this finds you well and moving toward a sense of peace after your recent loss.

Sincerely,

Michael Meadows

Ahadi read the letter a second time. Placing it on the table, she reached for the pile of articles she had printed, all written by Michael Meadows. They covered a wide range of topics; in fact, he didn't appear to focus on any single theme.

There were interviews with scientists, musicians, and NASA engineers; a couple of investigative pieces that brought him a degree of critical acclaim; a couple of exposés on elderly care facilities; a charming piece about a 9th-grade science fair in New Jersey; a really interesting travel article about Vermont (who knew that it took 40 gallons of sap to make one gallon of maple syrup? No wonder the stuff's so expensive!); and a couple of decent—as in, balanced—Op-Ed pieces.

Two things caught her attention about the writing: one, every article centered around story, rather than a barrage of facts, which she loved; and two, the broad reach of Meadows' work showed that he was driven more than anything else by curiosity.

Glancing over, she saw the letter from Sylvia Antonino, suggesting she meet with Mr. Meadows. She smiled; Sylvia was a consummate professional, but there was clearly more to this than the fact that Meadows was a good writer with a new take on the 'Presidency in Flux,' as so many jokingly called it at the time. Sylvia liked this guy.

What the hell, she thought. It's not like I have to be anywhere.

She picked up the phone and dialed a number in New York.

Part 4: Interview

Chapter 18: Arrival

The sun, golden-yellow, had barely cleared the orange wash above the horizon as I turned into the long driveway that followed the curve of the river for a good quarter of a mile. Tall reeds grew on both sides of the road, person-high, whisking the sides of the car and making me question the directions I'd been given—not to mention the suggested hour of my arrival. I drove along the dirt road, the grasses whispering, when suddenly the road widened and curved gently to the left, opening onto an oasis. A massive live oak, it's chest-thick branches drooping all the way to the ground as if the tree were leaning on its elbows, served as the center point of a flagstone roundabout. Beyond it was the house, a single-level ranch that wrapped around the curve of the oak, its bricks covered with the same green and gray lichens that encrusted the tree. Beyond was a vegetable garden that stretched into the distance, its greenery punctuated with the red and purple and yellow of its bounty. Rows of grapevines draped the hill that rose to the right of the house. Mist from the river drifted among the grapes.

I parked the car and killed the engine. As I stepped out, listening to the ticking of the cooling motor as I grabbed my shoulder bag, two dogs, a small black and white dachshund and a golden lab, came around the corner, barking but not threatening. I stooped to pet them. After two pats on the head the lab lost interest and wandered off; the dachshund rolled over on his back for a belly rub. I obliged.

"I see you've met Killer and Spike," said a deep, slightly southern-inflected voice behind me. "Whatever you do, don't stop rubbing that belly—he'll take your foot off at the ankle if you do."

Turning, I found myself face-to-knee with the lower half of a very large man. He was dressed in jeans and a golf shirt, covered by a windbreaker; I could see the clear pigtail of an earpiece disappearing under his shirt collar.

"I'm Al Gordon," he smiled, extending his hand. I took it (it swallowed mine), and he pretty much lifted me to my feet. "You must be Michael."

"Good to meet you, Al. I assume you're— "

He just smiled and put his arm across my shoulder like a log on a sawhorse. "Let's get you inside—she's ready for you. And dude, you must be on some kind of special list. She's been cooking for two hours making you breakfast. Hell, it was *two years* before she made me a bologna sandwich."

I wasn't sure how to respond to that, so I let him guide me to the front door. Opening it, he called into the cool darkness beyond, a darkness scented with fresh coffee, bacon, and cinnamon.

"Madame President, Mister Meadows is here."

"Be right there," came the reply, a recognizable voice echoing from somewhere in the house. I could see a comfortable great room at the end of the entryway, with floor-to-ceiling windows that provided a view to a stone patio with a fire pit and the river beyond. It was a spectacular setting.

My attention snapped back to footsteps approaching from what I assumed to be the kitchen. Ahadi Fadhili-Mason entered the hallway, her small size belying her much larger presence in my psyche. She had a damp towel thrown over her right shoulder, and a faint sheen of sweat glistened on her brow. Her smile illuminated the darkness as she approached, her hands extended to take mine. Her hair was streaked with gray, a beautiful contrast to her mahogany skin.

"Thank you so much for driving all this way to see me," she said, "and welcome to Raccoon Holler." Her brown eyes locked on my own, and her hands squeezed mine in genuine pleasure. A faint smell of bacon and cinnamon rose from of her clothing.

"The pleasure is genuinely mine, Madame President," I began. "I— "

She withdrew one of her hands and slapped my chest with the back of it.

"We're not on TV, young man, and I'm no longer president, so no more of that 'President' stuff. My name is Ahadi, or you can call me Haddie—that's what my grandkids call me. Whichever works. And by the way, I hope you're hungry. Come on. And Al, join us—I think I made enough to even feed you."

And with that, Ahadi Fadhili-Mason, president of the United States from 2025 through 2031, led me into her bright kitchen, fed me breakfast, and began to tell the story I had driven all this way to hear.

Chapter 19: Reversal

February 17th, 2024 was a routine day at the Johnson Space Center in Houston. The astronauts on board the International Space Station awoke to "We Are Family" by Sister Sledge, and after breakfast and a bit of exercise, they began their heavily scheduled day. Everything was proceeding swimmingly until 1800 GMT, when a transmission was sent from the ISS.

"Houston, Station."

"CAPCOM, Houston. Go for Station."

"Uh, Houston, we've got an anomaly."

"Say again, Station."

"Houston, we're getting some pretty weird readings here—instruments are showing an anomaly—hold one—"

"Station, CAPCOM—how copy?"

"Hold one, Houston. This is—this is strange…"

"We're holding, Station. What do you have?"

"Houston, we're getting really strange readings across the board. Navigation just flipped on every instrument."

"Station, say again—flipped?"

"Houston, every NAV system reads backwards. We've reset twice, no joy. China and Russia modules report the same. Hold one—Japan just confirmed, they've got the same anomaly. What the heck?"

Background noise in control room. "Hold one, Station—we're starting to get reports too—some kind of magnetic thing. May be solar. We're checking with USGS. We'll get back to you, Station—Houston out."

And so, it began.

It's called a Brunhes-Matuyama Event[v], and it wasn't the first time. Throughout the history of the planet, according to the geological record, these events occurred many times, the last one 780,000 years ago. For something of such magnitude, there was no sudden cataclysmic warning, other than some serious oceanic activity that resulted in coastal flooding and happy surfers. The Earth didn't suddenly start spinning the other direction, and the oceans didn't retreat into the depths. The only thing that happened was that GPS became useless, and compasses were backward, and a lot of electric motors didn't know which way to spin, and anything vaguely related to navigation, whether it be on a ship, plane, car, or iPhone, went haywire—because on that date, the Earth's magnetic poles decided to flip. North became south, south became north, and nothing would ever be the same again. But it wasn't the sudden change in polar alignment that drove a stake through the heart of status quo thinking; it was the magnetic realignment of a previously ignored feature of the human anatomy.

Iron is all over the human body: it's a required nutritional substance for good health. An iron atom is the central element—literally—in the hemoglobin molecule[vi], the complicated compound that makes it possible for the circulatory system to transport oxygen to the tissues of the human body. We've known for a long time that certain animal species, most notably birds and eels, have the innate ability to detect the Earth's magnetic fields, which they then use to navigate during their annual migrations, sometimes over thousands of miles. The phenomenon is poorly understood, but there are two theories as to why they are sensitive to the invisible flux lines that run from pole to pole. The first is that there are many species that have tiny flecks of magnetite in their cell membranes, and which are believed to be connected to the nervous system. These structures have electrical ion channels on their surfaces that are pulled open in the presence of a magnetic field[vii].

The second theory is that some species may actually be able to 'see' magnetic fields. Birds, for example, have compounds in their retinal cones called cryptochromes which have unpaired electrons. The spin of these electrons is affected when they are in the presence of a magnetic field, a phenomenon that birds may actually see[viii].

Until the poles reversed, there was little evidence to suggest that humans had any sensitivity to magnetic fields. However, research that was ongoing before the event has now shown that the alpha waves in the brains of human volunteers 'go quiet' when exposed to a magnetic field. The humans don't sense anything, but the alpha waves, which have been described as the 'background noise' in the human brain, definitely respond[ix]. Magnetite crystals were the most likely explanation, and as MRI scans discovered shortly after the reversal event, deep in the limbic brain, scientists began to notice tiny particles of magnetite that were, of course, magnetically charged, like all iron on the planet. They didn't actually discover them; they'd been known about for decades, but as far as scientists could tell, they had no physiological purpose. Some believed them to be evolutionary leftovers, like the appendix, so they were largely ignored. Ignored, that is, until what the National Science Foundation and the US Geological Survey termed the Mulvihill-McCooey event of 2020, named after the two scientists who first discovered the presence and possible role of the limbic ferroliths.

What they also knew was that the Earth's core was becoming increasingly, magnetically volatile. In 2019, the magnetic North Pole was moving—sprinting, as geophysical changes go—toward the northwest at 55 kilometers per year[x]. At the same time, the Earth's magnetic dipole—the clear line that divides a magnet's north and south poles—was becoming increasingly blurry[xi].

Satellite captures of the time showed with great clarity that part of the planet's magnetic field had already reversed in an area of the southern hemisphere, a phenomenon called the South Atlantic Anomaly. Geophysicists called it a reversed flux patch, and between 1960 and 2020 it doubled in size until it covered 20 percent of the planet's landmass[xii].

There were, of course, significant negative consequences from the polar reversal. As the flux reversal progressed, there was a period of time during which the planet's magnetic field's strength ebbed to almost undetectable levels. This allowed much higher levels of ultraviolet light to bathe the planet, resulting in galloping skin cancers, retinal damage, and what will most likely be significant numbers of genetic mutations. Because of this bombardment, some areas of the planet saw huge species die-offs and are on their way to being fundamentally uninhabitable.

Of course, it wasn't all bad, which was why I was here to interview the woman who was president right after it happened. There were a lot of people walking around at the time saying that because of the polar reversal, 2020 was the year that humans finally got 20:20 vision and began to see themselves for the bad neighbors they'd become on this planet. I had no idea; all I knew was that it messed up the birds and the bugs and the satellites. But it interested me, as much for the sociological and cultural aspects of the phenomenon as the scientific. I was here to get a first-hand account of what it was like to deal with the event's aftermath, from someone who actually used it and its impact as one of the greatest levers for societal change of all time.

Chapter 20: Assumption

Ahadi Fadhili-Mason was elected to the presidency as a long-shot candidate who rode into office on a bipartisan wave of abject disgust over the polarization of the nation and abdication by both major parties of their fundamental responsibility to serve the people as elected officials. Born and raised in Detroit, the child of a Tanzanian father and American mother, Fadhili-Mason graduated near the top of her class at Berkeley Law and quickly became a congressional representative in her home state. From there she secured a Democratic congressional seat, where she distinguished herself as the congresswoman with an undergraduate degree in life and a graduate degree in common sense. Many began to refer to her as the founder of the non-existent American Centrist Party because of her ability to pull from both sides of the oceanically-wide aisle. And while the party didn't officially exist, its mission did, at least in her mind, and more importantly, in the minds of her supporters. The presidential fiasco of 2020 opened the floodgates, and in 2025, she became the 47th president of the United States.

Her running mate, a progressive Missouri Republican (who knew there was such a thing) with a long history of centrist, common-sense thinking, began to feel dizzy in the final weeks of the campaign, and shortly after the inauguration was diagnosed with a rare circulatory disorder in his brain that made it impractical for him to continue in the office. With great reluctance Fadhili-Mason accepted his resignation and, pursuant to the 25th Amendment, nominated his replacement—her opponent in the presidential election, something that hadn't happened since the presidency of John Adams[xiii].

The 12th Amendment to the Constitution was proposed after the 1796 election in which John Adams was elected President and Thomas Jefferson was elected Vice-President. They were from opposing parties. Then, in the 1800 election, Thomas Jefferson and Aaron Burr tied, and the House had to hold 36 consecutive votes to break it. They were both members of the Democratic-Republican Party. Ultimately, Jefferson became President, and Burr became Vice-President. The 12th Amendment was ratified in 1804, making the Vice-Presidency an elected position. In that year's election, Thomas Jefferson was re-elected, and George Clinton became his Vice-President[xiv].[*]

All over Washington, legal scholars scoured the law for precedent when Fadhili-Mason selected her VP. The right wing was stupefied—they had no idea how to react to the decision—and after a series of intense, soul-baring conversations with the new president, the man from the other side of the aisle cautiously agreed to accept the position.

"Look," said the newly-elected president, shortly after taking office, to Scott Pelley of *60 Minutes*, "I'm doing this job, which I know is going to be a soul-sucking, bone-crushing experience, for one reason only: Change. Not political change, but deep-in-the-heart-of-America change. I'm tired of conversations about job creation, and empty promises about national unity, and slogan-based leadership about things like technological superiority and world-class schools and infrastructure and accessible healthcare. Enough talk: My goal is to complete one term in office, during which I intend to devote 1,460 days to the kinds of changes that people can feel proud of. If I can't get a few of those things done in four years, then I don't deserve the job. But I *do* deserve the job, so let's wrap this up so I can get started."

"But how will you do that?" countered Pelley. "You're not the first President of the United States to make those promises. Most have tried, and, with respect, most have failed."

"You're right," said Fadhili-Mason. "But the difference is this: four years. I don't intend to commit to four, two of which I'll waste planning the next four. Look, Scott—I want to be remembered for what I left behind, not what I did while I was in office. Legacy has to cook for a long time before it's edible, so I want to do the right thing while I'm in the kitchen. You watch me."

Scott Pelley smiled, and said, "We'll be watching, Madame President. We'll be watching."

Chapter 21: Institutional Voids

"It was all about institutional voids for me, Michael, at least at first," said the former President, reaching across my breakfast plate for the butter dish. "Excuse my boarding house reach. Long before I went into politics—in fact, before I went to law school—I decided to apply my undergrad degrees in political science and sociology to the professional services game. I went to work for Deloitte and hopped on the partner track. It wasn't long before I found myself in a practice that focused on sustainability projects in the developing world—you know, directing targeted investment to road and clinic building, agriculture development, that kind of thing. One of the challenges we ran into, again and again, was what we called institutional voids.

"Let me give you an example. A first-world western bank, maybe European, wants to tap into the rural African market. The middle class is growing there; people are making money, real money, for the first time, and they need a place to put it. But here's the problem. People in rural Africa—hell, AFRICA—don't trust banks. Why? Because they have an annoying habit of opening up, taking deposits, and then closing their doors and disappearing in the middle of the night with depositors' money[xv]. So, people bury their savings in a coffee can under their bed because they won't go near a bank."

She buttered the corner of a waffle as she spoke. "Because people don't trust banks, there's a huge social gap because of a lack of financial services. Without banks, you can't build social services, it's hard to give low-cost loans to people, you can't offer small infrastructure projects, people can't put their money to work to earn interest, and so you can't create wealth or prosperity for a very large segment of the population. In this case, the institutional void isn't the lack of banks—it's the lack of trust. What to do?

"The answer, as it happened, was cultural. We had to develop trust if we had any hope at all of bringing about the changes we wanted to see—and which we knew in our heart of hearts these people desperately needed.

"So, here's what we discovered. Please pass the bacon. There was plenty of trust already there, right under our noses. It was in the community. The village leaders, the elders, were trusted by everyone. So, they became recruits to ensure that people could get paid. Basically, what happened through little companies like TXTEagle[xvi] was that these older, trusted folks became the bankers for the community, for which they were paid a small stipend. Money was transferred to their mobile phones, and they would then transfer money to the individuals in the community for work that was done. These were primarily little tasks—for example, somebody agrees to help dig a well for four hours, that kind of thing. They also made micro-loans when people needed them. And because people trusted the village elder, there wasn't a problem. It didn't matter that there was a big bank behind the scenes that made it all work; the bank was invisible to the people who benefited from its services. So, before long, there was a full-blown financial infrastructure in place that actually worked. The mobile phone, which everybody has, even in the tiniest villages, became the ATM. Hell, they had mobile payment systems long before we had them here[xvii]."

Al walked over to the coffee maker, grabbed the pot and filled our cups. Nodding my thanks, I said, "So, you filled the void, and that created economic growth. Africa was definitely one of your success stories."

"That's not why I told you that, Michael," she smiled. "Africa doesn't have a monopoly on pain, poverty or institutional voids. I told you that story because that's what led me to make some of the first changes I made when I took office, starting with the tax plan. I'll get to that later. One of my dearest friends used to say that 'if you want something different, you have to do something different, because hope is not a strategy.' Well, I jumped into that philosophy with both feet, starting with education. And why? Because this country was a big leaking bag of institutional voids when I took office. Think about it: our roads and bridges were in dire straits; healthcare was an embarrassing disaster; corporations and banks had, for the most part, run amok because of a lack of consumer protection initiatives; and our education system was more concerned about building fancy campuses than they were about preparing people to go to work and create fulfilling lives. It was a very visible, very public disgrace, and after the work I did in the developing world, I knew that the first order of business had to be filling those voids. There was no other option."

"Your education platform was one of the most important—and let's face it, controversial—aspects of your presidency. But it worked."

"Of course, it worked!" she exclaimed. "Look: I took a shitload of heat—pardon my French—because I came out so strongly on the fact that college isn't the only way for people to get educated. Degrees don't fill institutional voids; skills do[xviii]. And skills come from education and training. Notice that I include the word training. Skills are what move a country forward and create competencies for life. Some of the best educated people I know—Lord, I don't know how they keep their shoes tied all day."

I laughed at that. "And some of the smartest people I know barely got out of high school. So, how did 'education' and 'training' differ in your mind at the time?"

"They're opposite sides of the same coin," she responded. "Education teaches us how to think about learning. Training teaches us the skills we need to create change. Both have their place, and both are necessary. Everybody fawns over the woman with the PhD after her name, but they sneer at the plumber. They sneer, that is, until it's Sunday night and they don't have any water. Suddenly that plumber becomes the most important person in their life."

"So true," I laughed. "So, you did some pretty interesting things right off the bat, I understand."

"I sure did. The first thing I did was create a new cabinet position called the Chief Infrastructure Officer, and I appointed Mike Rowe to the position. He thought it was a big joke when I called him, but once I explained what I was looking for, he was all in. See, everybody knew Mike as the guy who did the *Dirty Jobs* show, but how many people know that both of his parents were teachers, or that he has a degree from Towson in Communications, or that he was an Eagle Scout, or that he was a professional opera singer long before he got into television? Or that he runs *Mike Rowe Works*, a scholarship program geared directly at training? That man—what a force of nature. He was like a compassionate tornado."

"You are so right," I nodded. "I think the silverbacks would have killed him if they didn't already love him so much."

She laughed into her coffee. "But look at the results he got for being a non-politician. The first thing he did was take the STEM curriculum to task. I mean, here's the guy who became a household name by being the voice of the working guy, mister blue collar, and the first thing he does is change STEM to STEAM by including the Arts. That's what you get from an opera singer." She shook her head in amusement.

"The next thing he did, or I guess I should say that the next thing that happened, was that there was a renaissance in the Trades," she continued. "That was huge. Suddenly, and I still think it had something to do with that magnetic thing, although I can't underestimate Mike's influence, suddenly people started to look at blue collar jobs as really honorable professions. Look, my Daddy was a plumber. I used to go into his workshop and marvel at all those tools and valves and such and wonder how he knew so much. Well, with Mike at the helm, suddenly it was a good thing—a respectable thing—to be a food server, or a plumber, or an electrician, or a telecom installer, or a builder, or a bricklayer. People started going to school to learn how to be a professional waiter, because suddenly it wasn't a job you did because you couldn't do anything else—it was a job you did because it called to you. That was pure magic!"

"And if you don't mind me saying so," interjected Al, "I'm pretty sure that that was when the teachers had their day, too."

"Yes indeed," said Ahadi (by now I'd been admonished into submission—it was Ahadi, nothing else). "But that wasn't all Mike; he had help on that one. Again, we're pretty sure we can thank the Mulvihill-McCooey flux reversal for a lot of what happened, or for at least paving the way, because people just went a little bit wacky. The first thing that happened was that teachers woke up one day and went to work and realized that parents saw them very differently. There was respect there, and more than that, because the parents gave the teachers free reign to do what they needed to do in the classroom, the kids, for the most, started to show them respect. It took a while, but it was there. Suddenly it was good to be a teacher again. And on top of that, the damn politicians went all haywire." She laughed, shaking her head. "I've seen some weird shit in my time, but that topped it all.

They were knocking each other down to be the first to vote in funding to make sure that schools at all levels across the country had enough resources to do what they needed to do. Then the whole preschool thing started, and then they were going public, telling God and everybody how ashamed they were that they had cut funding to schools. If I hadn't seen it with my own eyes, I'd have put it right up there with unicorns and pixies."

"Can I take a little detour for a minute? I asked. "Will you tell me about the thinking behind your Cabinet Council of Learners? Because that was another pretty wild departure from the norm."

"Yeah, that was the result of a brainstorming session I had one evening over a bottle of Scotch with a few people," she began. "Let's see—who was there? Mike, of course; I think Rick Steves was there; José Andrés; the heads of the NEA and the National Teachers Union; and I think I might have had a few others. Yes—now I remember; Stephen King and Neil Young were there, too. Anyway—"

"I'm sorry to interrupt you, but I have to ask. We're talking about national education, and you're telling me that you pulled together an advisory council made up of a marijuana-smoking travel writer, a professional chef, a couple of educators from the NEA and the NTU, a horror novelist—"

"—And a musician—love me some Crazy Horse—and don't forget Mister Dirty Jobs. Yes, that's right. Why? Why all those non-experts in education, except for a couple? Well, let me tell you a story.

"One of the most influential books I ever read was called, 'The Age of Wonder: The Romantic Generation and the Discovery of the Beauty and Terror of Science,' by a guy named Richard Holmes. It's the only book I've ever read where I got to the last page and immediately went back to page one and read the whole thing again. You know what I learned in that book? I learned about Consilience. I learned that Ada Lovelace was the daughter of Lord Byron, the poet, and that she was good friends with Charles Babbage, who created this mechanical computer called the Difference Engine. But it never worked, until Ada got ahold of it and created the first working computer. The damn thing had something like 20,000 gears in it.

I learned that Lord Byron's good friend was an astronomer named William Herschel, who built the first really big telescopes in the world with his sister over in the UK. I learned about Humphrey Davy, a chemist who invented the explosion-proof mining lamp and discovered all kinds of things including the properties of nitrous oxide, and whose best friend was Samuel Taylor Coleridge, the poet who wrote the poem *Kubla Khan*— 'In Xanadu, did Kubla Khan, a stately pleasure dome decree.' Remember that? And I learned about Michael Faraday, who invented the electric motor and the transformer by day and wrote really compelling poetry by night[xix].

Then there was the poet John Keats, the 'Ode on a Grecian Urn' guy, who was also a medical student. And how about Mary Shelley, the physician who also wrote *Frankenstein*. And you know why her last name was Shelley? Because she was married to Percy Bysshe Shelley, the famous poet who wrote *Ozymandias* and *Ode to the West Wind*[xx].

"Do you see what's common here, Michael? Every one of these scientists—and they were giants of the time—was married to an artist of some kind, or whose best friend was one. And every one of these people stated clearly that their association with the other made their work better, richer, stronger.

"So, yeah—I had a weird team. But look where they took us. Today, all kids are strongly encouraged to spend a year after high school, doing a work-study program in a country where English is NOT the primary language. It isn't mandatory, but it might as well be—just about everybody does it, because if they do, the cost of their first year of university or trade school is comped. Sure, we got a lot of pushback about the tax burden. Do you know when that went away? It went away when those kids started coming back from their overseas programs with results. Keep in mind that they have to do a pretty big assignment that requires them to come back with ideas about fixing some aspect of our institutional voids. Some of those ideas had serious legs."

"Right," I conceded. "Just look at Detroit."

She shakes her head, takes a long drink of coffee, moves a bit of bacon around on her plate with her finger. "That poor city. Of course, I wouldn't say that now! But back then, it was a punching bag. High crime? Detroit. Bad water? Detroit. Crappy schools? Detroit. Racial shit? Again, Detroit. We managed to get it turned around, but it took some serious work. And we pretty much had to reinvent what it meant to be a city."

"Yeah," I conceded, "But it also became the model for cities all over the country, as near as I can tell."

"For a lot of them, yes," she agreed.

"Did you take an institutional void approach on that one?" I asked.

"Yes, I did. Actually, no. No, that's not true—scratch that. I built my whole campaign around institutional voids. But this was different—this was a problem of social voids."

I raised my hand to stop her. "Explain that, please."

"I'm not sure I can, but I'll try," she said. "Al, would you mind putting on another pot of coffee? You guys will drink a little more, won't you? She asked.

I smiled. "I never turn down good coffee, but I'm going to have to make room for more before I drink another drop."

She laughed, pointing down the hall. "Second door on the left."

I thanked her and went into the bathroom. When I came back, I noticed a framed photograph on the wall in the hallway that I hadn't seen before. It was big—easily four feet wide—an aerial photograph of Detroit taken after the city went through its "Smart Transformation." I'd seen similar photos in my research, but never one that showed so much— or at such scale. I was gobsmacked. I just stood and stared.

"It's quite a place, isn't it?" she said, putting a hand on my shoulder. "That area there, Dearborn Heights, was pretty much a war zone. The snarkier politicians talked about just bulldozing the whole damn city into the lake. Honestly, at the time, I had a hard time disagreeing. It really was a bad place."

"How did it change?" I asked. "I mean, what was the thing that really pulled it back?"

"Hang on." She walked away and came back with two cups of fresh coffee.

"It's easy to toss out phrases like urban renewal and gentrification, but those are just words," she explained. "What made the difference was the new Mayor. Degree from UC Davis in Precision Agriculture, Marine Corps vet, African-American, Iraq, Somalia, Afghanistan—all the garden spots. To him, 'dangerous Detroit' was amateur hour. But it was more than that. He was a Peace Corps volunteer for two years before joining the military, and his Dad was a minister in Dearborn. There was a whole lot of passion in that man—it came off of him in waves—but he also had a very, very finely tuned bullshit meter. He loved that town, but politics had failed it so many times that there just wasn't any trust left."

"Like your Africa example," I noted.

"In a manner of speaking, yes," she replied. "But it was more than that. Like I said, this was more about social voids than institutional. The people who lived in Detroit felt abandoned, betrayed, and ignored. Promises were made to them that were never kept. So, the new Mayor swept in, and the response was what he expected—same shit, different day. Not my circus, not my clowns.

"The thing is, he and I went to school together. So, a couple of months after becoming Mayor, he called me and asked for help.

"I don't need money," he said. "What I need is ideas. I need to plug into your idea factory to see what I can harvest."

"So, I introduced him to Mike for starters, and they had a few conversations. Then they added in a few more people: Elon Musk, my Chief Transportation Officer, Doug Standley, my Chief Applied Technology Officer, and Mary Slaughter, my Chief National Talent Officer. They decided to do a skunk works thing. They picked one neighborhood—I think it was the Old Redford District, south of Eight Mile Road—and said that they were going to work with the people there to do something radical. Then, if it worked on a small scale, they'd push to go big.

"What did they do? I mean, how did they get started?"

"Well, I shared a few thoughts to get 'em thinking. I told them about the whole institutional voids thing, but I warned them that this was more about social voids—things like trust, loyalty, compassion, collaboration, communication, creativity—a lot of 'C' words there—and that they had to fix those before they could go after the institutional stuff. Then I told them that if they wanted to fill the social voids, they had to actually demonstrate the qualities that would do so. In other words, if they expected collaboration in their test neighborhood, they damn well better be prepared to show the folks who lived there what cooperation looks like when it's done well. Actions speak louder than words, you know. It's the first rule of storytelling, or journalism, for that matter: show 'em, don't tell 'em.

"I also told them that being prescriptive would kill the whole thing before it ever got started. They had to reverse-engineer it for the folks in the neighborhood so that they could see *what could be*, instead of focusing on *what was*. That's always been the essence of leadership for me, you know. I'm a pretty simple person, and to me, a good leader is somebody who can paint a clear picture of what things COULD look like instead of what things DO look like. I mean, why would I follow somebody who doesn't offer me anything different at the end of the rainbow? It reminds me of a sign I saw once at Deloitte on a cubicle wall that said, 'Where are they? Where did they go? I have to find them, I'm their leader!'

"There was a guy who used to work at Apple way back in the beginning. His name was Alan Kay, and he was a member of the brain trust when they first got started. Very smart guy. He gave a talk a long time ago, and during that talk, he said something really interesting. He said, 'The best way to predict the future is to invent it[xxi].' I've never forgotten that; so, when we first started talking about Detroit, I shared that quote with them. I told them that the only way this would work was if they could work with the folks in Redford to invent the future."

I thought for a moment before I spoke.

"Detroit's a big place, and with all the problems they had, I'm surprised they could even figure out a place to begin," I challenged. "How did they get off the ground?"

Ahadi smiled and nodded. "They listened," she smiled. "they listened, and they paid attention. The Mayor first went into the schools. And when I say the Mayor went into the schools, I mean *the Mayor went into the schools.* By himself. No entourage, just him, a handful of questions, and a boatload of listening. He asked the teachers what their biggest challenges were. He asked them magic wand questions— 'If you could wave your magic wand and change one thing in the classroom, in your school, in the neighborhood, for your students, for their parents, what would it be? What would this place have to look like for you to wake up in the morning an hour before the alarm clock goes off because you can't wait to get to work?'

"Well, they unloaded on him, and they said all the right things—at least, they did once he got them to open up. He had to give them permission to dream. And he had to listen to their dreams. And then once he heard them, he had to give them space and resources to make those dreams real."

"Wow—no pressure," I half-laughed. "So, what kinds of things did they tell him?"

"Pretty much what he expected," she replied, "although there were a few surprises. You familiar with Maslow's Hierarchy of Needs? Yes?" I nodded. "Well, most of the things they hit him with were from the lowest levels of the hierarchy. Food security. Safety. Total lack of self-esteem. And then there were the issues with the parents: Job insecurity. Feeling hopeless about being able to take care of your family. Racial crap. They pretty much checked all the boxes for a first-class shit-show."

"Not the kind of stuff you knock off in a half-day workshop," I observed.

"And especially," she emphasized, "not the kind of stuff you knock off when government gets involved. Ever hear the expression, 'A camel is a horse designed by a committee'? Change 'a committee' to 'government.' So, after meeting with the teachers, the mayor decided to meet with the kids, starting with the high schools. He asked the teachers to recommend a handful of students that he could meet with that showed promise. They didn't have to have great grades, or even be on a college track. He wanted leaders, influential kids who could carry a message back if they chose to, or kids who demonstrated a special skill that others admired—science, writing, wood shop, automotive repair, music, whatever. He ended up with about 25 kids who agreed to meet with him. So, on a particular day, after school, the Mayor sent a bus to the three or four schools—I can't really remember how many there were—to pick up the kids. It drove 'em down to city hall. The Mayor met them in the lobby and took them up to a fancy meeting room that had a brass plaque on the door that said, 'Redford Skunk Works.' There was a board room table, and at each seat there was a professional nameplate for each person—Mr. Jackson or Ms. Almendale or Mr. Smith. There was also a pad of paper, a set of pens, a lanyard with an empty transparent access card holder, and a Mac Air laptop. He invited 'em all to sit down at their places.

"Look," he told them. "I'm gonna put my cards on the table. I need your help. You're here because you're smart, outspoken, opinionated, willing to work hard when you want to, and respected by your peers. You all live in Redford, which means you know it better than I do. It also means that you know what's working and what's not in the neighborhood.

"This city has become the country's punching bag, and as far as I'm concerned, that's bullshit. Do we have problems? Sure—all cities do. But if we do the political thing and spend our time telling people how wrong they are about Detroit, that's a waste of calories. We have to *show* them they're wrong. And the way I'm going to do that is by reinventing Detroit, one neighborhood at a time, starting with Redford.

"But here's the thing: I'm not going to do it: You are. I need you to be my advisory board. I'm going to give you a bunch of questions that I need answers to, and I need you to get the answers. And by the way, this is not a volunteer mission: I'm going to pay you a good salary to do this, because I expect professional behavior for professional pay. And before you ask, no, you don't get a break on schoolwork."

One of the girls raised her hand and asked, holding up the empty badge holder, "What do we do with this stuff?"

"OK," he told her, "first, you don't have to raise your hands. This isn't school. The answer to your question is that if you agree to be on the task force, your paychecks will start in two weeks, and you'll be given a cardkey that lets you into this building any time you want, and into this room any time you want. In fact, the only people who will be allowed in here are me and you. Nobody else: This is our show, and only our show. And those laptops in front of you are yours to keep.

"I need serious help here, folks, and I'm not going to get it from the politicians I normally have to work with. I want to work with people who give a shit about their neighborhood, and who are willing to help me reinvent the city. Your job is going to be helping me figure out what that looks like. So: are you in?"

"Wow," I breathed. "So, what happened?"

"Everything happened, Michael," she said. "At first, the kids were suspicious, but once that first paycheck arrived, they were pretty dedicated. The Mayor gave them spending money for transportation back and forth to City Hall and gave them a budget for things like interview recorders and such. Then he gave them his questions, which were pretty much the same questions he asked the teachers and told them to ask them to people around the neighborhood. On their own, they had to gather the information, and then prepare a report for him.

"The answers were pretty much the same as what the teachers said—food, jobs, racial issues, all that stuff. So, the next assignment he gave them was to prioritize the wish list, and then put together a plan to fix the thing at the top of the list, which turned out to be food security."

"And that's what led to this," I said, pointing to the area in the picture south of 8 Mile Road.

"Not at first," she said. "First, they decided that if food is a problem for a lot of people, then they needed to make it available to them. But this is where we get back to the whole social voids thing: they had food shelves, but people avoided them because of the stigma of being poor and having to be on the dole. So, the kids came up with a pretty interesting idea: they'd turn one of the school fields at each high school into a farm field and grow food for the neighborhood. But there was a catch: to qualify for food, you had to work on the farm.

"When the Mayor heard about this idea, he reached out to me, and I put him in touch with Doug Standley, my tech guy. It turns out that just to the east of the Redford neighborhood there's a community college with a pretty strong IT and telecom program. Doug, who built lots of high-tech Ag programs in partnership with universities and cities all over the world, went to the college and offered to help them get started with an Ag Tech program, IF they'd agree to help the kids with their farm startup. They agreed. He also told them that if the program showed success, they'd have the right of first refusal for a follow-on initiative that would be even bigger than the farm."

"And this?" I asked, pointing to the photo again.

"THIS is what happens when a plan comes together," she laughed. "The high schools agreed to the plan, because it would help them offset the cost of subsidized meals for kids living below the poverty level. It also taught skills that those kids and even some of the adults could take away and use to get a job. Some of them did, especially when Mary Slaughter, my Chief Talent Officer, got involved. The next thing that happened was that a partnership arose sort of organically between the high schools and the community college. Thanks to Doug's help, the community college started a Smart Agriculture program that taught farmers and would-be farmers how to use technology to improve crop yield, predict conditions that could affect the crops, reduce water usage, and cut down on the costs associated with fertilizer, insecticide, seed, and so on. The kids applied for grants from tech companies for what they wanted to do, and some of them came through, which helped them offset the cost of the technology. The grape growers over by the lake were the first to jump on-board, but they weren't the last. Word got out pretty quickly, and soon everybody wanted a piece of the action.

"Meanwhile, the kids were going gangbusters on what they called their "No Harm Farm." Community members worked the crops; the kids got lessons on business, agriculture, technology, botany, chemistry, marketing, and sales; and pretty soon, lo and behold, the stigma went away. People worked for their community farm and were proud to be part of it. And then, magic happened. In their second year of production, they ran a surplus. They had more food than they could dole out. So, they—and when I say they, I mean the kids—started a barter program with an Illinois cattle ranch to trade produce for meat. And, they opened a little farm stand.

"What happened next was just this side of magic. As you know, my Chief Transportation Officer, Elon Musk—Good Lord, that man was a handful, but smart! —Elon had a look at what they were doing and suggested the neighborhood repurpose some of its transportation infrastructure to support more farming. After all, these kids were running a surplus on a farm the size of a high school soccer field; what would happen if they had more space?"

"And that's when this started to happen?" I asked, pointing once again at the aerial photograph on the wall.

"That's when this started to happen," she confirmed. "Elon assigned a team of people to work with the city people in Detroit. They looked at traffic patterns in Redford, road usage, car ownership, availability of public transportation, home vacancies, and a slew of other things. They looked at a map, and they made a decision. A six square-block area with high numbers of empty houses would be their first project— right here," she said, pointing at the map. Major east-west roads formed a ladder with north-south streets forming the rungs, but every other north-south street was no longer a street—it was farmland. And some of the houses had been converted to storage for equipment.

"You know how people talk about the Law of Unintended Consequences?" she asked me.

I nodded.

"Well, Detroit pretty much rewrote that law. In those days, smart cities weren't here yet, but everybody was talking about them—how streetlights would go on and off when you walked under them, that kind of thing. But once things started happening in Redford, and the press found out about it, 'Poor Old Detroit' became 'Pretty Cool Detroit.' And as soon as things started happening, I let the dogs out. Doug and Elon and Mary started talking about how Detroit could become a truly smart city, and that's when they showed the world what they and the kids had been doing, under the radar, for the last couple of years. That little college—I think it was called Wayne County—and the high schools—built a technology program for agriculture. They did analytics, and networking, and IoT, and food science. And they had already wired Redford as a smart community. They tracked water usage and sewage output, built pathogen detectors to track infections in sewage, turned Wayne into a smart campus, and a whole bunch of other things. Michael, it put that little place on the map. They had a big grand opening to show the world. I was there to congratulate them, and I'll be damned if Al Gore and Bill Gates didn't show up, as well. And sure enough, my old friend Scott Pelley was there with a smile on his face. We spent a couple of minutes together, and he just shook his head and laughed.

"Well, you did what you said you were going to do, Madame President. I told you we'd be watching. And here we are. So, what's next?"

Well, I just smiled at him and said, "Scott, you'll know when I do."

Chapter 22: Course Corrections I

Ahadi took me by the arm and led me toward the back of the house. "Before it gets too warm, let's take a walk outside. I'd like you to see what we're doing here. We've got quite a little farm going of our own."

We walked out the back door onto the patio. It was ten o'clock, and the chill had left the air. I heard people talking in the vineyard, and recognized Al's voice as we approached. He came over to check on us, see if we needed anything.

"We're good, Al; go back to whatever you're doing," she said, patting him on the back.

"He's probably the first member of a presidential security detail that also gets to be a farmer," she laughed.

"He seems like a great guy," I replied.

"He's the best," she nodded with a smile. "Al's been with me from day-one. I'm pretty much the only family he's got, so we're joined at the hip. When David died, he stayed with me. He's not my husband, but he might as well be. We pretty much share a brain."

Fifty feet away, I could see Al, surrounded by a handful of farm workers. He was speaking with them in easy, fluent Spanish, waving his arms around, and they all laughed at whatever joke he was telling. One of them saw us standing nearby, smiled, and waved. Ahadi smiled and waved back.

"Can we talk a little more about your education initiatives?" I asked. "I mean, you did a lot of things while you were in office, but I don't think anything had as much impact as those did."

"Well," she chuckled— "let's give credit where it's due.

The flux reversal had a lot to do with what I was able to get done. Remember, I suddenly found myself in a situation where people were actually willing to listen to what I had to say. It was like everybody took a Mister Rogers pill and pretty much overnight, everything changed. So, I made hay while the sun was shining.

"The first sign that things were off was when people started treating each other nicer. It was just weird. Instead of parents defending their kids' bad behavior in school like rabid jackals, they started giving teachers the benefit of the doubt. They volunteered in the classroom. I'm telling you: the teachers didn't know what to do. And when the politicos started throwing money at the schools to atone for their bad behavior, it was like Christmas in July."

"Yeah, I studied that for a year and still don't understand it," I replied, shaking my head. "But based on what I read, you didn't waste any time."

"No, I didn't," she said, walking toward a tall, leaf-covered structure in the distance beyond the rows of grapevines. "Nobody knew if this was going to last; hell, for all I knew, I'd wake up and realize it was all a bad dream. So, I figured I might as well jump in with both feet."

We had now reached the leaf-covered structure, and I saw that it was a frame supporting hop plants. "Making beer, are you?" I joked.

"I'm not, but a little brewery downtown is, using my hops. They have an IPA that will make your socks roll up and down called 'Madame President.' It's just a little bitter, and it packs a wallop. I've got some here; I'll give you one later.

"By the way, that reminds me. You probably didn't notice, but one of the blocks in Detroit got turned into a hop farm, and the kids got a contract with a brewery in town to make some kick-ass beer. The deal they made was that in exchange for the hops they provided to the brewery, they'd get a percentage of the profits from the sale of the beer, and it would go toward the farm, their food programs, and if anything was left, a scholarship fund. In fact, I have the same deal here; the profits I make on the hops go to international relief programs and domestic education initiatives. Bottom line is that I learned a hell of a lot from working with the folks in Detroit—things that helped me with my own programs."

"If my understanding of history is correct, you started with the prisons, right?"

"You're damn right I did," she said, sternly. For the first time, I saw a tiny sign of the toughness that she'd come to be known for during her presidency. *Get in my way at your peril. The last person who did hasn't been found yet.*

"I don't have to tell you why, either," she continued. She was on a roll. "We talked about institutional voids and social voids, but our prison system was in a league of its own. It was a disgrace—inhuman. Department of Corrections, my ass. There was no correcting going on; the system was an excuse for private contractors to make money on the backs of the incarcerated, many of whom had no business being there.

"Look—I'm no Pollyanna. We had some baaaad assholes locked up who didn't deserve to ever see the light of day again. But when a kid gets put in prison for stealing an apple because he's hungry, or a bottle of aspirin because his mama's sick, he's not a criminal—at worst, he's a Robin Hood trying to do the right thing in a world that's stacked against him from the get-go. He's desperate. So, yeah, I went after the prisons."

"Pushback?"

"You're damn right there was pushback. All that happy pill stuff from the flux reversal only went so far. So, I pulled together the Cabinet and told 'em I wanted a plan on my desk within a month that would help us flip the whole system on its head. Mike Rowe led it, because even though he was technically my Chief Infrastructure Officer, more than anything else he was the country's Chief Common-Sense Officer. Nobody has a bullshit meter like Mike's, and he wasn't afraid to use it—it didn't matter who was in the room. Mary Slaughter led the whole talent development part of the project. What a force of nature SHE is.

"So, what Mike and his folks did was look at the whole situation and reverse-engineer it back. After a couple of months of studying it—and they worked around the clock, I was told—they came to see me in the Oval and told me to sit down because they had a ludicrous idea that couldn't possibly work but that it was the best idea they could come up with. I'll never forget that conversation; I've never seen a more energized group of people.

"What they told me was that they started with the outcome and worked back from there. By the time a kid— and such a high percentage of the incarcerated citizens were kids, and, no surprise, kids of color—by the time a kid leaves the prison system, he's screwed—he doesn't have a snowball's chance in hell of making it in the outside world. He's vilified, he's branded, he's marked, and on top of that, he's like Rip Van Winkle: while he's been locked away in a box, the world has moved on around him, so he might as well be stepping out of a rocket on Mars. He can't get a job; he has no discernible skills; he can't fit in anywhere except among the people he should be avoiding; he can't make friends or become part of a community; the only thing he's prepared for is to commit another crime and go back into the system.

"Mike Rowe said it best when he told me that they had identified what they called 'the crap triangle': Poverty on one corner, poor self-esteem on another, poor preparation on the third. He called it the cause-and-effect from hell. Kid grows up in poverty because the social system puts him there. That same system stacks the deck against him by making it nearly impossible for him to get a decent education, so he can't learn a skill, or a trade, or get a degree. He lives in a dangerous neighborhood through no fault of his own, so he doesn't live—he survives. He's hungry all the time, so he can't concentrate, and if he IS in school, his grades suffer. His family is in desperate straits because they can't get jobs either, so substance abuse and violence creep in. He's black, or brown, or from the wrong neighborhood, so he MUST be a criminal. And pretty soon, guess what—he starts to believe the shit that people say about him. He's so desperate to be somebody that he becomes an easy target for gangs and other ne'er-do-wells who offer him community, fucked up though it may be—pardon my language."

"Sounds like the never-ending problem in the Middle East with the recruitment of young men into radical groups," I observed.

"That's because it's exactly the same thing. People want to belong; we're tribal. We're social animals. The problem is that we *are* animals, and we'll behave like one if the social community part isn't available to us.

"So, Mike proposed something radical, and impossible, and unavoidable. He and his group concluded that there really is a linkage between the three things on that triangle. First, a lack of education and marketable skills makes it impossible for a person to play a role in a capitalistic society, and like it or not, good or bad, that's how the world works. Second, without a skill, it's impossible to play in the economy. In other words, if you can't do something that society needs, you can't make money, buy a house, start a family, live a full life. Third, if you can't do those things, if you spend your whole life with your face pressed against the glass door of civil society but they won't let you in, your self-esteem goes away.

"'But watch,' he said, 'Watch what happens when we grind off the corners of our triangle of crap. We make sure that every kid—EVERY kid—gets three square meals a day. We reinvent education so that it creates people who have options, because they have skills. We kill this stupid idea that becoming a plumber, or an electrician, is what you do if you're not smart enough to get a degree—that's nonsense.' Man, he was on a roll.

"The more Mike talked, the more energized the conversation got. 'The next thing we do is work with companies like LinkedIn and Salesforce to create a platform to connect graduates to jobs. And I don't just mean people with degrees. I'm talking about welders, plumbers, telecom techs, IT people, bakers, truck drivers, and all those other trades that people sneer at but can't live without. We do everything we can to connect a candidate to a job so that they can make money, feel good about themselves, and put a stake through the heart of the crap triangle.' In fact, they started a little campaign that said, 'No more blue-collar jobs. Now they're blue-sky jobs, because the sky's the limit.'"

She smiled at the ground as we walked along a path that led toward the river.

"When the group finished their presentation to me, Mike looked over and said, 'There's one more thing.'

'OK, I replied, what is it?'

He looked over at the group, who sat there, half-smiling and half wetting their pants.

'We start with the prisons. We want to turn the prisons into schools.'

"Well, I didn't see that coming, so I asked him to say more. Mary laughed and said, 'Yes, Mike, say more.' That got a big laugh out of the whole group, let off a little pressure. Remember, the poles had reversed, and because of those ferroliths in everybody's head, the whole world had gone squirrely. Pretty much anything was possible, even though we had no idea how long it might be that way. So, because I encouraged him, he hit me with both barrels.

'Look—Madame President—the prisons don't work. The whole system is set up to pretty much guarantee recidivism. You know that poster that says, 'The beatings will continue until morale improves'? Well, that pretty much sums up prison life. It's beyond horrible. But when we dug into it, it turns out that it's worse than we thought.

'Let me first say that there are people in prison who *should* be in prison—no one's denying that. But there are a lot—and it may be the majority of them—that shouldn't be. Should they be in some kind of correctional program? For the most part, yeah. But locking them up isn't the answer, not if you want to actually make a difference.

'So, we went looking for options, and we found one. It's called Restorative Justice, and it got started among the Maori of New Zealand, believe it or not[xxii]. You may wonder why we picked a program from a society that still ate each other in the mid-19th century but go with us for a minute.

'This system that they came up with recognizes that education is key to a civil society. And in fact, city police departments around the United States are already using it, and here's how it works. When somebody does something that we would consider to be criminal—and we're talking non-violent crime, now—they have to go in front of a council of their peers that includes the person or people they harmed when they committed whatever crime they did, representatives from the justice system including police and attorneys, uninvolved members of the community, sometimes even people who committed a similar crime and went through the program themselves. They have to listen to each person tell their story, how the crime affected them, what the consequences have been, and so on. They're asked to make a statement, which the others listen to.

'At some point in the process, the law enforcement folks and the attorneys have their say, which is to explain what the alternative to the program is—and they pull no punches. They explain what the person would have to go through if they were remanded to court, how much it would cost, what the impact would be on their family, and that there would be long-term consequences, starting with jail time and ending with a criminal record. They also make it very clear that this is a one-time offer: Take this opportunity or suffer the consequences.

'They then jointly decide what kind of restorative action the person has to engage in to pay for their offense, and it usually involves doing some kind of research, community service, financial compensation over a period of time, and so on. But what matters isn't the process, Madame President.

What matters is that it works. Less than four percent of petty criminals brought before a Restorative Justice board commit another crime[xxiii]. *That's a 96% success rate.* I'm pretty sure the numbers from incarceration are just about the opposite of those.'

"Well," Ahadi continued, "I was pretty speechless. So, I went back to the cryptic comment he made about converting the prisons into schools.

'Right. So, if the crap triangle is real, and we're pretty

sure it is, then the only way to escape from it is to blow through one of the corners. So, we figured that we'd start with education, and what better place than in a prison, where you already have your target audience? When you look at these people, most of them never finished school—hell, a lot of them barely made it out of junior high school—and it's not their fault. So, we decided the best course of action is to take them back to school.

'Let me also go on record for my colleagues before they throw shoes at me and say that we're not stupid. This hare-brained idea doesn't imply that violent criminals or serial criminals can all be rehabilitated; that's naïve. But for non-violent criminals, there's a different way to achieve the goal of a forward-looking corrections system. If a lack of education is one of the main factors that leads to poverty, and poverty leads to low self-esteem, and low self-esteem leads to desperation, and desperation leads to criminal behavior, well, I say we cut the head off the snake. Let's go full-on and give these people what they need—an education, a skill, a craft, a trade, and then let's get them a job. We're gonna keep them so damn busy working and earning money that they won't have time to get into trouble.

'Oh, one other thing. I'm not channeling Studs Terkel here. I'm not suggesting another make-work WPA program that the right wing will crap all over. We've got roads and bridges that are so old they're downright dangerous, our schools are falling apart, our telecommunications infrastructure is sub-par and that's being kind, we've got huge gaps in the ranks of the first responders, teachers have way too many kids in their classrooms because there aren't enough of 'em, our national parks need work, and we've got a major deficit in the trades. So how about we build a system where instead of being paroled, you graduate? Wouldn't that be a better outcome? And by the way, we're thinking of a

'Have Gun, Will Travel' model,' referring to a television show from the 50s. 'But in this case the model is 'Have skill, will travel'. We're gonna create a skills library that people can check people out from who have the skill they need.'"

The WPA reference wasn't lost on me. Created in response to the Great Depression of 1929, the Works Progress Administration was part of Roosevelt's New Deal and was formed to put people to work on public infrastructure projects like roads and buildings. But it also spawned other projects that created magic. For example, The Federal Writers' Project published nearly 300 books and launched the careers of some of our most cherished authors, including Loren Eiseley, Ralph Ellison, Saul Bellow, John Cheever, Zora Neale Hurston, and Studs Terkel. Without the WPA, it's likely that many of these authors' works would never have seen the light of day. But it wasn't just writers. Part of FDR's plan included the Civilian Conservation Corps, the folks who built a lot of the infrastructure in the nation's national parks. A lot of it's still in-use, although it's getting pretty long in the tooth.

Of course, that's the beauty of 20:20 hindsight; detractors called the WPA a 'make-work project,' and derided it at every turn. But the way I looked at it, the country was desperate, and as Mike Rowe pointed out, desperation leads nowhere good. Assessing the value of the WPA as a make-work program was short-sighted; assessing it for the results it created was something else entirely.

"One thing we haven't talked about," I asked, "is the role that your vice-president played. What you did there, picking a VP from the enemy camp, was a pretty radical move. Why did you do that? I mean, what were you trying to accomplish? Some would argue that you let the fox into the henhouse."

She nodded, thinking. "Keep in mind that I wasn't immune from the effects of the Reversal," she began. "When it came to how I thought about the opposing party, I had my own fair share of jaundice when I started out. But I knew that business-as-usual wasn't going to cut it. It wouldn't work, and the people wouldn't stand for it.

"I did a lot of soul-searching before I selected my VP, and the conclusion I came to wasn't where I expected to end up. Look: When it comes to politics, we have a terrible tendency to engage in a lot of othering."

I interrupted. "I don't know what that is."

"Simple. There's Us, and then there's The Others. We look at those that are different from us and think of them as 'those Others over there.' Political alignment, skin color, race, creed, gender, age, whatever. What that leads to, and it's another piece of the whole tribalism thing, and by the way, it's usually sub-conscious, is that they're The Others, so they don't matter as much. It's not that they don't matter—it's that they don't matter *as much*. There's a difference. Whatever happened to 'We, the People?' It doesn't say 'us and them.' Or E Pluribus Unum? From the many, one? Same message.

"I had this epiphany when the time came to select my VP. Keep in mind that I had already picked somebody from my own party, but he got sick and I had to fill his shoes. People kept telling me to pick somebody who would bring value to my presidency. That word kept coming up: Somebody who would bring value, somebody with the right values, somebody whose values were in alignment, and so on.

"What happened was that I fixated on the word, but I also got fixated on something else—a different word. *Loser.* People were referring to my opponent in the election as 'the loser.' He wasn't a loser; he was the other side's best candidate because he demonstrated adherence to the values that they stood for. How is that a loser? And by the way, do you know what the word 'value' means? I looked it up, and I've never forgotten it. It comes from Latin, and it means 'the qualities that make you strong.' Same root as 'valor.' So, I got to thinking: If I choose not to see my opponent as a loser, and I believe that his values are what make him and what he stands for strong, then why would I not want to adopt and represent those values? After all, a bunch of people in the country seem to be aligned with them, so why would I toss them out, just because they don't align perfectly with my own? To do so is to reinforce the myth of 'Us and The Others.'

"The truth is that the values—*the real values*—of the other party are very, very strong, and very, very real. An inclination toward fiscal conservatism. A belief that the Federal government should be kept as small as possible. A belief that with capitalism comes the ability to climb high and grow strong through hard work and commitment to ideals. And a strong commitment to states' rights, to a reasonable balance between the decision-making power of the States vs. the decision-making power of the Feds. There isn't a single thing in there that I disagree with. So, I took a deep breath and offered him the job. And *he* took a deep breath and accepted. One of the best things that ever happened.

"That was the beginning of a whole new era, and the hits just kept on coming. Here," she said, plucking a handful of grapes and handing them to me, "try these—they're a Cab hybrid we developed right here."

They were delicious. We continued toward the river; it was a really beautiful piece of property. Al was way off in the distance, doing something with a tractor.

Chapter 23: Farming and Food

"So, was this the beginning of the whole social program makeover that people still talk about?" I asked. We were approaching a small building at the far end of the vineyard which housed the smart agriculture electronics and the complicated valve system that fed water, nutrients and pest control solutions to the farm and vineyard.

"Pretty much," she began. "Like I said, we had no idea how long the other side was going to play nice with us, so we just kept pushing the boundaries, waiting for them to call foul. But they never did. They asked a lot of questions, they pushed on a few things, but for the most part, they listened. Michael, that was the key—*they listened.* Polar reversal or no polar reversal, that's always been a problem in politics. Everybody hears you, but few of 'em actually listen to what you have to say. But that changed. Even when they disagreed, they listened. That was the best thing that came out of the whole flux reversal thing."

"So, how did you go from prisons to the whole social program reinvention? I mean, that's a huge leap, even for you. And how did you avoid the whole left-wing make-work raise-taxes thing?"

"Well, it wasn't easy," she laughed. "I'm pretty good at connecting the dots, but a lot of folks can't see the animal in the picture even when the dots are all connected. So, we had to go back to that whole reverse-engineering concept that I mentioned earlier and paint them a picture so that they could see where we wanted to go. You can imagine that some of the right wing thought I was trying to push a left wing, socialist-communist agenda on them until I rolled out the tax plan that went along with it. That's when they really sat up and took notice—we'll talk about that later.

"Anyway, the more we looked at the problems in the country—and I mean, the real problems, not that first-world nonsense that so many people used to complain about—we found that there was a common thread running through just about all of them. I knew that if I could get my fingers on that thread and pull on it, I could fix the whole damn thing. So, I started unraveling this hairball and before long, I figured it out—with help from the Cabinet, of course. We had a good start on education, and prison reform was well underway. We had the success story from Detroit that we could talk about. But we still had some serious voids to fill. People were still hungry; for God's sake, the wealthiest country on Earth, and people were starving. Totally wrong. We had a welfare system that people treated like an ATM. No job? No problem. Just have another kid. Ka-ching! A bigger check from Uncle Sam.

"So, we went after that whole entitlement thing. Look—sometimes, bad things happen. Even the most successful people in the world can find themselves in trouble financially, for things that are no fault of their own. So, we have to have a safety net to take care of people when that happens. But that safety net needs to have an expiration date associated with it, otherwise we're back to the ATM machine problem. And by the way, I'm not talking about extraordinary circumstances here; back when COVID hit in 2020, it seems like half the country was out of work. That wasn't their fault, and the government stepped up initially, for the most part. Here, I'm talking about everyday life.

"We took a long, hard look at the system, and we decided we'd try something different. We kept unemployment available so that meals wouldn't be missed, and kids wouldn't stress, but we built a framework around it. When you get an unemployment check, you also sign up to get skill-assessed and put into the library—remember the skills library I talked about that we built with LinkedIn and Salesforce? Well, it worked—it worked really well. And if there was no job available, you had the option to be trained with a new skill that would build on whatever you did before becoming unemployed. So, if you were an IT manager, maybe we train you to be a Big Data Analyst. Or a Python Programmer. Or an app developer. If you're a welder, maybe we train you to do sheet metal fabrication. In other words, yeah, we'll catch you in our net and we'll protect you, but you have to show us that you're swimming like hell to get out of the net if you want to keep the protection.

"Another option that was available was going to work for Mike's group, the infrastructure people. Their whole mandate was to fill institutional voids like decaying roads and bridges; an inferior rail system; inadequate power infrastructure; a broken education system; preparation for the trades; cybersecurity; IT and telecom infrastructure design and rollout; and so on. But here's where the magic happened. These jobs weren't just for what an old friend of mine used to call 'the can't-hardlies,' people who can't do anything else. These were purpose-built attack teams made up of highly skilled engineers and architects, student interns, and skilled craft and labor, many of them freshly graduated from prison or school and ready to make their mark on the world. It wasn't a make-work program; we needed this! Did you know that in the 1930s, it wasn't uncommon for trains to run at over 100 miles-per-hour? You could go from Chicago to Denver in 13 hours. In 2020, our fastest train, the Acela, ran at an average of 81 miles-per-hour. We've gone backwards[xxiv].

"Michael, let's head back to the house. It's almost lunchtime, and I'm getting thirsty. I'll get lunch started and pour us some iced tea, and we'll continue this conversation in the kitchen. Is this what you were looking for? Has this been helpful?"

I flipped through my notes and looked at my pocket
recorder to make sure it was still running. "This is more than
helpful, Ahadi," I smiled. "I can't thank you enough for
taking all this time to talk with me. I've got the beginnings of
a great story here. And that, by the way, talking about lunch,
is a perfect segue to another topic. You did some amazing
things for farmers and food distribution while you were in
office. Can we talk about that? And I'm not talking about the
downtown Detroit farmers."

"The flux reversal full moon strikes again," she laughed.
"That whole farming thing was a real travesty. For more than
20 years, the government told stories to farmers and other
small businesses out of both sides of its mouth. 'We're going
to create great jobs in middle America,' they'd spew. Then
they erected trade barriers that evaporated the farmers'
overseas sales, and then turned around and gave subsidies to
mega-corporations and looked the other way when those
huge companies began to hollow out the middle of the
country because the smaller farmers couldn't compete with
their large-scale efficiencies. Jobs just evaporated—in fact,
whole lifestyles went away. Please understand, Michael, I've
got nothing against big companies. For the most part, they
get big because they're good at what they do, and why would
we punish success? But a lot of them got so big that they
couldn't see the forest for the trees—or in some cases, didn't
want to. They were like Shrek in a china shop—stuff's gonna
get broken. And when you add in the fact that the
Republicans deregulated just about everything they could
when they controlled things, it was hard to hold anybody's
feet to the fire. Everybody hates regulation until you explain
to them that the word means 'protection,' and more to the
point, 'consumer protection[xxv].' Anybody who doesn't
believe that should go back and have a look at the banking

crisis in 2008 and the extraordinary steps that were needed to get us out of it. By the way, that's why I de-politicized all the regulatory bodies—the FCC, the FTC, the FDIC, the FDA, the EPA, and the CPSC, just to name a few. If you think about it, even AT&T was broken up as a way to protect the consumer way back in 1984. Here's a little factoid I remember from way back when. In 1983, a 9600 bit-per-second modem was the size of a large Fedex box and cost $40,000[xxvi]. And remember, you needed two of them to make a circuit! Remember also, we're talking about 9,600 bits-per-second. The slowest DSL on Earth today gets at least two million bits-per-second or something like that.

"Anyway, part of the reason for that was the AT&T monopoly. They controlled service, R&D, manufacturing, which meant that they and only they were in a position to manufacture the things. So, when a customer complained about the cost, AT&T would say, 'Well, then you should go to the competition—oh, wait, there isn't any competition—oh well, it sucks to be you.' When the Justice Department busted them up and allowed full-blown competition, it wasn't more than a few years before innovation and competition made those prices laughable. So yeah, I kind of like regulation, and I'll advocate for it, but I'm also very quick to point out that the goal of regulation is not to create competition; it's to create a fair playing field for everybody, so that ultimately the consumer is served by a sound business environment. They can mandate competition as way to achieve that if they deem it appropriate, but it's a means, not an end.

"Anyway, we hired a bunch of those farmers to help us design the program that's still working just fine. One of the things they recommended was that we ask farmers to set aside a portion of their land for crops that would become Community-Supported Agriculture—CSAs—in exchange for an attractive tax benefit, of course. People could work on the farm to earn CSA credits, but they also had to learn a trade related to farming or ranching.

"And this had implications for your immigration policies too, didn't it?" I asked.

"Yes, it did. Everything's connected. I'll get around to that in a minute."

We had reached the back patio and were headed for the door.

"Grilled cheese and tomato okay with you?" she asked.

"One of my favorites," I smiled. I definitely wasn't going to lose any weight on this project, I thought. "Tell me how I can help, okay?"

"Just stay out of the way," she replied. "Here, you can set the table. Plates are up there," pointing to a cabinet as we entered the kitchen. "Silverware's in the drawer next to the dishwasher."

I began collecting everything I needed.

"Al will join us as well, I'm sure, so set the table for three," she called over her shoulder.

Chapter 24: Course Corrections II

As I set about preparing for lunch, I thought about the sequence of events that had led me to this story. The planet's magnetic poles flip, and people go kind of crazy when those little iron things in their heads re-orient.

Of course, it wasn't just people that went gonzo. Birds and bugs and a boatload of other animals that for eons have depended on the planet's invisible magnetic flux lines to guide their migrations suddenly found themselves in trouble—in fact, quite a few species were now in jeopardy because they went the wrong way—north in the winter, and vice-versa. Of course, we had already pretty much done them in with our own human stupidity and greed, but that's the subject of another book. Bugs and birds don't go out of their way to be deliberately mean to each other; that's exclusively a human trait, so when the poles flipped, the impact was pretty insane. It's still going on, so who the hell knows where it will end up.

But true to form, a few forward-thinking people, like the woman who stood at the stove in front of me frying up a batch of grilled cheese sandwiches with tomato, jumped at the opportunity to reset things. As old Wayne Gretsky used to say, 'You miss one hundred percent of the shots you don't take.' So, Ahadi Fadhili-Mason took her shot.

Her voice pulled me back from my daydream.

"Before we get into immigration, which was a mess of the highest order, I want to circle back to the prison conversation because I don't think I did it justice earlier.

"In 2020, there were more than two million people in

prison in the United States. It had become a goddamn industry in its own right, and I had a real problem with that. First of all, let's talk practicality. It took a million people to run the jails and it cost $80 billion a year to do so. Do you have any idea how many people you could educate and train with that kind of money[xxvii]?

"But here's the deal," she said, flipping the sandwiches in the pan. "The whole system was based on a bunch of myths and legends that had no connection to reality, but the prison industry's marketing machine was pretty damn good, so people believed them. For example, there was this widely held belief that private prisons—meaning, corporations that ran prisons for profit—were the heart of the problem. You know— 'let's build a business that feeds on the misery of others.' But that was bullshit. At the time, only about eight or nine percent of all prisoners were held in private prisons; the rest were in public jails[xxviii]. Even so, incarceration had become big business. For example, city and county jails often rented out space—cells—to the US Marshals, Immigrations and Customs Enforcement, state prisons that didn't have room, that kind of thing. And then on top of that, they jobbed out all the services to private contractors. So, telephone service, healthcare, the commissary, and the cafeterias were often privatized, and the cost of using those services got passed on to inmates' families, who couldn't afford to pay them because they charged waaaaay above market price[xxix].

"And here's another thing. I can't believe I remember all these facts, but they got into my gut and I couldn't get rid of them. Prisoners did get paid for working in the prison laundry, cafeteria and so on. Yeah, they got paid—anywhere from one to four dollars per day. Per day! Look—I get it— they're in prison for a crime against society. But how the hell are they supposed to return to a civilized society as a civilized human being if they're treated like they're subhuman?

"One more thing and I'll shut up about this and let you ask questions—and eat." She shoveled the sandwiches onto the plates with a spatula. "The idea that people who commit violent crimes can't be rehabilitated is wrong. If somebody goes to prison for a violent crime, sexual or otherwise, they're gonna be in there for a long time. That means that they aren't kids when they come out. It turns out that people who go to prison for violent or sexual offenses are among the least likely to re-offend. One of the reasons is their age. Violence tends to peak during adolescence and then drops as people get older[xxx]. That makes them much more likely to respond to a program designed to give them a working skill when they get out."

The door opened just as she was putting the plates on the table. Al walked in with a big smile on his face. "How's that for timing? Am I good or what?"

"We'll see how good you are after you've washed your hands," she scolded, smacking him with her dishtowel. Chuckling, he headed over to the sink.

"So, Michael," Al asked over his shoulder as he was drying his hands, "Why this project? If I'm not interrupting progress here…"

"Not at all," I replied. He sat down and joined us. "For all kinds of reasons, Ahadi's presidency was—unique? There are plenty of words that describe it. And sure, she got a lot done because of a natural phenomenon that no one could have possibly predicted. Let's face it—that was an enormous advantage."

"An advantage that made it possible for me to do the things I did," Ahadi interjected.

"I don't disagree," I nodded, picking up my sandwich, "but with all due respect, Madame President—sorry, Ahadi—it was more than that. You did something that most politicians never do—in fact, something most business leaders don't even do. You demonstrated what leadership is actually about."

"OK, now I'm intrigued," she smiled. "What remarkable thing did I do, other than make a few changes?"

"Yeah—a few changes. Let's go with that," I smiled back.

"Look—I have this personal belief about leadership that's a lot simpler than what most people think. Everybody's of the opinion that leadership has to be complicated and elusive, but I don't think that at all. I don't think you have to be a president or the CEO of a giant corporation to be a leader. In fact, I've seen people living in tiny villages in Africa who had no electricity, no running water, no sewage, not even a salary, but who were exceptional leaders. Why? Because they did what you did throughout your presidency: They took the time to show people what could be, rather than what was. They painted a picture of a future that people longed for, a detailed, rich picture, and then they enrolled people to help them make it real. You did that every time you undertook a new initiative. And yeah, you had the flux reversal in your corner, but if you hadn't made the effort to create a new status quo for people that was better than the one they already had, flux reversal or no flux reversal, you would have had a much harder time getting things done, because there would have been no compelling reason for people to get behind you."

I turned to Al, who was sitting quietly, listening. "Al,

that's why I took on this project. What Ahadi did can't be described in words very well, but I'm sure going to try."

He nodded, crunching a handful of chips. It was quiet in the kitchen for a while as we sat there, talked out and thoughtful. At last, Ahadi spoke.

"Thank you, Michael. That was very kind of you, and it means a lot to me that you would make that observation about my presidency. Many years ago, Justice Sandra Day O'Connor said that the impact that any one of us makes during our lifetime is similar to the hole we leave when we stick our finger into a bucket of water. Just a few ripples that quickly fade away[xxxi]. But I wanted my ripples to count for something."

"Well, I said, "I think your ripples were more like ocean swells. Can we go back to our farming conversation?"

"Sure," she replied. "There isn't much more to say. But one of the things I went after was the problem of food waste, which to my way of thinking was just criminal. So, we designed a program—actually, strike that—I need to be clear here. A group of kids in a hackathon designed a program that allowed farmers to list their surplus output for redistribution to communities with a need, and an AI-driven, cost-effective transportation system that facilitated delivery—in exchange for labor or some other fungible resource. It didn't make it to the national level—too much scale to deal with—but at the local level, it worked really well.

"And speaking of local, there's another ag-related thing we worked hard to fix. Water. Water's a huge issue, but at the time it wasn't getting anywhere near enough attention."

"Say more," I urged.

"Most of our water—most of *everybody's* water—gets stored deep underground in porous rock layers called aquifers. They're huge. The biggest one is called the Ogallala-High Plains Aquifer, and it stretches from South Dakota all the way down to northern Texas. That's eight states, all of them heavily farming-dependent. But here's the deal: between 1900 and 2008, farming sucked 89 trillion gallons of fresh water out of that aquifer, which is two-thirds the volume of Lake Erie. It was a crisis, because we were pulling water out faster than the aquifer could recharge itself with rain and snowmelt. In the hydrology industry, they talk about zero day—the day the wells run dry in a region because of depleted aquifers. Well, we knew way back then that in Kansas, for example, that day was 50 years away—at which point the aquifer would be 70 percent depleted[xxxii].

"Now, some of the depletion is drought cycle. If we had dry seasons, then we didn't get rain, or snow, so the aquifer naturally shrank. That's just the way of things. But what we also discovered was that we were making it worse. And when I say 'we,' I mean government."

"How? I asked.

"Subsidies. Back in 2020, everything was looking pretty good for farmers. Crop production was up, farm incomes rose almost six percent, and corn had a bumper year. But what people weren't seeing was the dirty side of the subsidies that the government was paying. In 2020, farm subsidies increased 65 percent, to something like 38 billion dollars. That number was used for things like covering losses from Trump's mindless trade wars and for COVID relief. Meanwhile, the price of corn was way too low to cover the cost of growing it, so the subsidies made up the difference. So, farmers worked harder for less production. Essentially, they were being paid to overproduce, which meant that they had to buy more farm equipment, seed, fertilizer, soil treatments, and pesticide, which under normal circumstances would be good for the economy—but it was a house of cards.

It also meant that they had to suck more water out of the ground, which was a major factor in depleting Ogallala.

"The bottom line was that they were paid to overproduce, which put pressure on natural resources like water, and at the same time, because they flooded the market at the encouragement of the government, they also drove the price of the commodity down.

"So, what we had was a bunch of people in Washington who've never seen a farm, making long-term decisions about an industry they know nothing about. And just to make my point, we found a study—a very good, very accurate study—that clearly showed that between 1980 and 2010, when farmers increased their irrigated land use, the increase did nothing to increase income, improve healthcare, or provide better education for the people living there. It was a travesty.[xxxiii]"

"So, what happened?" I queried.

"Reality happened," she responded, tersely. "Look, sometimes we need subsidies. We're a big country, with a lot of hungry people. But the whole farming and ranching industry got flipped on its head. The giant corporate farms began to run things pretty much with impunity, and they figured out how to work the system to take maximum advantage of the subsidies, while at the same time putting farmers into a precarious place with no long-term future. You ever hear the term, 'Precariat?'"

"Sure," I responded. "That's one of the words they used back in the day to describe the platform economy— companies like Uber and Lyft and Airbnb because their 'employees' made so little money for so much effort that they were always in a precarious place, financially."

"Correct, Michael. Well, our farmers were in the process of becoming the next wave of Precariat workers. Again—

nothing against big, successful companies, but we're talking about national food production, here. So, we took some pretty serious steps to try to set things back on track.

"The first thing we did was not what people thought we were going to do, which was to regulate the use of groundwater. That would have been totally counterproductive, and it would have turned the farmers against us. We also didn't go after the subsidies—like I said, we needed them, especially given the margins that farmers have to work with.

"But here's what we did do. We moved subsidy monies around so that we could pay farmers to leave tracts of land that were ecologically sensitive untouched. Less farming, less water use. Then, we put programs in place to encourage farmers to produce crops that required less water.

"At the same time, Doug Standley put together a team to develop water monitoring and usage technology that would be available to farmers at a low cost, but that would help them maximize yield while reducing water use.

"We did all of this under the Federal Farm Bill, which among other things, funds national anti-poverty programs like SNAP. At the same time, we made sure that community subsidies would offset tax revenue losses in farming communities, since they weren't farming as much land.

"Where we did play a bit of a game was when we looked at federal farm credit. Remember that technology stuff that Doug was leading? Well, we figured out a way to provide very attractive financing rates for technology-based equipment that reduced water consumption and encouraged a—how do I say this—more gentle approach to farming as far as the land was concerned. And we set the rates higher— substantially higher—for equipment that did nothing to reduce human impact."

"And what about taxation? Did you make any changes there?" So far, there hadn't been any discussion about tax changes related to farming or water use.

"Oh, yeah," she said. "The way things were set up back then, when the water level in the wells dropped, farmers could claim deductions for that! And, they could depreciate their irrigation equipment—the very same equipment that was emptying the aquifer. So basically, we were rewarding them to destroy their own businesses. It was lunacy! So instead, we replaced all that with a tax credit that they could get if they took steps to reduce groundwater use, and a 'modified' depreciation schedule for low water use irrigation infrastructure. It worked."

"Incredible. You must have had some seriously good people working with you on that. And, if I remember correctly," I asked, reaching for a pickle, "one of your foreign policy efforts was also farming-centric, right?" I asked. This was an rea I was anxious to explore, because I'd seen the results of it firsthand during an earlier project in Kenya.

"I see you've done your homework," she smiled. "You're talking about Africa, right? So, here's the story. The reason California is such an agricultural gold mine is because of the geology of the area. That Central Valley where everything grows is miles deep with some of the most fertile land you can possibly imagine. Cut a picture of a sweet potato out of a magazine and bury it in Salinas with a little water, and I swear, a sweet potato will sprout.

"Well, we wanted to improve our long-term relationships with African nations, as a hedge against other players getting too-well established there, and what better way than to create jobs and make those places more self-sufficient, without relying on extractive industries like oil and gas, uranium, or trace elements.

"It turns out that the center of the African continent—what they call the Rift Valley—is just like California's Central Valley. It's full of incredibly rich soil, which means that the entire Central Valley of the continent could produce food on a huge scale. But there were two main differences between Africa and California, other than the obvious. One, in Africa, the infrastructure just wasn't there; the roads were merely suggestions, there were very few dependable deep wells, the business stuff like banks and transportation companies were pretty much non-existent, and the technology base for high-end agriculture didn't exist. But it's the second difference that really mattered. Africa's Rift Valley is *14 times the size of California's Central Valley,* which means that with the right investment, Africa could quite literally become the world's breadbasket[xxxiv]. So, our focus was on fixing that."

"So, we're back to institutional, or social voids again?" I asked.

"That's right," she nodded. "I recruited my Three Musketeers: Standley for technology, Musk for transportation, and Rowe for infrastructure, skills development and plain old common sense."

"So, what did you do, exactly?" I asked.

"Well, once again, we hopped on the polar reversal train and rode it as far as we could. People were behaving, even the politicians across the aisle, so we went after this one big-time. Elon knew that we had to create infrastructure if we were going to make this work, so he and I went to the United Nations, where, for the first time, they actually were—united, I mean. I explained the overall goal and went through some pro forma numbers that my Chief Financial Officer pulled together, and Elon told the affected countries that we would draw up a plan that would include infrastructure designs, technology requirements, labor, and timelines. Meanwhile, Doug Standley got on the technology thing. He and his team started calling the project The Smart Rift Valley, because his intent was to instrument the crap out of the place to keep costs down and yield up. That's what he eventually did, by the way.

"While all this was going on, Mike Rowe was working with UNESCO and the Gates Foundation to create a skill development program for all the nations that touched the Valley. There are seven of them, and they were among the most desperate countries on Earth: Eritrea, Djibouti, Ethiopia, Sudan, Tanzania, Uganda, and Kenya. Hell, most people can't find those countries on a map—they're hard pressed to point at Africa with any confidence—so building compassion for them wasn't gonna happen easily.

"At the same time, Mike started putting the word out to the programs he had developed, most of them in prisons, indicating that he needed a whole raft of people—surveyors, designers, supervisors, electricians, plumbers, solar specialists, truck drivers, specialists in smart ag, telecom engineers, builders, road workers, pavers, and logistics specialists—to work on a major project in Africa. Not only would they be doing the work they'd been trained to do and getting paid a handsome salary to do it, but they were also going to be training the Africans how to do those jobs so that they could become truly self-sufficient. Win-Win, all the way around."

"But I can't imagine that this was all sweetness and light," I said. "There had to be some rough spots along the way."

"Oh yeah," she replied, reaching for the jar of bread and butter pickles on the table. She couldn't get the lid off, so she passed it to Al, who popped it open for her. "Thank you. Yeah, there were some rough spots, all right, especially when we started talking about how we were going to pay for all that foreign investment. I mean, the reversal made people nicer, nobody's denying that, and made them more reasonable to deal with, but it didn't make them stupid. We still had to justify everything we did, and not everything got through. But at least they were willing to listen, ask questions, and consider what we had to say, instead of dismissing our ideas out-of-hand, just because we sat on the other side of the aisle.

"When I think about it today, what we proposed seems insane, but it passed—I was caught completely off-guard. Basically, we looked at the defense budget, which, at the time, was about $700 billion[xxxv]. So, we asked that one-half of one percent of that be allocated to non-military aid for Africa. That was three-and-a-half billion dollars that we were able to use to create a stable, self-sufficient Africa, and that was half of what we already gave the region in foreign aid every year[xxxvi]. Some of the investment came through technology transfer, some of it was in training and education, but regardless, it worked. The deal we made was that we would only agree to make the investments we promised if they would agree to pony up farmers willing to play along, and the labor required to build the infrastructure. Well, they fell all over themselves getting in line to take part, and in the first year we laid the first modern rail tracks in the region, built 2,500 miles of paved roads, dug hundreds of wells, trained thousands of people, and built countless buildings.

"But it was in the third year that things really started to happen. That was their first crop year, and the excitement was electric. Not only did Africa produce a bumper crop, they signed their first in-region contracts, mostly with South Africa, Namibia, Morocco, and Botswana, followed by contracts from Europe and western Asia. And when Doug got involved and put in the Smart Agriculture technology to help them save cost by reducing water use and cutting the cost of seed, fertilizer, and pesticide, that shit got real. We had friends—real friends—in Africa for the first time. And the friendships continue to this day. Because one of the things that came from that, besides a massive food production machine and a whole lot of self-respect, was demand for other skills. We continued the agriculture training, but we added business, logistics, supply chain, soil chemistry, animal husbandry, road planning and maintenance, refrigeration, wastewater management and treatment, telecommunications, and IT support. We brought in the Peace Corps and even a few VISTA volunteers to help. We built farms, but what we really built was a self-sustaining education and training sector that began to extend all over Africa. That was the real magic."

"There's another piece of this story—the biggest piece, I'm thinking. I have a feeling you know what I'm talking about."

Ahadi smiled, nodded. "You're talking about Matumaini?"

I smiled back. "Sort of hard to ignore, I think."

She laughed. "In for a penny, in for a pound, I guess. When we started working on the Africa food project, the day came when we looked at each other, shook our heads, and collectively questioned our sanity. There were so many things we screwed up along the way, but thankfully we found most of them as they happened and managed to dig our way out—no pun intended."

"Is it true that Matumaini wasn't part of the original plan?" I asked.

"Yep," she replied. "It came later. At first, as we've already discussed, we were pushing to create opportunity and self-sufficiency. Those countries are incredibly poor, and opportunities for change were just non-existent the way things were at the time. So, our idea was pretty simple: export skills to the countries that needed them, build infrastructure to fill institutional voids, and then provide what they needed to get the farms started.

"The problem was that our idea was *too* simple. We saw the opportunity—help them feed themselves and create a stronger market-based domestic economy, become economically independent, and join the global economy—but we didn't take into account the unintended consequences of what we were trying to do. And that bit us in the ass BIG time."

"How so?" I queried.

"Well, when we first came up with our grand idea to build farms and roads and such in north-central Africa, we were so starry-eyed over the possibility of turning what we perceived to be a wasteland wilderness into an agriculture center, we didn't bother to ask about secondary or tertiary impacts to the region that might not be all that great. It's that old physics thing, 'For every action there's an equal and opposite reaction.' Or, if you prefer, John Muir: 'When you try to change any single thing, you find it hitched to everything else in the universe.'"

"Can you give me an example?" I asked.

"Yep—I'm getting to that," she replied. "There were really two major things that hit us full in the face that we had to deal with. The first was the potential impact on wildlife, which we didn't think about initially. Stupid. Wildlife tourism brings billions of dollars into east Africa, and there was a very good chance that by building the farms and roads we initially wanted to build, that we'd disrupt migration patterns and put entire species at risk, which could also affect the ecological balance of the region and disrupt food supplies for people who depend on game to live. And, of course, we could screw up the tourist industry, which has been a dependable source of revenue for decades. So, we had to bound the initiative to ensure that we didn't disrupt migration corridors, and that meant bringing in specialists in wildlife biology and wildland management to ensure that we didn't fix one mess by making a bigger one.

"The second thing was a much bigger challenge—and took some serious horse-trading that in a lot of ways is still going on. At some point along the way, we got a call from a hydrologist at the US Geological Survey. This guy's job was to study how water flows across and through gigantic land masses—we're talking country-size areas. So, there we were, clapping ourselves on the back about our wonderful farming idea, and this guy comes out of nowhere and tells us that we're making a big mistake. So, we invited him in, and he sat us down and made us aware of some things we didn't know about that were kind of important.

"Turns out that the geology of the whole Rift Valley is pretty dynamic because it is *a rift valley*. Thanks to plate tectonics, the two sides of the valley are slowly pulling apart, and the valley is getting deeper. In fact, a lot of it is below sea level. The deepest parts are in Ethiopia in a place called the Afar Depression. It's sort of where Ethiopia, Djibouti and Somalia come together, and in some areas it's more than 400 feet below sea level. Just for comparison, that's almost 200 feet deeper than the Badwater Basin in Death Valley.

"Because of the way the geology and hydrology of the region work—and the fact that the Afar region is so far below sea level—the Rift Valley is in the early stages of flooding, which means that it will ultimately become a huge,

185

shallow, inland sea. You can imagine the havoc that would create.

"Of course, it's not like we're going to wake up in a couple of weeks and find a new Salton Sea in the middle of North Africa. The flooding is going to take thousands of years. But: brackish water is already starting to seep into the aquifers in the region, and some of them are in worse shape than others. The Afar Depression is the first place that will flood, but long before it does, it'll become even more uninhabitable because the wells will stop producing freshwater. The area is already a nasty alkali flat that doesn't support any life to speak of, other than sand fleas and salt flies. Long-term, we can help them with desalination infrastructure, but in the meantime, we realized that we had to do something to help establish a viable economy in the region.

"So, we stopped everything and pulled together a team of people that were a hell of a lot smarter than any of us about this stuff. We presented what we'd found and what we were concerned about: damage to tourism if the farms messed things up, negative impact on the ecology of the area, destruction of habitat and species die-off, and so on. Then we told them about the problem of saltwater incursion, which wouldn't happen any time soon but *would* happen over time. We answered all their questions, and then proposed a completely different approach. We would still do the farms, but we would make a radical change that would eliminate the problems we listed. We're not there yet, but we're within about three years."

The change was the Matumaini Canal.

"Loren Eiseley once wrote, 'When man becomes greater than nature, nature, which gave us birth, will respond.' So, here we were, planning farmland and roads, and the water we'd be piping to the crops would eventually kill them as it became more and more brackish. That was just nature responding.

"One of the project team members was an engineer who understood big, hairy projects. He had a great idea: 'Rather than make nature an enemy and try to fight her in a battle that we absolutely cannot win, let's turn her into an ally.' He explained his idea, and we unanimously agreed that it was the most ridiculous, outlandish, unrealistic idea imaginable— we loved it. He made it clear to us that building giant farms wasn't the answer. So instead, we built Matumaini.

"Matumaini Canal was indeed a ridiculous, outlandish, unrealistic, and breathtaking project. If the overall goal of our Africa foreign policy—and I'm not even sure that's the right term—was to create opportunity and self-sufficiency for the people who lived in the region, the answer wasn't farming— it was industry, only one of which was farming.

"Here's what we saw when we looked at the whole thing a little differently. That whole region that sits just to the west of the Horn of Africa, which includes Djibouti and the bulk of Ethiopia, is not exactly desirable in terms of its ability to grow crops—or anything else, for that matter.

"So, we got to thinking: What if we could figure out a way to create a variety of job types, not just farmers and ranchers? What if we could actually create light industry that would help to turn that wasteland into useful, productive space, but that wouldn't damage the ecology of the region or disrupt the wildlife populations?

"What we ended up creating was a multimodal transport system. Water's the cheapest transport mode, as long as there's water where you need to go. Rail carriage comes in second in terms of having the lowest ton-per-mile cost. Then we have trucking. It's not the cheapest form of cargo transport by a long shot, but it has the advantage of being super-flexible for doing last-mile delivery and pickup.

"So, by building an intermodal system, we combine the best of all three transport modes. You load a cargo container at a shipping site somewhere in the interior onto a tractor-trailer, truck it to a nearby railhead, load it in rail cars for carriage to the port, and then transfer the cargo to ocean-going ships for global transport. And of course, you can reverse the process for the movement of goods into the interior."

"Sounds like a boil-the-ocean initiative," I observed. "But you just said that there was nothing there—I mean, in the area where you wanted to do this project. What did you call it, the Afar Depression? I'm having trouble understanding where the multimodal idea comes in."

"Well, here's what happened," she replied. "When we started looking at the area, we had to keep reminding ourselves that our goal was to incubate industry and by extension, jobs. To do that, we needed a way to get raw materials in and products out, which at the time was incredibly difficult if not flat-out impossible. Still is, to a large extent.

"Well, moving raw materials and finished product requires some kind of transportation. But let's go back even farther. Not too far south of the border with Eritrea, there's a town in Ethiopia called Aksum. It's quite famous, because there's a church there called the Chapel of the Tablet where the Ark of the Covenant is supposedly stored. Anyway, one of the things that the area is quite well-known for is soapstone carvings. The market for those carvings tends to be pilgrim tourists who come to see the churches in the area, or archaeologists who come to study there.

"So, maybe one of these artists sells three or four of these carvings every month. The problem is that they tend to be kind of big—not life-size leopard big, but bigger than a dinner plate, and heavy. It isn't going to fit in your suitcase or carry-on. So, they ship it home for you, which could take weeks because it has to make its way to Djibouti or Addis Ababa for shipment. Small market—accidental market, if you really think about it—and complicated. And, small market equals small revenue.

"So now, we make a few changes. First, we build up our transport infrastructure so that it's easier for a craftsperson or artist to get their goods to market. Then, we bring Internet access into the region. You can imagine that Elon was all over that with his Starlink[xxxvii] project. But that isn't enough: we also have to teach people how to use it, so we make sure that schools are part of the overall project, because if the kids can learn how to access the Web, they can teach their parents. And they don't need complicated computers—all they need is a decent mobile phone. Once they have that, these people can build Web sites to advertise their products, and the next thing you know their market goes from some dumb archaeologist who got lost on the way to find the Ark and instead finds this guy selling soapstone carvings, to Crate and Barrel calling to order 500 of the damn things—which can then be easily plopped on a truck, which takes them to the train, which takes them to the port for shipment. Suddenly the guy's market goes from lost tourists in the desert of Ethiopia, to the entire planet."

"And you think you can do that?" I asked. I had to say, I was pretty skeptical. This sounded way too good to be doable.

"Not only can we," she countered, "we already have. Look, I'm a firm believer in the old adage that says that the best way to become a leader is to find a parade and get in front of it. We did a pretty comprehensive infrastructure survey before we got started and saw that there was already rail service there. It was spotty, but the makings of a decent track system were already in place. It was all over the map in terms of how well it had been maintained, how well it was managed, the number of available route miles that were actually available and working, and so on, but it was a start, anyway. We knew we could renovate and extend the existing rail lines, as needed. So, while the engineers and surveyors were looking at the route options for the canal portion of the project and for whatever roads they would have to build, another group was looking at the rail infrastructure and what they would have to do to bring it up to speed. Look, there are some seriously nice trains in Africa—tonight when you've got nothing else to do, have a look at South Africa's Blue Train that runs from Johannesburg all the way to Dar es Salaam in Tanzania, or the Shongololo Express, which runs between South Africa, Mozambique, Namibia, Swaziland and Zimbabwe. Even Morocco has some *seriously* decadent train journeys. So, it's not out of the question that a capable rail infrastructure could be built up north that would serve the needs of the tourism industry as well as it would serve industrial transport."

"Sure," I teased. "Seems to me that 'The Maneaters of Tsavo' was all about lions eating the people who were trying to build a rail line in that general area. You should have no problem getting people to work on that part of the project."

"Okay, smartass," she retorted, "Just for that, you're on dishes tonight."

I laughed. She could definitely dish it out as well as she could take it. I was really beginning to like and respect this woman.

"Okay, but seriously, tell me about hooking together all the different transport modes."

"You have to keep in mind that there were a bunch of moving parts to this thing. And don't forget, it isn't done yet—it's still a work in progress. We wanted to build on top of what was already there to help keep the cost down for all the funding agencies that were involved. That meant rail and roads. If they were there, we'd make them better; if they weren't, and we needed them there, then we'd build them. But why reinvent the wheel? If we've got perfectly serviceable rail lines, or paved roads, then let's use them. That's the approach we took."

"And the canal?" I asked.

"We decided to build a canal system that would push maritime access deeper into the interior, because the cost-per-transported-ton of cargo moved over water is so low. But we didn't want to have to tunnel through mountains or install locks, because that would push the cost through the roof and nobody would buy off on it, with or without the flux reversal. So, to avoid the cost and complexity of building a canal system with locks, we opted for a route that would keep the canal at sea level, similar to what they did with Suez. Our engineers decided that the best thing to do would be to connect the northern portion of the Gregory Rift, which is the eastern arm of the north end of the Rift Valley—it looks like a 'Y'—with the Gulf of Aden, because the Gregory Rift is way below sea-level. It's part of that Afar Depression. And of course, as we continue with the current cycle of planetary warming, and as polar ice melts and sea levels rise, the incursion of water into the Depression will just get worse. So, why not use it to our advantage?

"Think about it. Let's say you build tractors in Germany and you want to sell them in the interior of Africa. You transport them to a port on the Mediterranean and put them on a ship. The ship sails east, then turns and heads into the Suez Canal, then into the Red Sea. At the bottom of the Red

Sea, the ship lands at a modernized container port in Djibouti, where it passes into the Matumaini Canal and heads south, deep into Ethiopia. At some point it offloads the tractors onto flatbed train cars, which transport them into the interior, where they're loaded onto tractor-trailers for transport to their ultimate destination. Meanwhile, trucks loaded with sugar beets and potatoes and onions and squash make their way to the railroad's intermodal terminal, where the refrigerated containers of produce are loaded on trains, which pass them off to a cargo ship, which returns via the canal to Djibouti. From Djibouti the vessel heads into the Gulf of Aden, enters the Arabian Sea, and goes wherever the hell it needs to go to sell its cargo."

I was a bit puzzled. "But in that scenario, do you really need the canal? Seems to me that you could just make do with the railroad."

"We could," she smiled, "but that's where the magic, not the devil, is in the details. Initially we had the crazy idea of building a canal that would run from Djibouti all the way down to the bottom of Tanzania, providing an inland waterway almost as long as Africa. Thankfully, we had engineers with working brains on the team that shot that idea down before it could be seriously considered. After all, the Suez Canal is 120 miles long; Panama, 50. Under that original design, Matumaini would have stretched roughly 3,000 miles from end-to-end, and would pass through big river basins, Lake Albert, Lake Edward, Lake Kivu, Lake Tanganyika, and Lake Malawi, and would have been the largest terrestrial engineering task ever attempted. 3,000 miles—that's LA to Milwaukee. Or Kabul to Beijing, if you prefer. I'll admit, the dreamer in me loved the idea, but again, that's why we have engineers.

"So, instead, we scaled back—WAY back—and went for the multimodal transport idea.

"Let me start with the roads, since they do play a key role for the trucking part of this dance. The roads in Ethiopia—to be fair, in most of the Region—are not great. In fact, a lot of them are merely suggestions, and those that are considered to be major roadways require serious intestinal fortitude to use. They're not for the faint of heart; let's just say that the drivers there are—creative. But for commercial big-rig drivers, who are accustomed to dealing with that kind of thing, they worked fine, although some had to be improved because of increased traffic and because in some cases there just weren't roads where we needed them for the project.

"As far as the rail part of the equation was concerned, it was very interesting—and timing played a huge role in our design. As I said earlier, there were existing rail facilities in the region, but they were kind of spotty. Don't get me wrong—what was there was actually pretty good, it just wasn't as ubiquitous as we would have liked. What we proposed, and what the team ended up agreeing to do, was to build a feeder route system that would interconnect new rail routes with the rail infrastructure that was already there. In fact, the Awash-Hare Gebeya-Mek'ele Railway, which was a big project funded by Credit Suisse, has been under construction now for some time, and it's close to being finished. It isn't part of this project—it started long before we did—but it's designed to serve as a northern extension of the Ethiopian National Railway System, connecting Awash to Mek'ele. It's pretty much a straight north-south shot. Our goal was to connect to that system—another example of find a parade and get in front of it.

"Anyway, the new lines that we built as part of the Matumaini project connected existing and new rail lines in Ethiopia to the rail systems that already served west Africa, and provided the access required for the new agricultural activity that was getting started on the plateau west of the

Afar Province so that they could get their product to market. As the area evolves and grows and as business there diversifies, additional connections can be built, as required.

"Meanwhile, the beginnings of a new port facility were constructed midway along the new Awash-Hare Gebeya-Mek'ele Railway, because that's where the new inland sea will rise up to. It took a lot of doing, because basically we were building a port facility in the middle of the desert. But Gretsky always said that the key to winning was to always skate to where the puck is going to be, not where it is."

"Find a parade..." I chuckled.

"Exactly—yet another example. That inland sea, which they're now calling the Afar Sea, will be about 400 feet deep once it fills, and it'll be fed by the Awash River. Ultimately, that 'sea' will be used for all kinds of things, including additional port facilities with roads and rails running in all directions, salt production, as a desalination reservoir for freshwater production, as a headwater for hydroelectric, and of course, as a turning basin and staging point for the maritime vessels that come down the canal to drop off and pick up cargo."

"I have to ask," I interrupted. "Downsides? You're flooding a lot of territory; there have to be disadvantages."

"To be sure," Ahadi replied. "And in fact, some of them are still under dispute, although at least they're all talking to each other. The area mines a lot of trona, which is basically sodium carbonate, a chemical used to make paper, textiles, glass, and some kinds of soap. They're still working the numbers on that, but there are other sources—Wyoming, I think, has big deposits of the stuff. Much more controversial, though, is the fact that this is the area where "Lucy" was discovered, the skeleton that's supposed to be the oldest-known human. The area's a major activity region for paleontology and archaeological work, and there are valid concerns about losing access to critical research sites. Again, they're working on how they can preserve the most important areas while still moving forward. Heritage sites are critical, and I want them preserved. But people matter too, so finding a balance was always front-and-center in my mind.

"So, what we're doing to take care of the historical sites is kind of like what they did when they built Aswan on the Nile. Included in the cost of the canal is funding to help the scientists working in the area hire and acquire all the resources they need to thoroughly explore the area before the flooding begins. And by the way, it will be highly controlled: at the southern end of the canal there's a huge coffer dam that prevents the area from flooding prematurely. It has big bypass channels on either side, so that when the time comes to let the water flow, it will happen slowly and deliberately.

"We also have to talk a bit about the *positive* unintended consequences here. Once we flood the canal and start using it, something interesting happens. Water will evaporate from the surface of the channel, and from the surface of the slowly expanding Afar Sea, which will cause weather patterns to shift slightly, resulting in more rain in the dry central region of the Valley. It won't be that much more, but it'll be welcome.

"Meanwhile, land along the canal on both sides is going to be set aside specifically for farming, extending a few miles out on either side of the canal, forming a long green belt with access roads alongside so that vehicles can get easy access. Eventually, the plan is to build a rail line alongside the canal as well, so that the crops can be moved to market quickly to avoid spoilage."

"It seems as though Ethiopia gets the bulk of the benefit from this massive plan," I mused. "Why does that make sense?"

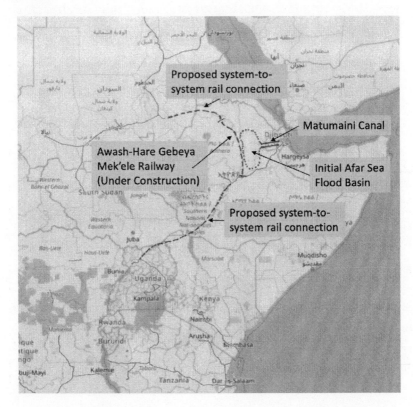

"It's a good question," she replied. "First, Ethiopia is, by north African standards, pretty stable economically and politically. They're strong western allies. But way back when, they went to war with Eritrea, and in the process, they lost access to ports that they had been granted access to under a previous treaty. After the war, that access was never restored. But they have good relations with Djibouti. The canal provides greater access to interior east Africa and guarantees expanded access to railroads. As a result,

Djibouti's presence as a major port is expanded, and new ports are established in the Afar Sea, which gives them another reason to accommodate the canal because of increased commercial port business. And, Addis has become a major banking center on the continent as Kenya's fortunes faded, and their national airline is actually very good, so Ethiopia is poised to become a global player.

"Another thing to keep in mind is that Ethiopia is one of the largest, if not the largest, producer of coffee in the world. This can only help them expand what is already an extremely lucrative industry.

"Of course, additional rail connections, especially to the south and west, will develop as commercial interests and economics provide funding.

"We also implemented an acre-for-an-acre program," Ahadi continued. "We made it a requirement that all the countries that will benefit from this infrastructure investment must set aside an acre of perpetual wildland for every acre that gets put under agriculture. That's non-negotiable. And as you probably already know, the canal, once it's complete, will be managed by a multinational corporation owned by the countries it passes through and will be administered by the UN."

The canal was still years away from being fully operational, but it was taking shape. It was a massive project. Once complete, Matumaini will be roughly 80 miles long, stretching from the Port of Djibouti deep into the desert, with huge wildlife 'overpasses' that provide a means for migrating animals to move east-west.

"Obviously, I'm very much aware of a lot of this," I replied. "You'd have to be living on Mars to not be aware of the canal construction. What I find really interesting about this, based on the research I've been doing in your Presidential Library—amazing facility, by the way—is all the little side projects it has kicked off, none of which, if I'm not mistaken, were part of the original plan. Talk about unintended consequences!"

"Once again, we're back to institutional voids. Nature abhors a vacuum—especially human nature. Once word came down that we—meaning all the global entities involved—were really serious about doing this, the opportunity engine kicked in and ideas started exploding like popcorn. Planning to build a canal and connect it to the railroads? Gonna need power. Suddenly, ZESCO in Zambia and UEGCL in Uganda appear at our door, ready and willing to run power lines into the area. And if we're gonna have power, then we need telecommunications, so infrastructure builders started showing up like cluster flies. Got telecom? Then we can build expanded towns and villages, and schools, and clinics, and municipal infrastructure. Before long, we have the makings of a productive region that can actually support people, create jobs, educate kids and adults alike, and keep them all healthy. Oh, and that also means that Doug Standley can do his magic with smart agriculture technology manage water and all the other things that can be optimized in a complex environment with resource challenges like the one we decided to build in."

"That really is astounding," I sighed, thinking about the prospect of another book on the horizon. "Before we leave this topic, while we're still discussing food and foreign policy, can we talk about your little take on what people took to calling your 'New and Improved Marshall Plan'?" I asked.

"Ha!" She laughed. "I think that was the most memorable thing I've gotten credit for—it was definitely the most fun, even though a lot of people got upset. Basically, we knew that there was no way in hell we were going to get to Iran, North Korea, or Venezuela through ideology—that would have been a complete waste of time, even with the ferroliths thing. So instead, we did a flanking maneuver. What did all those countries have in common? Well, they all had ideologues running the country who preached the evil ways of the west. Apparently, we were massing on the border to eat their children, that kind of thing. So, I figured, what could we possibly lose? It's not like they'd attack us for what we did."

Nope, I thought—they didn't attack us—at least not physically. But boy, did they howl. Under the cover of darkness, high-altitude bombers based in Seoul, Diego Garcia and Puerto Rico made overflight after overflight, dropping ordinance all over Iran, North Korea and Venezuela. The 'ordinance' consisted of tens of thousands of packages of non-spoilable food, kid's toys, first-aid kits, and little solar-powered shortwave radios. And every package was marked, 'A GIFT FROM YOUR FRIENDS IN THE UNITED STATES, CANADA, AUSTRALIA, AND EUROPE.'

"I'll never forget it," she said, chuckling and shaking her head. "That horrid little fat man in North Korea damn near had a stroke. He told his people not to eat the food, that it was poisoned, that it would make them sterile, that kind of happy horseshit. But guess what: When you're starving, and somebody drops food on your roof, you eat it. Nobody got sick, people still had babies, so suddenly we weren't the evil empire anymore. We did that for about a month, and it was the most fun I had outside of a bedroom the whole time I was President."

"And what about that whole 'kidnap the North Koreans' thing[1]? Was that real?" I asked. Of course, I knew the answer before I asked the question.

"I can neither confirm nor deny..." she began, taking a bite of her sandwich. Al looked at me and winked.

---

[1] Please see the Appendix for a screenplay based on what is rumored to have happened.

Chapter 25: Jobs

By now we had finished eating and were enjoying a final glass of iced tea before leaving the table to clean up after lunch. Al took the plates to the sink, and I insisted on doing the dishes. He then left to continue his work in the vineyard. Meanwhile, Ahadi took a break to make a few phone calls and check email. After the dishes, I did the same.

When she returned, we refilled our glasses and went out to sit on the patio. The heat and humidity were fierce, but it was comfortable under the awning that she rolled out with the push of a button.

"If you don't mind," I began, "I'd like to leave Africa—unless there's something else you'd like to cover—and talk about a few other domestic agenda items."

"Nope," she replied, "we covered the Africa story. I'm pretty proud of what we did there, because it was a great example of an apolitical cooperation agreement between multiple countries, that actually worked."

"Well, let's talk about something else that worked," I began. "I want to talk about job creation, manufacturing, and innovation. I don't need to remind you that that was a pretty contentious area at the time that your presidency began."

"Let's call it what it was, Michael. It was a train wreck. Donald Trump did more to damage the image of the country than any president in history, and Biden spent a lot of his time in office doing damage control and recovery. He did restore a sense of honor and decorum to the office, which was important. He wasn't able to move things forward as much as he wanted, but it wasn't for lack of trying, but because of political obstruction in a still divided country. So,

I had a lot of catch-up to do, and honestly, if the reversal hadn't happened, I don't think we'd be having this conversation right now."

"I hear you, but with or without the flux reversal, you did make a difference," I responded. "You promised jobs in the Midwest, and you actually followed through, which was quite a win—especially given the damage control that you had to do at the same time."

"Well, thanks for that, but it took an army. When I think about Mike's Triangle of *Caca,* it all goes back to training and education. That's the center of all the misery we wanted to fix. We knew that there was an immediate need for jobs in the center and south of the country (I mean, we needed jobs *everywhere,* but those regions were hurting the most), so we decided that we'd better start kind of small, prove in a model that works, and then go big. So, we started with Iowa, mainly because they jumped on board—volunteered, really—the minute we announced our plan, and offered to help. But one state wasn't enough, so we added Missouri and Tennessee."

"And why those states, specifically?" I asked.

"Well, as I said, Iowa was easy, because they offered. And, they already had a head start on infrastructure—that place is covered with optical fiber because of all the call centers that are there. But we picked the other two, Missouri and Tennessee, for a completely different reason. Geography."

"Meaning?"

"Those two states share borders with more states than any others[xxxviii]. They both touch eight, including each other. So, we figured that if the plan we ultimately put together worked, it would be easy to extend it across state lines. It just seemed like a good idea. Not to mention the fact that they both have a lot of rural areas and were both job-challenged.

"So, we reached out. Like I said, going back to the triangle, we knew that it all started with education and training. We pulled together an idea fair. Basically, we invited universities in the region, technology think tanks, some Silicon Valley people, some folks from Austin, a bunch of students, folks from professional services firms, and a few others, and we just gave them the podium with a set of instructions: reverse-engineer this thing. Imagine it's three years from today, and everybody here is STUNNED at how well it worked out. There are new jobs, people are working, and tech companies are flocking to the middle of the country to establish beachheads. How did we get there?

"Well, the chemistry was there, and so was the energy. All we had to do was stay out of the way. I remember Mike telling me that they were chastising each other every time one of them said, 'Yeah. But…' instead of, 'Yes, and…'" And when the kids kicked in and started throwing around technology ideas, well, that was the real beginning of things. As soon as they started talking about that, the whole thing went from concept to reality."

"So, what happened first?" I asked.

"The first thing that happened was Iowa," she explained. "Iowa—that funny little puzzle-piece state in the middle of the country. Like I said a minute ago, they jumped in and offered to be a guinea pig for some of the ideas. Their argument was pretty good: 'We're already the contact center capital of the country, and we have 130 telephone companies in-state—not to mention fiber everywhere[xxxix].' So, their state government took a huge leap: They began to market themselves as 'The Silicon Cornfield.' Because of all that telecom infrastructure, the state positioned itself as the maker space capital of the United States and began to offer incentives to tech companies to relocate there. They also attracted satellite campuses and commercial educational institutions, which focused on training programs to educate the local population on jobs that were required to support the newfound industry base.

"In response, Missouri, Tennessee, Nebraska, South Dakota, Minnesota, Wisconsin, and Illinois, some of which surround Iowa, jumped on-board and announced their own cooperative efforts.

"Things took a real turn when Missouri and Tennessee, our first two focal points, worked together to build a sort of a think-tank in Chattanooga. They staffed it with a combination of recruiters, industry reps, technologists, and teachers from colleges, trade schools and universities, and began to hold virtual meetings called 'What-Iffers.' Mary Slaughter helped a lot at the beginning to get those going. Those meetings, which happened every two weeks, each had a theme, but the goal, the outcome they were looking for, was always the same: 'Based on this conversation we've had today about whatever the theme was, what new jobs should we be developing training programs for?' Sometimes the themes were specific industries, like farming, or ranching, or financial services, and sometimes they focused on a particular technology—like robotics or AI.

"Let's say a What-Iffer was held around Artificial Intelligence. The question they wanted to answer at the end of that meeting was, 'What kinds of training programs do we need to develop right now for AI jobs that won't be here for another three years or so? It turned out to be a tough exercise to go through a lot of the time, because a lot of these technologies were moving targets. Some of them weren't even commercial yet. But AI was a good example, because there was also a lot of fear and uncertainty about it. People were worried about losing their jobs to robots and machines and such, and let's face it, some of that fear had merit."

"Say more," I encouraged.

"Jobs have always gone away—that's just the way of things. Machines will never replace people, because they lack so many of the things that make us human: compassion; creativity; curiosity; the ability to deliberately collaborate. Of course, the other side of the argument is that robots regularly replace things that people *do*, and that's where the controversy starts.

"This may surprise you, but in 1950 they held the first ever conference on Artificial Intelligence at Dartmouth College[xl]. The people who attended were some of the smartest people in the world, people like Marvin Minsky and Claude Shannon, and while they were there, reporters asked them how long it would be before we had a machine that could think like a human. They said, '20 years[xli].' Well, it's now—what—almost 100 years later? And the experts are still saying '20 years' when they get asked that question.

"So, things aren't moving very fast, apparently, but robots *have* displaced a lot of people, because in reality, robots don't replace people, they replace some of the things that people *do*. But when you ask the real experts, they tell you that a lot of jobs will *never* be replaced by machines. Yeah, yeah, I know, never's a long time. But the jobs they're talking about tend to be creative jobs, like artists, writers, musicians, electricians, plumbers, designers, and scientists; jobs that require the ability to make strategic decisions, like executives, diplomats, economists, and sociologists; jobs that require empathy, like nurses and other caregivers; and a lot of jobs that haven't even been invented yet.

"But there are always going to be jobs that go the way of the dodo bird—or that, at the very least, will be seriously disrupted. I mean, just look at the positions that have already been affected by technology: bookkeepers and accountants, retail clerks, editors and proofreaders, couriers and delivery people, IT support, market analysts, advertisers, and office receptionists.

"Look, I get it: people fear technology; they always have. But before we all start worrying about Skynet taking over the world, let's remember that jobs have always gone away as new technologies have arrived. Factories used to have people called 'lectors' who stood in the middle of the factory floor with a megaphone and read the newspaper to the workers to keep them entertained while they did their work. Now they all have iPhones and earbuds. Computers used to be people. Pinsetters at bowling alleys used to be people, not machines made by AMF and Brunswick. Knocker-Uppers were people who walked around with a long stick, knocking on people's windows to wake them up for work—the first alarm clocks. I'd love to have that title on my business card, by the way. Ratcatchers, lamplighters, and switchboard operators are all long gone, because technology evolved[xlii]. So yeah—jobs will disappear—and new ones, better ones, more relevant ones, will arise to take their place.

"Every wave of immigration that's happened throughout history always followed the same pattern: whoever arrived next, whether it was the Irish or the Germans or Latin Americans or the North Africans or the Syrians, immediately became socially inferior to whoever came before them. It's pecking order stuff. Well, I think we're watching a new wave of immigrants creep in, called Artificial Intelligence and Robotics and Machine Learning, and it's causing a backlash that looks just like the backlash that happens when the next wave of human immigrants arrives. 'Robots are going to take our jobs!' Yep, they're going to take SOME jobs—not all. Why? Because robots are really, really good at doing mindlessly boring, repetitive, precise tasks. And, unlike people, they don't get tired; they don't get bored; they don't ask for time off; they don't go on strike; they don't want a raise; and they don't get repetitive stress injuries from doing exactly the same thing, precisely, thousands of times a day.

So, yeah, machines will take that away. But in the process, we're going to need robot designers, programmers, installers, troubleshooters, integrators, electricians, metalworkers, security specialists, and a bunch of jobs that we don't know about yet. And we're going to need people to build and design the networks that hook them all together. And we'll need people who can design and install the data generation infrastructure—Internet of Things—that will guide the robots. And we'll need people who are trained to analyze and make sense of all the data that those things generate. The list goes on and on. So, will some jobs go the way of the dodo bird? Sure. But others will rise up like a phoenix to replace them. And they'll be better jobs."

"That's really interesting," I responded.

"Don't start thinking I'm some kind of bit-weenie, Michael, because I'm not," she laughed. "The one thing I've always been good at is knowing what I don't know and then surrounding myself with people who do. Who cares where the knowledge comes from, as long as we get to the answer we're looking for? But I picked up enough from Mike and Doug and Elon to be very, very dangerous—and very excited."

Chapter 26: Immigration

"As long as we're on the subject of immigration, could we talk about that for a bit?" I asked.

"Oh, so you want to open Pandora's Box, huh?" She laughed. "That was a lot of fun. Uphill most of the way, but fun.

"Immigration is like ascendency in a corporation. If you don't bring entry-level people into your company on a regular basis, and then allow them to develop and grow and move up the ladder, everything gets complacent and stale. You've got no source of fresh ideas, or new ways of doing things, and you get into a situation where all you're doing is reinforcing the status quo. When that happens, you're leaving the door open for a competitor to come in and eat your lunch.

"Well, the same is true with a country. People seek refugee status for a bunch of reasons, but, as the word implies, they're seeking refuge from something. That means that they've faced adversity and learned how to deal with it. Or, they're just looking to better their lives by coming to a place that rewards hard work and integrity and commitment, and family values and innovation. I don't know—call me crazy, but I want those kinds of people coming to live here."

"What about the 'criminal element' argument?" I asked.

"Doesn't hold water," she replied. "We've already got plenty of criminals, and they didn't come in as refugees. They're home-grown. We don't kick them out of the country when we catch them. Will there be some criminals in the mix? Of course. But they're a vanishingly small percentage of all the people who are trying to be here. What does it say on the pedestal of Lady Liberty? 'Give me your tired, your poor, your huddled masses yearning to breathe free, The wretched refuse of your teeming shore.' To shut down an entire program of hope because of a few assholes is incredibly short-sighted and mean—and that's not who we are."

"Your programs were pretty far-reaching—and more than a little bit unusual," I challenged.

"What does that bumper sticker say, Michael? 'Well-behaved women rarely make history'? Well, forgive me for being poorly behaved. I wasn't out to make history; I was out to make a difference for a bunch of people who had no one in their corner. That's where the 'Bring Your Job to Work Day' came from."

I nodded as I made notes. Bring Your Job to Work Day was one of the more controversial—and successful—programs that Ahadi Fadhili-Mason managed to put through during her term as President. It was designed to overcome as many of the objections to immigration as possible and put into place a model that would attract much-needed talent from abroad. Given the aggressive plans that Fadhili-Mason's Three Musketeers (Standley, Rowe, and Musk) had put into play, along with their D'Artagnan, Mary Slaughter, it became clear pretty quickly that a diverse range of talents was needed, and they weren't necessarily available domestically. The country needed skilled laborers for the farms, of course—nothing new there—so after a brief but thorough background check, immigrant farm workers were granted temporary visas to enter the country at the beginning of the agricultural season. While they worked, they were taught English and American civics by VISTA volunteers. If they worked for five consecutive years without a legal problem, they were fast-tracked to citizenship, if they wanted it. Not all did, interestingly.

"One other interesting thing that came from this—small scale, but really interesting—was that a bunch of kids got together to set up programs under which these new Americans were enrolled to help teach their own language to local kids, as a way to broaden cultural inclusion," she added. "But it led to some really interesting work opportunities for would-be exporters."

The second part of this was longer-term and had to do with the looming national infrastructure crisis. Most of the country's critical infrastructure—roads, bridges, tunnels, power, water, sewage, and so on—was built in the fifty years following World War II. That investment allowed the country to rocket ahead economically, but World War II had ended almost 100 years before, and much of that infrastructure was in need of work[xliii]. Back in the 2020 timeframe, Canada, as an example, spent about 2.9 percent of its GDP on infrastructure; the United States spent 0.6%, and the complacency was catching up with the country as bridges began to fail, roads became substandard, and water systems, especially in urban areas, became increasingly unable to handle the demand for fresh water or waste treatment[xliv].

So: Under Fadhili-Mason's guidance, workers were brought in on provisional visas to build roads, bridges, dams, water management systems, and so on. Some had specific skills related to the project they would ultimately work on; others were laborers, and after five years, if they behaved, they were also given the option of fast-tracked citizenship, something most of them jumped at. And of course, former inmates who successfully completed their education or sentence or whatever you want to call it, had the right of first refusal for the jobs, because we didn't want to disadvantage our own citizens.

What this also did was create a pool of skilled labor that could be tracked and deployed, as needed, anywhere in the country. We made it easy for them to send money home to their families, but also made it easy for their families to join them after a year of 'good behavior,' if they wished.

"As part of the process," she explained, "Mike and Mary pulled together a team of people who designed a training program for the New Americans. If they already had a desirable skill, we augmented it; if they didn't, we provided them with the training they needed to develop one.

"So, some of our prison graduates became teachers after learning their skill, and they then taught the skill to new members of our society. I *defy* you to show me a downside to that model. Oh—and they had the option to set aside a percentage of their earnings, which I—meaning the government— agreed to match, for higher education. So, if they saved a thousand dollars for college, I'd give them another thousand—but they *had* to use it for education, trade skills or college—it didn't matter. Again—who the hell loses, here? By the way, this was why I pushed hard to make the changes I did in public school curriculum. You may recall, or you may have read, that I pushed pretty hard for a few changes to the classes that kids had to take in order to graduate from high school, especially after that 2020 shit-show."

"Absolutely," I nodded. "You forced through a requirement that kids had to have classes in civics, debate and civil discourse, and demonstrable skill as a practitioner, as a graduation requirement. And now that I think about it, an engineer friend I know attended a college in the mid-70s that required graduates not to pass a laundry list of classes, but to complete projects and then demonstrate their competency in their field—that kind of thing."

"Yep. And you know where that came from? After I graduated from college, I took a trip to Europe and ended up spending a lot of time in Spain. One day, I wandered into a bar in Madrid and felt like I had walked into a street fight about to break out. People were yelling and screaming at each other, waving their arms around as Spaniards do, veins sticking out on their necks, and then they'd stop, drink some wine or beer, talk about their families or dogs or kids or whatever, and then go back to this intense arguing. I'd never seen anything like it. It's called a *Tertulia*. Basically, the Spanish *Tertulia* is a gathering of people, usually in a bar or restaurant, often including university professors and other intellectuals, but not exclusively. They eat, they drink, they get rip-roaring drunk, and they argue issues from every side. It's a great example of how people with radically differing views can come together, argue loudly, listen to each other, and walk away friends. And it's a spectator sport: people come just to watch and learn[xlv].

"So, I asked that kids be required to take a course in the Tertulia. I don't mean that literally; what I mean is that kids should be able to engage in a spirited debate with someone who believes things that are different than what they believe, without judgment, and walk away friends to go look for girls or drink beer or whatever. Instead of seeing a differing point-of-view as a threat to their personhood, as a ridiculous trigger warning that will scar their sensitive souls for life, they see it as a way to learn, a way to broaden their perspective. They shouldn't be ruined because somebody has a different belief than they do—or, God help them, if they discover that their beliefs are wrong. What a concept. Oh, and there was one more thing. I advocated for a course in world geography. Call me crazy, but when kids hear the name of a country mentioned in conversation, they should be able to at least envision the continent that it's on. I mean, kids tossed around the word Timbuktu all the time, but how many of them knew it was the name of a real city, that it was actually spelled

Tombouctou or Tumbutu, that it was in a country called Mali, and was located in north Africa[xlvi]? Pretty much none of them. So, I wanted to create that awareness."

Chapter 27: The Environment

"Can we talk about environmental stuff?" I asked.

Her face visibly darkened at the question, and I saw a rare flash of anger sweep across her eyes.

"Sure—I mean, that's pretty much the only thing people wanted to do about the environment, anyway—talk."

She shook her head in what I took to be a sign of disgust—or perhaps, resignation.

"If there was one area where I feel like I failed, it would be the environmental changes I tried to bring about," she said. "Everybody's quick to jump on the clean air, zero emissions, alternative energy, energy-independent, low carbon footprint bandwagon, because it looks good and sounds good and takes slogan leadership to a whole new ineffective level. But when it comes time to pay for it or get behind the hard decisions required to make it real, or shift industrial dependencies, well, now, let's slow down—let's not get ahead of ourselves. But isn't getting ahead of ourselves exactly what we *should* be doing?

"Just think about this for a minute. By doing nothing, all we do is reinforce the status quo. Do you know what that phrase actually means? It means 'the current state of affairs.' Well, the current state of affairs was pretty damn ugly. In his zeal to take care of his cronies, Trump and his brain trust deregulated heavy industry, killing hundreds of environmental protections. Years of work to clean up the environment, down the drain. The man was a disaster. In the late 60s, Barry Commoner, the country's first real ecologist and the founder of the modern ecological movement, made dire predictions about the negative impact people were having on the planet. But we didn't need him to tell us that. Lake Erie was so polluted from industrial runoff that it was biologically dead. And in 1969, the Cuyahoga River caught fire. Let me say that again: *the river caught on fire.* The air above Los Angeles was so polluted that the chemicals in the smog above the city would actually capture images of the city in the clouds, like photographic film. That is some serious shit.

"So, there we were, in the middle of my term. Funding for alternative energy, like wind and solar and nuclear, was stalled out. Pollutants were once again accumulating in the atmosphere and water. And, the planet was getting warmer, which had all kinds of downstream effects. Now, look: I read the books, did my homework. I know that the planet naturally cools and warms, and that has nothing to do with humans. I get that. But I also know that humans make it worse—I get that, too. The science is there, it's proven beyond doubt, and when it comes to what I believe, I side with the science every time. For example, smokestacks spew carbon and heavy metals into the air because we still mine and burn a lot of coal in this country—not to mention elsewhere, like China. Elemental carbon isn't poisonous, per se, but it settles on everything. It's black, so it absorbs heat and accelerates the melting of the polar ice and the permafrost, along with the greenhouse gas effect and the natural warming of the planet. That means that more freshwater pours into the oceans, which changes the salinity, leading to mass die-offs. And, because we're pumping so much CO_2 into the atmosphere, we're also acidifying the oceans, which leads to MORE mass die-offs. It's a double whammy. We change the salinity, we change the pH, oh, and now let's make it a *triple* whammy: we warm things up. All of a sudden, all those species that have adapted to existing oceanic conditions discover that their neighborhood has gone to shit. So, they leave—because they die.

"And as long as we're talking about that, here's what else happens. Everybody sits around wearing their bracelets made from recovered oceanic plastic and lamenting the death of the rainforests because they're the lungs of the planet. Really? Oh, they're important, alright—it's tragic what Brazil's leader did down there. But here's the dirty little secret: 80 percent of the planet's oxygen comes from the ocean, not the rain forests. In fact, 20 percent of oceanic oxygen comes from one single organism, an oceanic alga that nobody's ever heard of called prochlorococcus. And guess what—it's dying, because we're screwing up the ocean.

"Shall I continue? When the planet warms, and the permafrost melts, it releases methane gas in huge quantities, because it's been stored in the deep ice for centuries. You think cattle and concrete produce a lot of pollutants that contribute to global warming? Think again. And those heavy metals in the atmosphere, like mercury? We still don't know all of the health risks they're causing today.

"So, yeah, I went after the environmental thing hard and fast. But as I said earlier, I'm not stupid. I knew that going after the oil and gas and coal industries was a waste of my time, because they employ too many people and, let's face it, they also provide a big slice of our energy. And to be fair, some of them are investing pretty substantially in alternative energy development, so I don't want to paint them all with the same brush.

"Another problem we have is that even today, way too many people don't have the whole picture. They love to wave the wind and solar flag, but they don't understand that you can't put solar panels on your roof and a windmill in your vegetable garden and voila, suddenly go off the grid.

You can't run your fridge or your oven using solar—there's just not enough current for that. You still need a feed from the power company. But: you *can* do good things for the environment by feeding power upstream to the power company, which reduces their need to burn coal or natural gas to spin turbine generators. It's an offset model. You get a credit on your bill, and the environment gets a credit in the greenhouse gas department. Everybody wins.

"I guess the thing that pissed me off more than anything was the fact that the fossil fuel industries wouldn't even consider some of our ideas. Yeah, they were all quick to talk about their R&D in alternative energy and carbon capture, but they were pretty much dead set against even considering strategies that would reduce the use of oil and gas, or for that matter, coal.

"Honestly, I don't blame them; oil and gas employs hundreds of thousands of people, supports a zillion ancillary industries, and is the reason a lot of countries have managed to become industrialized nations."

"And," I added, "crude oil is about more than gasoline. I did a piece on all the things that come out of a barrel of oil besides what everybody knows about, and I was shocked: paint, all kinds of plastics, anesthetics, toothpaste, even some drugs. So, I can understand why moving away from oil and gas is an uphill battle."

"Absolutely, which is why my goal was never to 'move away.' All I wanted to do was *reduce* our use of crude, not eliminate it altogether. I believed that if we could reduce our dependency on gas and diesel-fueled vehicles in favor of electric, we'd be ahead of the game. But there's no way in hell we can eliminate the use of crude completely—that's asinine. Sure, we can use plant-based technology to make plastics, and drugs, and all those things you mentioned, but there's a cost with that as well. And remember: plastics are used for a lot more than just plastic bags that kill turtles and whales. They're also needed in clothing, heart valves, artificial joints, the list is pretty much endless.

"But coal is a different story. First of all, when I was in office, the coal industry employed 50,000 people. Just for the sake of comparison, Starbucks had just shy of 300,000 Baristas serving coffee all over the country. My point is that we mined coal for two reasons: because we had power plants that were designed around it; and, because we've always mined coal. It's a way of life more than it is a job. People cling to it because it's part of their identity, like any job—not to mention that in many of our coal mining regions, like West Virginia, there were no other jobs to be had. So really, we had two problems. One was jobs, in a region of the country that's already got the deck stacked against it, economically, and the other was the environment—the need to reduce coal dependency and move to a cleaner fuel.

"There's another factor that we have to consider as well. Like crude oil, some coal mining will have to continue, not to produce coal to burn for power and steam production, but to produce coke, a vital part of the production of steel. Without coke, the carbon inserted into the iron crystal can't be done.

"What I tried to do—and I wasn't as successful as I would have liked—was a couple of things. The first was to figure out a way to decommission the country's coal-fired plants, which was an enormous job. I didn't want to turn them off and tear them down; I wanted to figure out a way to reconfigure them to burn something else, like natural gas. Not ideal, but much cleaner than coal. That, of course, would mean ending those 50,000 mining jobs…"

"And replacing them with what?" I asked.

"Exactly—that was the problem. Germany tried it back in

the day—meaning, tried to shut down the coal plants—and it turned out to be more than even Angela Merkel could do, as influential and powerful as she was. The pushback from labor unions and local governments pretty much stopped her in her tracks. What she ended up doing was paying a subsidy to the coal industry to offset the cost of refitting the plants and paying the workers. It worked out to a couple of billion Euros, but it gave her the runway she needed to get things moving in the right direction.

"For us, it was a huge undertaking, because there were about 240 coal-fired plants in the US. Germany had 40. So, we entered into the world's largest due diligence effort, trying to understand the cost-benefit equation from a purely apolitical point-of-view. We looked at the cost of raw materials production, including extraction and refining; the cost of transportation of finished product to the plants; the environmental cost, in actual dollars, if we continued to burn coal, including things like carbon sequestration, impacts to healthcare, that kind of thing; the cost of retrofitting the plants to natural gas; the secondary cost associated with the hit that the coal industry would take, in terms of revenue and lost jobs; and, the very real cost to the communities that are so dependent on coal for their livelihood, including everybody from the miners to the operators to the deli down the street that they all buy their lunch from. Know what we learned? I'll bet you can guess."

"It was cheaper, long-term, to move away from coal," I guessed. Although it wasn't really a guess.

"Yep—and not by a little bit. Remember when Trump pulled us out of the Paris Climate Accord? Talk about short-sighted pandering. He said that it was unfair to America because it would kill jobs in coal. The part he missed, and which he would have understood if he knew how to read, was that bringing back coal as a fuel wasn't the same as bringing back jobs related to its production. The problem is that natural gas is cheaper than coal to produce, and we've been drowning in it for years, even now. One of the reasons that the jobs started to go away in the coal industry was because of that—natural gas was cheaper, so coal's market share took a huge hit, which meant cutting costs for the employers—and the first thing to go was the most expensive thing, people.

"But it's more than that. Between the mid-1970s and the great recession of 2008, there was a big boom in coal production and consumption. In fact, the number of tons of coal that were extracted increased by 865 percent during that period. But here's the dirty little secret—as if there's any other kind with coal. The number of miners that produced it fell by half. Miner productivity increased by 350 percent, not because they ate their Wheaties, but because of robotic automation and the fact that a lot of the extraction operations went from old-fashioned underground mining in Appalachia to open pits in Wyoming and Ohio. And get this: The Federal government was paying the coal industry more than $300 million annually in subsidies—but that money didn't create jobs. It made the industry more productive by *eliminating* jobs, because the companies invested in technology, not job creation."

"And did they see any benefits, once they started talking about it?" I asked.

"Oh yeah—and they started seeing them pretty quickly. Once they started retiring coal-fired plants, it didn't take them long to realize that wind and solar are actually cheaper than coal, oil and gas, or nuclear—and that's without factoring in Federal subsidies.

"The thing is that what drove them to change more than anything was a growing dependency on cheap natural gas. But it still pollutes. We wanted them to go farther."

"But can a solar facility generate as much power as a gas or coal-powered plant?" I asked.

"It depends. There's a solar facility near Yuma, Arizona called Solana that generates 280 megawatts, enough to power about 70,000 homes. And the good news is that because they're 100 percent solar, they avoid producing 470,000 tons of carbon dioxide every year that would otherwise make it into the atmosphere.

Then there's the Ivanpah facility in California, way out in the Mojave Desert. It produces something on the order of 377,000 megawatts, but it also uses natural gas to supplement its output, a fact that got it into trouble in its first few years of operation. It's still orders-of-magnitude better than coal, though.

"I'll tell you what I find so interesting about all of this—which is why I still remember all these facts from so long ago. We can burn coal to produce electricity. We can burn natural gas to produce electricity. We can burn oil to produce electricity. We can split atoms, or take advantage of quantum physics, or harness the wind, all to produce electricity. What's interesting to me is that with the exception of wind and hydro and one flavor of solar, in every case, we produce electricity by heating water to produce steam which creates pressure which spins a turbine which generates electricity. We're talking James Watt, technology that was invented in the 1700s! That doesn't make it bad, but we sure don't seem to be moving very fast. Then along come wind and sun, and they're the bad guys? Really?

Here's what else pisses me off and just makes me shake my head. George W. Bush started an extensive jobs training program in Appalachia, which was expanded under Obama. It collapsed in 2017 when Trump proclaimed the return of King Coal. But it didn't collapse because he defunded it; it collapsed because coal industry workers, including laid-off and unemployed workers from closed mines, stopped going to the training program! They bought into Trump's nonsense that the good times were coming back, and they didn't have to work at finding new jobs or training in new skills. He gave them an easy way out, and they took it."

"I know this frustrates you, but you definitely moved the needle on environmental issues," I said.

"Not enough—I should have put more emphasis there. But we were juggling a lot of balls, as you know. We made good progress; I just wish we could have done more. Thanks to a recommendation from Doug Standley, I pulled Bill Shireman into the picture as my Chief Environmental Officer, because he was pretty successful at bringing warring parties together, especially over environmental issues. So, he gets a lot of the credit for what we accomplished—and none of the blame for what we didn't. That, I place squarely in the lap of inertia."

Chapter 28: Dawning Realization

Ahadi poured the few remaining sips of her iced tea into the grass next to the patio table and stood. "Michael, I don't want to cut off this conversation, because it's important. I have to make a few calls and do a few things before dinner, so with your permission, I'll leave you here for a bit and we can pick this up later. Feel free to wander around, or you're welcome to work here or at the kitchen table—whatever you need. I'm glad you're staying over; in fact, if you like, I can show you where the guest room is, and you can unpack and relax—whatever you need."

"You're too kind, Ahadi," I replied. "I think I'll sit here at the patio table and make some notes while I get my thoughts together. But if you need me for anything, I'm here. I'm pretty good with a kitchen knife."

"Oh, don't worry—I'll put you to work later," she chuckled. "Meanwhile, make yourself at home. But if you need to rest for a bit, your guest room is the first door after the bathroom."

"Thank you so much—and thank you again for the kind invitation to stay over. I wasn't expecting that when we first spoke, and I don't want to be a nuisance."

"Not at all," she replied. "It's a pleasure to have you here. I'll see you in a few. Just holler if you need anything or go find Al—he's still out there messing with that tractor. I told him not to buy the damn thing, but does he listen? No…" Her voice disappeared down the hallway.

The brand-new Moleskine notebook I had brought with me was four pages away from being completely full of hastily-scrawled notes from the day's conversation—and it was barely two in the afternoon. The cover was stained with grape juice from our foray into the vineyard, and I had plucked a couple of hops to press in its pages.

I pulled the SD card from the digital recorder and inserted it into a slot on my laptop to copy the sound files I had captured. Once the copy was complete, I checked them to make sure they were audible—they were—and slid the write-protect switch on the card into the 'protect' position. I then placed it face-down in my card wallet and inserted a fresh card and batteries into the recorder, ready for whatever came next.

The research I'd done prior to scheduling this interview was a journey in its own right and had taken most of a year to complete. Between Ahadi Fadhili-Mason's headstrong nature, the people she surrounded herself with, and the polar reversal and its physiological aftereffects, she had everything going for her in terms of being able to get things done during her presidency. And she did. But what was just as impressive, and to be honest, baffling, were the things that happened that were directly related to the magnetic reversal and that had absolutely nothing to do with politics, or reform, or any kind of social agenda. They just happened. For example, the bulk of the world's people, for reasons that are still unclear, became disenchanted and left the ranks of organized religion in massive numbers. To be clear, they didn't become less spiritual—in fact, it could be argued that they were actually more spiritual than they were before the reversal happened. They embraced their spirituality, their belief in something bigger than themselves. But they went through a period of deep consideration that led most of them to conclude that organized religion had become a systemic way to legally accumulate vast amounts of money and power. This caused The Church—and it was an equal-opportunity phenomenon, no single religion was spared—to decline in relevance and become a shadow of its former self. Hollywood's idols desperately clung to Scientology, but the numbers weren't there, and the organization became a second-rate publisher of third-rate science fiction books.

And that was the other thing: Heroes died. Not literally, but all those folks who had enjoyed the trappings of fame for the simple reason that they were famous, suddenly weren't. Sports figures and actors and socialites and rock stars were respected for their skills and abilities if they had them, but they weren't revered anymore as demigods. But what nobody expected to happen was that other whole segments of the population suddenly rose to the occasion and took their place. Scientists and engineers and architects and nurses and doctors and college professors suddenly found themselves surrounded by hordes of admirers. *My God,* they thought. *We're cool.*

And then there were other things. Like holy shit, the NRA. Where the hell did THAT come from?!?!? From out of nowhere, a popular rebellion starts, and the National Rifle Association is given an ultimatum. In response to the growing number of shootings in the country, they're given 45 days to come up with a solution that will curb the problem. As one legislator said, 'Since you're committed to keeping guns available in the country, you will now be legally committed to making them safe. And don't give us that crap about people, not guns, killing people. That's why we regulate cars so carefully.' If after 45 days they did not come up with a solution, they were told, they would be declared an illegal organization and all funding would be denied to them. If you want to be part of the solution, don't be part of the problem.

"You look deep in thought," a voice rumbled behind me, causing me to start. It was Al, wiping grease off his hands with a red rag—although there was so much grease on the

227

rag already, I didn't see how it could possibly help.

"Just pulling my thoughts together," I replied. "Lots of moving parts in this story."

"Yeah, she's something," he chuckled.

"I guess what I'm wrestling with is just how lucky we, the country, whatever—how lucky we were that all those moving parts came together when they did. I mean, the changes that happened on her watch are like a century of history in six years. But they were changes the country desperately needed—hell, they were changes the *world* needed."

"Look, Michael," Al responded, "I've been with her from day one, and I've watched her go from being this doe-eyed novice to a savvy, passionate, leader—and somebody who could savage an opponent without even trying. That's one of her better qualities, by the way. But here's the deal. She looked at the country, and what she saw, wasn't pretty. And she would have tried to do the things she did with or without the polar reversal.

"What she saw was fear—people were scared. Not because they thought we were going to have a civil war or something like that—they were scared of themselves, of what they'd become. And in some cases, they were scared of what they would *never* become. But she knew that a lot of that fear was just ignorance. This is a big country, with a lot of people who are very, very different. Some of them are well-educated, some are not; some are wise beyond their years; some are filled with hope, but some live lives that are utterly hopeless, with zero chance of escape for themselves or their kids, and they know it.

"So, what we knew—what SHE knew—was that ignorance leads to fear, fear leads to a lack of trust, and a lack of trust leads to social disconnect. And that's a dangerous state of affairs."

"But what were they really afraid of?" I asked him.

"Each other. Government. The unknown. Loneliness. Poverty. Hunger. Endless racism. As Goose said in Top Gun, the list is long and distinguished. And by the way, ignorant doesn't mean stupid—it means unaware. To try for something better, you have to know there's something better out there.

"So, when she took over," he continued, "she set her sights on education as her number one target. She told me once that 'education kills ignorance, and what blossoms in its place is curiosity, which leads to inquiry, and inquiry leads to understanding and insight. Understanding and insight lead to acceptance, and perceived differences disappear.' I've never forgotten that—she said it late one evening when she was wrestling with her Cabinet and trying to figure out where to start. This was before the reversal really kicked in, and government was kicking her ass around the block. I told her that she was the best thing that had happened to this office in eight years, and that she would see her way to doing the job well. I told her that she had a lot to learn, but that she was obviously a fast learner. She shook her head and said, 'If only the country was.' But this was her formula from day one. She used to say, 'If I can just plant a seed of curiosity in the nation, if I can just get a few people to say 'maybe' instead of an outright 'no,' then we have a chance, and the nation will cure itself.'

"She always said that what had historically made America a great country—not in the Donald Trump sense, but in the sense of hope and promise and cohesion—was the presence of a large and prosperous middle class. But while she was campaigning in New Mexico one time, a woman came up to her and really unloaded. Not in a rude way; it was more like she was desperate and needed to vent to somebody who was willing to listen. One thing she said really hit Ahadi—and hard. She said, 'America is no longer a democracy with a vibrant middle class. It's a whorehouse that has gone condo.' Wow. The woman said that self-respect, self-worth, and national values that everyone could get behind had disappeared, because everybody was out for themselves. Community was no longer a priority. The poor at the bottom of the pyramid were growing their ranks, and the elite rich were growing theirs. The middle class was being hollowed out, which meant that we were becoming, at least, from a societal structure perspective, another banana republic, like Venezuela, or El Salvador, or Cuba.

"That was what drove her, and that was when she began to formulate a plan for her presidency. And, that's when the Mulvihill-McCooey event really began to affect things."

"And was that when she started thinking about reinventing the rules of government?" I asked. "Because what she did there was really a 'go big or go home' moment."

"No, that came later. Like everybody, she went into the office starry eyed, but it took about a week for her to realize how Washington works. In fact, I gave her a coffee cup one time that said, 'NON ILLEGITIMI CORBORUNDUM.'"

"Meaning…?" I asked.

"It's fake Latin," he laughed. "It means 'Don't let the bastards grind you down.' She still has it in the cupboard in the kitchen. Anyway, once it dawned on her what a nest of snakes Washington was, she started thinking about what she could do to improve it. If nothing else, she could leave the place a little bit better than it was when she arrived. But she never thought she'd be making amendments to the

Constitution and basically overhauling the world."

What a great way to put it, I thought. Once she got on the government overhaul bus, there was no stopping her. First stop was the 22nd Amendment. The problem? The constitution provides for two four-year terms as President for any one candidate. But they always spend the last two years of the first term campaigning for their second term, during which time nothing presidential gets done. So, it was really six years. Easy fix, she said: a single six-year term. And the campaign season lasts six weeks, and there's a severe cap on political contributions.

Second stop: a visit to Amendment 20, Congressional term limits. Those old silverbacks saw a money machine that they could draw from anytime, so she put a stop to that damn quick. And nobody stopped her. Twelve years max, then somebody else gets to come in and shake things up.

"But she did other things, too, that were not quite as dramatic as rewriting the Constitution, but still important," I added.

"Oh yeah—like kicking the damn lobbyists out of Washington." He laughed, shaking his head. "You'd think she'd cut their arms off with a nail file, the way they screamed. And I guess, in a way, she did. But she held her ground, and the next thing you know, she's holding the equivalent of a job fair for lobbyists so that they could peddle their influence, but in the bright sun of reality and in carefully controlled conditions. It was great."

I thought about what Al had said for a moment before asking my next question.

"Al, you're as close to her as anyone—in fact, from what I see, closer than anybody. I know that you were the head of her protection detail. What matters is that you were close to her, both physically and emotionally, throughout her career, and now, way beyond it. She flipped the country on its head, which I'm sure pissed off a lot of people, Polar Reversal or not. Did she ever have doubts? I mean, were there ever times when she seriously questioned what she was trying to do?"

Al thought for a moment, looking down at the ground between his shoes and rubbing the palms of his hands together. "The only time I ever saw her doubt herself was when she went after healthcare," he said.

Chapter 29: Life and Taxes

"That whole thing had become such an evil circus; it was like trying to unravel a ball of barbed wire. Insurance companies, pharma, the tort lawyers, the doctors ... everybody wanted a piece of everybody else's flesh.

"She had a meeting one time with a group of healthcare advisors, and after going back and forth with them with zero progress, she stopped the meeting and asked if any of them had ever read the parable of the five blind men and the elephant. None had, so she told them the story. Five blind men are asked to go over and examine an elephant, and then come back and describe the animal. One feels the animal's broad, wrinkled ear; another, one of his tusks; another, one of his tree trunk-like legs; another, his ropy tail; and the last, his trunk. Obviously, they came back with five different but definitive descriptions of what an elephant looks like. They were all right, and they were all wrong.

"None of you has the whole picture," she told them. "You're all looking at one piece of the puzzle. But that's not the real problem: as smart as you all are, none of you is willing to look beyond what you want to see. You're supposed to be my advisors, my thought leaders, but instead what I'm getting is opinions and sound bites.'

"So, she cleared the room and started over. She sat down with a few of her closest advisors, people she really trusted— and you know who they are, we've been talking about them all day—and a bottle of Scotch and asked them one question: Has healthcare *ever* been good in this country? Has there ever been a time when people felt as if the system was out to help them, rather than gouge them?

"Well, they talked about that for a long time, and what

they decided was that the system was at its best back when doctors made house calls, and it was pretty obvious that their goal was to care for patients, rather than for their bank accounts. Not that they don't deserve to be paid well, but when a doctor starts to get rewarded based on how *little* time he or she spends with each patient, something's wrong.

"They also got off on a sideline conversation that actually turned into a big part of the greater conversation. Somebody said, 'yeah, but back then—what are we talking about, the 50s? 60s? All the technology a doctor needed fit in that little black bag they carried around. Today we have MRI machines and cat scans and robotic surgery systems that require entire hospital wings.'

"But that line of reasoning got shut down pretty quick. 'That's not relevant. We're talking about care quality, not the tools that help you deliver it,' somebody said. 'The quality of care is about the caregiver and the system they work in; the tools are just gravy.'

"Anyway, they talked for days about this, and they finally made a decision. Instead of trying to build a system from scratch—actually, instead of trying to fix the broken system, which would have been a disaster—they decided to look at all the world's healthcare systems and see if there was a way to pick the best of each, and then from those pieces try to cobble together a healthcare model that would actually work for everybody, or nearly everybody. We're not talking free; Ahadi isn't one for rainbows and unicorns and pixies. One way or the other, you have to pay for it.

"But the way they decided to do it was a stroke of genius. The number of insurance company executives who became instantaneously incontinent when she released her plan was a beautiful thing to see. She told the country that she was going to leave the existing healthcare system alone, and that it would continue to work the way it always had. But: She was announcing an alternative plan that would compete with existing plans, and that it would be outcomes-based with a focus on wellness. In other words, to the extent possible, the plan would keep people as well as possible as a way to hedge against the cost of treatment when they got sick. The rates would be set according to lifestyle. Now, obviously there are things that can't be anticipated, and coverage for those wasn't affected. But if somebody has never smoked, gets lots of exercise, eats reasonably well and drinks moderately, why shouldn't they get a break on their healthcare costs?

"So, they put together a bi-partisan committee of people that included economists, tax specialists, hospital administrators, social workers, law enforcement folks, first responders, sociologists, and of course, nurses, doctors, and psychologists. They also pulled in Melinda Gates, somebody from Warren Buffet's organization, a handful of high-end, bleeding-edge technology specialists, and a few folks that did things like medical software. And then, they set out to reverse-engineer the crap out of healthcare. But first, they set some ground rules.

"First, politics was strictly prohibited—that was non-negotiable. As Ahadi said on the first day, 'park your jackasses and elephants outside the door.' Second, the use of the word 'but' was strongly denounced. Third, the goal was to discuss healthcare as we wanted it to be, not as it was.

"So, they picked a day in the future. I don't remember what the date was, but it was five years out from the day they started, and they said that this was the day that they were working toward. Then, they began to throw ideas on the board. The ideas were pieces of the healthcare system that were considered at the time to be broken, which was pretty much the whole damn ecosystem. There was no editorializing; nobody was allowed to say, 'we'll never fix that, so let's leave it out of the discussion.' *Everything* was fair game.

"Before long, the walls of the room were covered with hand-written sticky notes. Eldercare. Prescription drug costs. The influence of big pharma. The cost of insurance. Mental health. R&D. Privacy and confidentiality. The rules that decide what's covered and what's not. Hell, childcare was up there. Health maintenance and prevention. Availability of good-quality rural care. There were probably thirty or forty notes on the wall, and they were all big problems."

"How did they decide to use this particular technique to attack the problem?" I asked.

"It came from a book that Ahadi read a long time ago about a guy who was the CEO of one of the big telephone companies in Canada. His name was Brian something-or-other, and he was apparently a take-no-prisoners kind of leader—as long as taking no prisoners served his company and customers. Canfield—his name was Brian Canfield, and he was at a company called TELUS.[xlvii]

"Apparently, when he was elected to the CEO job, one of the first things he did was to gather up a bunch of people from all the different organizations in the company—finance, engineering, sales, marketing, billing—and turn them into a task force. And by the way, he apparently made it clear that he didn't want old farts—he had a strong preference for younger employees who wouldn't be intimidated by working with the CEO on a regular basis. If I remember the story correctly, he stuck them all in a big room that had whiteboards on all four walls, and he gave them an assignment.

The assignment was simple: Pick a process in the company that you all agree is broken. Maybe it's billing, or service provisioning, whatever. But pick one. And when they had one selected, he told them to flowchart the process on the whiteboards. But there was a twist: He told them to flowchart the process the way it SHOULD work, not the way it DOES work. So, they took about three weeks, and they basically redesigned the process from the ground up. And when they were done, they called him back into the room. He looked at their drawings, asked a few questions to make sure that he understood what they had done, and then asked them to get out of the way. He then brought in the business unit leader that owned the broken process, gave the person a few minutes to look at the drawing on the wall, and told him or her that they had two months to make the current system look like what was flowcharted on the wall, or he'd find somebody who could. This is all from memory, but I think that that group ended up redesigning something like 30 systems before they were done. Amazing what can happen when you empower people to make decisions about something important, without fear of 'yeah but' blowback[xlviii]."

"So, that's what this group that Ahadi pulled together did for healthcare," I asked.

"Yeah, pretty much, although it was a lot more complicated and not quite as dramatic as the Jerry Maguire moment I just described. But it worked. Once the group realized that their conversation was a what-if conversation, where anything goes, they rolled up their sleeves and got to it. Hell, they had nothing to lose, but everything to gain."

"OK," I asked. "So, they have this list of problems, this wall full of broken pieces. What next?"

"Well, next, they went on safari. That's what they called it—an excellence safari. They went hunting for healthcare systems around the world that did at least one of those things well. Look, Pollyanna wasn't a member of the committee;

they knew that a lot of what they hoped to do was a mirage, but they had to try. And hell, all they had to do was fix one of the things they identified, and the whole country would be ahead, you know? So, they broke into small, multifunctional teams, and they headed out. And man, what they discovered was amazing."

"It worked?" I asked. "they found things that they could steal?"

"'Steal' is probably the wrong word, but they definitely found examples of healthcare done well and brought back as many ideas as they possibly could. And if the ideas were such that they could be implemented here, then they made whatever minor changes they had to and made each one part of the overall plan."

"Can you give me some examples? I mean, the kinds of things they found?"

"Sure, although you should talk to Ahadi—she can give you more of the details than I can. I just remember being wowed by the whole process, since I was sort of the fly on the wall with a gun in my armpit."

"Details about what?" Ahadi emerged from the house where she had been working, with a freshly filled glass of ice water in her hand. The awning gave us plenty of shade, but it was still hot and muggy on the patio.

"We were talking about healthcare," Al explained, "and Michael was asking me for some examples of the kinds of ideas you and your folks brought back from the safari you took when you went out hunting for healthcare done right. I told him that I could share a few that I remembered but that he should talk to you. And since you're here ..."

"Yeah," she said, joining us at the table. "Talk about tilting at windmills. I got so sick of hearing people say,

'Look—this is just the way it is.' But once we came back with a handful of best practices—and by the way, we also found a boatload of worst practices; we didn't have a monopoly on those by any stretch of the imagination—people started to see the possibilities. To be clear—nobody believed that we could actually *do* the kinds of things we found, but they were at least willing to admit that other places did certain things better than we did."

"That's where Al and I were when you came out. Like what?"

"Sorry to interrupt your train of thought, but let's see. We found a lot of really good things going on, and one of the ones we liked best was what Israel was doing with primary care. They may be under a constant threat of invasion, or annihilation, or whatever, but did you know that that country has one of the highest life expectancy rates in the world? At the time it was north of 80. But here's the best part: the percentage of their GDP that they spend on healthcare is one of the lowest in the world among developed nations. When we looked at them, they had four health maintenance organizations that had the responsibility to both acquire and sell primary care services. Care is available 24 hours-a-day, and in addition to hospitals they have a huge network of urgent care centres, evening clinics, and home health services available[xlix].

"Another area where we found great things being done was the whole universal care thing. Without exception, we found that the very best example of this was the care provided by the National Health Service in the UK. They did it first, and they've been doing it for a long time, so I'd expect them to do it well. Doctors and other healthcare professionals are well-paid, and every person in the country gets top-of-the-line healthcare, regardless of how much money they have—or don't[l].

"Another area I really wanted to explore was mental health, which was just one big, fat, paralyzing stigma in this country. Sick is sick, I don't care what part of the body is causing it. So, we ultimately got to Australia, and holy cow, were they doing it right. As part of their own national health service, they invest a lot of money into intervention and cause research, they do really aggressive outreach and counseling, and they provide home treatment, outpatient treatment, and crisis care. They're damn good at it[li].

"The whole medical technology arena was another area we wanted to look at, because things like healthcare that touch people and that have a bunch of moving parts are only as good as the technology that makes them work properly. That particular search took us to Singapore, and I got to be part of that team. Al was with me. Wow: national health records, shared data across the country with *all* healthcare facilities, and exceptional analytical systems to create insights around things like epidemiology, etiology, genetics, and so on. Granted, they're a tiny island nation, but so what—a country is only as big as its data networks, right? I mean, if I can do a videoconference between Maine and San Diego and Guam in real-time, I should be able to create a universal, secure, totally private and confidential medical records database[lii]."

"Okay, I'm blown away here," I said, shaking my head in wonder. "These things are amazing."

"Yes, but be careful," Ahadi retorted. "Just because a country does data analysis well doesn't mean they have the best record for affordable care or equal access to it. That's why we were very careful to say that we weren't out to copy a system; we were out to find the best parts of every system and see if we could build a Frankenstein that actually worked."

"What are some other examples that you found?" I asked.

"Well," she replied, "India has a model that prioritizes cost-effectiveness over cost-reduction, which means that they can provide better care with less people. They also have a world-class referral system[liii]. And while we were doing our research, India made a lot of waves when their hospital system partnered with a handful of manufacturers to build prosthetics and implants because the traditional manufacturers refused to lower their prices[liv]. Switzerland lowered the boom on funding; at the time, they spent 11.5 percent of their GDP on healthcare, while we spent 18, yet they have great clinical outcomes, great customer service numbers, and an average life expectancy that's higher than Israel's[lv]. Oh, and France leads the world in choice—as in, there isn't any. I don't mean that the way it sounds. What I mean is that if you get sick, or need surgery, or whatever, you can go to any doctor, or clinic, or hospital, anywhere in the country, without restriction. Healthcare is healthcare. And their patient satisfaction scores, and clinical outcomes, are very high[lvi].

"We had great results from our work in Africa around agriculture, but honestly, we didn't expect to find centers of excellence in healthcare, especially given the region's rampant HIV numbers, not to mention malaria, Dengue, Ebola, starvation, and the rest of the Africa hit parade. But we did. What we found in Africa was activism: lots of it, and very, very effective. They have broad education and awareness programs, knowledge-sharing systems for pregnant mothers, prevention programs, and so on. Basically, it's what we based so much of our administration on: Education fixes just about everything, and they were doing it right[lvii].

"Another thing we found there, and we also found it in Brazil, was aggressive, proactive, immersive community outreach. The poverty in those places is staggering, so people don't seek out medical care, and when they finally do, it's often too late. So, the cost of rural healthcare is through the roof. So, what do they do? They have teams that go out into the townships and into the favelas every week to do checkups, wellness care, immunizations, chronic care, and so on[lviii]. They figure that if they can deal with an illness before it gets serious, then they save huge costs that they would otherwise incur when the illness gets really bad and the person has to be hospitalized, or have surgery, or whatever.

"I'm almost afraid to ask, but was there anything that *we* excelled at?" I queried. I wasn't sure I wanted to know the answer, but I had to ask. For a while there—a long while— the only thing we excelled at was being the world's punching bag and the butt of everybody's jokes. Surely there was something.

"Oh yeah…there sure was. We came out on top, and by a huge margin, in R&D. A lot of that had to do with the funding model that emerged over the last century or so for university research programs. Our ability to develop drugs, prosthetics, critical care equipment, analysis technology, that kind of thing, is unparalleled. Nobody does it better. So yeah, there's at least one area where we're still in the game[lix]."

"OK," I asked, "There's one area we haven't talked about yet, and it's huge. What about eldercare?"

"That's easy—Japan. All Japanese citizens get compulsory long-term health insurance, which is kind of like Medicare here—65 and over. But *unlike* Medicare, it includes unlimited community services, residential care, nursing care, and home care. They also have special group homes for patients with dementia, which allow people with progressive mental health issues to be cared for in a home-like environment, under medical supervision[lx]. It's phenomenal."

I shook my head. She made it sound so easy, but I knew otherwise. But if there was ever an argument for curiosity, this was it.

"OK. So, you traveled all over the world and collected all of these how-to-do-healthcare-right examples. Then what?"

"Don't think it was easy," she laughed with a bit of sarcasm. "In fact, they're still trying to sort out the mess I created. Remember, the best way to become a leader is to find a parade and get in front of it. So, we went looking for parades, and we found them. Basically, we came back, shared what we learned, and then started on the hard part."

"Implementation?"

"Oh, God, no. First, we had to do some serious marketing. Even though people were loving on each other like never before, and acting all reasonable, that only went so far. We had a bunch of pieces, so first we had to throw them together to see if they aligned at all. The group started calling the whole exercise 'health tectonics' because of all the movement.

"We had to walk a really fine line. We weren't asking people to agree to implement each piece; all we were trying to do was get all the members of the panel to agree, yay or nay, on whether each piece had merit. That was incredibly hard, not because people were being difficult or political or just being curmudgeons, but because of the incredibly difficult task of getting people to consider a different reality than the one they already had.

"But that's where Reverse-Engineering the Future came in. I remember the day well: I asked the group how many of them had ever played fantasy football, or Dungeons and Dragons, or any of those other role-play games. Most had, but a few hadn't. To them, I asked the question, 'Have you ever read Harry Potter or Tolkien, or for that matter, any children's books?' And of course, they had. So, I told them, 'Look—every time you do any of those things, you're suspending your belief in reality and allowing yourself to be run entirely by your imagination. Reality is still there; it's just been turned off for a little while. Well, this is the same thing. All I'm asking you to do is imagine a different reality for a few hours. We're going to play fantasy healthcare: no tricks, no political bullshit, just pretend. Can we do that?'

"Well, they could, and they did. It took some doing, but we managed to get on a roll after a few hours by following the rules laid out in the *Reverse-Engineering the Future* book. First, any sentence that started with 'But' was outlawed—the word 'And' had to be substituted. And if anybody pushed, they had to go through the trout stack."

"The what?" I queried. "The *what* stack?"

"The trout stack. You need to read this book, Michael—it'll save your bacon. Great ideas in it, straightforward and practical, and they really work. The trout stack works like this. If somebody has an objection to something we're doing or talking about, they have to offer a solution that they believe is better. And then they have to go through the stack."

"I'm lost." I was. "Can you give me an example?"

"Sure," she replied. "Let's see. Let's use the example of the care teams going into the *favelas* in Brazil to take care of the poor. Now, imagine that somebody in the group has a problem with that. They say, 'But that will never work here.' The instant they've said that they're put into the stack. Al, play-act it with me so that Michael can see how it works."

"OK," said Al, with a grin on his face. Looking at me, he

said, "You're gonna love this."

Then he looked her in the eye and said, "Madame President, that will never work here, and you know it."

"Why?" She replied.

"Because it sounds like social medicine."

"Why?"

"Because it's the government over-reaching again, and people will object."

"Why?"

Because sooner or later, it's gonna turn into upward pressure on the tax base."

"Why?"

"Because it's going to cost a bunch of money to do these things."

"Why? —OK, you can stop."

"Good," laughed Al, "because I was about to turn into a trout."

I was still lost.

"Here's what happens, Michael. Everybody agrees to go through this process up-front, because it works. It's really simple: If Al and I had taken this all the way through to the end, with me asking 'Why?' over and over again, he'd eventually get to a point where he'd open his mouth to answer my latest 'why' question, but nothing would come out. In other words, he'd be moving his jaw, but not saying anything. He'd look like a trout. When that happens, he's reached the end of his ability to respond, he's exhausted all objections, so you go back to the very last answer that Al gave to one of my 'why?' questions, and that's the strategy for resolving why the care teams won't work in the United States. It works every time if you go all the way through it, but it really pisses people off because it forces them to think about their own positions and to consider that they may be wrong. But once you get into it, and a few people agree to go through it, it stops feeling like a personal attack and starts to feel more like a step toward something good and important. Anyway, it's detailed in the book; you really need to check it out[lxi]. Like I said, we call it the trout stack because the person's mouth is moving like a trout's, but they're not saying anything."

"So, where did that take you?" I asked. "I mean, I can't imagine you just waved your magic wand, and everybody fell in line." I smiled so that she'd know I wasn't being snarky.

"Why Michael, what are you implying? Witchcraft? Sometimes it felt that way, but I assure you, nothing of the sort. All I had to do—and I say 'all' because I'm vastly understating the difficulty—was get them to accept that a different option doesn't mean that the current one's wrong.

"See, the beauty of this whole process is that it forces you to let go of how things are done today, and only think about how they might be done differently—and better—in the future. Basically, Reverse-Engineering requires that you think only about what could be, not what is. And the reason it works so well is because it eliminates the 'Well, now, you see, that's not how we do things here' challenge. Your goal becomes one of designing what could be, not building a case for why it can't be."

"It almost sounds too simple," I countered. "I mean, you were attacking one of the biggest political hairballs ever created. What else did you use?"

She smiled, and looked at Al. He smiled back, saying, "I know exactly where you're going."

"Yep," she said. "There was another book that we all read that you need to add to the stack I'm building for you. It's called, 'Orbiting the Giant Hairball.' I tell everybody who asks that if they work for a company of one or more employees, they need to read this book. The guy who wrote it was a former Hallmark executive. His title—as in, it was on his business card—was 'Chief Creative Paradox[lxii].' Basically, what he says in the book is that all companies start out with the same noble intentions: make money, create good products and services, make their customers happy, take care of their employees. And if they do those things, the company prospers and grows. The problem is that as it grows, it eventually reaches a place where it's so big that it's not the same anymore—the boss doesn't know everybody, you have to dress up, no more dogs in the office, that kind of thing.

"Anyway, the author, Gordon Mackenzie, points out that as soon as the company gets to a certain size it becomes unwieldy, and somebody in the chain of command decides, with all the right intentions, that because we've gotten so big, we now need some rules. And guidelines. And protocols. And regulations. And procedures. And principles. And standards. And maybe some formal recommendations. He says that every one of those is like a hair, and as they get added, the hairball gets bigger and bigger and bigger. He also points out that people are removed, but hairs are *never* removed. Then he reminds us of something that we all learned in basic physics: that any sufficiently large body creates its own gravity, including this gigantic hairball that just keeps getting bigger. And when that happens, the job of the hairball is to suck everything in its path into itself. This is the old Star Trek thing about the Borg— 'resistance is futile.' So, Mackenzie's book is about the fine art of orbiting close enough to the corporate hairball to stay connected and effective, but far enough away to maintain objectivity and not get tangled in the hairball.

"So, you can imagine—and this is why we were smiling when you used the word—there's no bigger hairball on earth than the United States Government, and the biggest tangle of all is healthcare. We had no illusions about magic wands or dancing pixies. All we really wanted people to do was get comfortable with regularly asking the question, 'What if?'"

"And it worked?" I asked. "I mean, I know it worked, but were you comfortable with the way it went?"

"For the most part, yes, although there were a few times when I just couldn't fathom the stupidity of people. To object to a change on political grounds, rather than on some reasonable objection, never sat well with me. And that's why I also worked so hard to revise government—you know, term limits, reasonable regulation, that kind of thing. But even now, all these years later, healthcare is still a work-in-progress, which I guess is okay as long as they keep biting off reasonable chunks of the elephant to chew and swallow.

You can't go after something as big as a national healthcare system and treat it like a single moving part that can just be adjusted. We had to look at all of the subsystems, all of the different functional modules, and work on them one-by-one, then figure out how to glue the parts together. But once we got the lobbyists under control and managed to reduce the influence-peddling, things began to show promise. Basically, we ended up with a system that sat alongside the existing healthcare programs as an option that people could select if they wanted to. The idea was the same idea that a lot of forward-thinking corporations do, which is to create a subsidiary that has one responsibility—to compete with the mother ship. It's a wholly owned competitor. At one level, it doesn't matter who wins, because they're different pockets in the same pair of corporate pants. But at a different level, it's profoundly important, because one wins over the other because it's more effective or efficient."

"And of course, it wasn't free—there was cost associated with the new program. And actually, there was cost associated with a *lot* of things you did—not being critical, just making a point. Can we talk about how you convinced all the players involved to accept your payment structure? I'm referring, of course, to your tax model."

"Well…that was a riddle, wrapped in a mystery, inside an enigma, as Churchill once said to describe the Soviet Union[lxiii]. What we found was another five blind men and the elephant problem. Only in this case, it was all about using the same standard to measure the overall impact of the various tax models we looked at. I pulled together a group of very intelligent, well-informed, reasonable people, as apolitical as I could find, people who had probably forgotten more about finances than I'll ever know—they were that good. I told them that we were going to blue sky this whole tax code thing, and once again, we—"

"Let me guess—you reverse-engineered it," I offered.

"You're catching on, my friend," she laughed. "Before we talk tax code, which is right up there with watching grass grow and paint dry on the index of mesmerizing activities, I need some wine. Will you gentlemen join me?"

"I would love to join you, Ahadi," I replied, "but would it be rude of me to ask to try one of your Madame President beers first? I haven't stopped thinking about it since we were out there by the hop racks."

"Consider it done. Al, would you mind?"

"Not at all," he said, rising from his chair and gathering the iced tea glasses on the table. "Be right back."

From the patio, I could see the river in the distance, and could just make out the superstructure of a tug pushing a string of barges down-river. "This has to be one of the most beautiful pieces of property I have ever seen in my life," I told her. "And it's so quiet and peaceful. Have you lived here long?"

"In a manner of speaking," she replied, smiling. "This was my grandmother's place on my Mother's side of the family. Climbing in that live oak out front is one of my earliest and fondest childhood memories—or it was, until I fell out of the damn thing and broke my arm, trying to branch-walk. I think I was nine. Anyway, we bought it and rebuilt it, until my husband died. But Al stepped up, and he basically ran the place and managed the workers for me. I mean, he's my protection detail, but the only thing I need protecting from out here is mosquitos."

Al arrived with a bottle of red and the promised beer, ice-cold and dripping with sweat, one for each of us. "Drink it while it's cold," he told me, as he poured wine for Ahadi.

"And pace yourself—it has a serious kick to it, much like its namesake."

Ahadi smacked him on the arm for the wisecrack, smiling all the while. The can was silver, with a black silhouette of the former President, surrounded by the name of the brew. It was indeed ice-cold, very hoppy, and zowie, what a kick. I drank deeply before stopping and placing the can on the table. "Wow," I said, my eyes wide.

"Told you," he chuckled, as he drank from his own can. "I'll join you and we'll have wine later. It's local—as in, from right over there," pointing at the vineyard that girdled the house.

Ahadi raised her glass. "To new friends, and warm

relationships."

I raised my can. "And to the kindness of those who were strangers less than twelve hours ago."

"Here, here," said Al. We drank.

"Okay, tax codes," Ahadi began, taking a long drink from her glass. "We looked at three different models: what we had at the time, which is sometimes called a progressive tax; the flat tax idea, which comes and goes in popularity; and what a lot of people called the fair tax. So, I'll explain what we found with each, and then I'll tell you how we got to a solution that more-or-less worked.

"I'll start with what we already had, the progressive tax model. It's pretty simple: you set a base tax rate at the lowest income level, and then the percentage of tax charged to each citizen increases according to their income. But there are some other factors that give the government control over tax revenue. For example, you can keep the tax rate flat—unchanged—over a period of time but increase tax revenues by playing around with things like exemptions, deductions, tax credits, and so on."

"So, it's all a game," I observed.

"Yep—it's a game, but done for the right reasons most of the time. People bitch and moan about it, but it's always been the most commonly deployed tax system, at least in the developed world. Italy, Japan, Australia, France, China, Germany, Canada, the UK—they all use a progressive tax. It tends to be popular because those most able to pay, meaning the wealthier end of society, pay a higher tax percentage. Conversely, the tax rate is low for those at the other end, which hopefully gives them more of an opportunity to escape from poverty and join the middle class. Couple that with the education and training initiatives we built, and you have the makings of something pretty good.

"The downside—and there's always a downside—is that the people at the top of the economic ladder complain that they're taxed unfairly because they end up paying more as a percentage of their overall income. But there are ways for them to play the game too, and they do. So, it isn't perfect. Spoiler alert—none of them are.

"So, next on the list is the idea of a flat tax. A flat tax is exactly that: everybody pays the same percentage, regardless of income. So, if you make $100,000 a year, and the tax rate is 15 percent, you pay $15,000. If you make $10,000 per year, you pay $1,500.

"The strongest positive argument for a flat tax is simplicity. 'How much did you make? Multiply it by 0.15. Write a check for that amount and send it to this address.' Simple! And by the way, flat taxes are typically only applied to regular income, not to capital gains or investment revenue. Hell, some people argue that we could kill the IRS if we went to a flat tax. By the way, Russia uses a flat tax model.

"The downside, and this one is real, is the burden a flat tax places on the lower end of the income scale. If you're making $100K, having to pay $15K is a pain-in-the-ass, but it won't mean you have to pick between paying the heating bill and feeding your kids. But for lower-income folks, it could mean exactly that. If you're only making $10K, and you have to pay 15 percent of that to Uncle Sam, that's huge. Or think about the impact of buying groceries. Five dollars for a gallon of milk to a wealthy individual? Doesn't even show up on the radar. But to someone who's struggling? That's a lot of money. Or, what if they have a special needs kid, who needs special foods, or medications, or whatever? All in all, the model has problems."

"Earlier you said that the rich people at the top figure out ways to get around paying huge amounts of taxes under a progressive model. Aren't there ways to protect the folks who are poor with a flat tax approach?" I asked.

"Absolutely, although as far as I know, it's never been done," she said. "But to get around that problem, tax people have come up with ways to deal with it, at least, in theory.

For example, they talk about a whole slew of deductions and exemptions, but the minute they do that, it starts to look an awful lot like a progressive tax."

"Gotcha," I nodded. "So truthfully, a flat tax pretty quickly becomes an offshoot of a progressive tax. So, what about the third option—" I consulted my notes— "The fair tax?"

"Well," she said, nodding, "the fair tax is pretty interesting, but it's a radical departure from the other two. Instead of taxing income, it taxes consumption. In other words, all income taxes as we know them go away, and are replaced by a tax on the things you buy. But here's what makes the model interesting: certain things, certain purchases, are tax-free. So, you set a fair tax rate—say, 25 percent—and it gets billed based on the stuff you purchase. Payroll and income taxes go away, so you get to keep your whole paycheck. And since you have control over what you buy, you also have control over how much you pay in taxes. And since a lot of things would be tax-free or low-tax, like food, drugs, childcare, that kind of thing, we protect the most vulnerable. And the government still makes its money."

"And … the downside?" I asked.

"Ah, yes, the downside," she laughed. "I did say there's always a downside, didn't I?" She sipped her wine, set the glass back on the table. "The biggest downside is that it had never been done before, by anybody anywhere. Everybody's afraid of the boogeyman, especially the one that has the government tattooed on its hide. And then, there's the burden of minutiae. For example, under a fair tax plan, instead of the federal government collecting taxes, that job is shifted to businesses, since the tax accrues on what you buy rather than on what you make."

"So: what did you do? Did you reverse-engineer again?" I asked.

"Sort of," she replied. "We actually started with a number—a big number, but a number. We took a swag at what we needed to generate in the way of tax revenues to run the government reasonably and responsibly. Then, we took a step back and asked ourselves, 'What do we intend to do with all this money?' In other words, were we collecting it for the right reasons? And as it turned out, for the most part, we were. Sure, there was waste and pork, but in the grand scheme of things, we were okay. But what I really wanted to do was guarantee some degree of equity in the final result— meaning that I wanted to protect those who needed protecting, while at the same time dangling a carrot that would legitimately give people the ability to get out from under what amounted to guaranteed poverty, either because their skin was a certain color, or they were born in a particular zip code. You have to remember, Michael, that the tax code was one of the first things I went after, because it was legitimately, genuinely, broken. That fruit was hanging so low you'd need a backhoe to get to it.

"Finally, we asked ourselves what we could fix in the way of social challenges with the tax revenues we proposed to collect. We looked long and hard at the kinds of lives people were living at all layers of society, from the poorest to the richest and everybody in between.

"That exercise actually sent us down a bottomless rabbit

hole, because poor people and rich people were there in increasingly large droves to look at. But guess what: there wasn't much in the middle. In other words, all those myths and legends about the middle-class disappearing? They weren't myths—they were fact. And you know why that's a problem? Because economic prosperity in a healthy country should look like the standard bell curve. There will always be a small number of disadvantaged people living in poverty, and there will always be a select few wealthy people who got there for any number of legitimate reasons, but there should *always* be this big hump in the middle that represents everybody else. Why? Because national economies are built on the backs of the middle-class. That's where all the jobs are, that's where things get designed, and built, and innovated, and invented, and tweaked, and perfected. It's where things get marketed and sold. The middle-class is the economic engine of a country. When it's working well, it pulls people out of poverty and spits out the occasional newly minted millionaire on the other end of the bell curve. But along the way, it creates a happy, healthy, strong, driven-to-succeed, successful group of people who feel good about themselves, but who are constantly striving to be better, because they can be. Think about it: Bill Gates and Steve Jobs and Larry Ellison weren't rich kids who invented amazing things; they were geeky college students who had cool ideas that they then managed to turn into products, which in turn made them boatloads of money. They were part of that middle-class bell curve. And you know why the middle-class can do that? Because it's the place where education, and opportunity, and promise, and compassion, and curiosity, and hope, and need, come together—along with the bulk of the people in the country.

"The United States has always been referred to as a mixing bowl—a place where people of all backgrounds come together as one. It's the story that this country was founded on, and I believe in the power of that story more than I believe in anything else about the place. But there's another mixing bowl that's every bit as important, and that's the one we're talking about. When I looked at America's bell curve, it was upside down. Instead of a big lump in the middle, there was a big U-shaped hole, full of nothing. I had the poor on the left, the wealthy on the right, and not a goddamn thing in the middle. Meanwhile, the very rich and the very poor were growing at rates that made me puke the first time I saw the numbers.

"So, I called in the dream team—Mike and Doug and Elon and Mary and Phil and a few others—and I sat them down and drew the upside-down curve on a whiteboard and said to them, 'We need to fill this hole, and I mean right-goddamn-now. Eighteen months from now I want to see a hill there, not a hole. What do we do?'

"Well, they went away, and the next thing you knew, they were coming back to me with all kinds of ideas, and that's where it all started. In fact, it was Mike who really kicked things off with the whole training and education push and his triangle of crap and the cause-and-effect chain we talked about earlier, about how criminal behavior is directly linked to a lack of education and the opportunities it destroys.

"Anyway, we decided that we'd start with the tax code. It was a hell of a windmill to tilt at, but hey, Don Quixote would be proud. We dismissed the flat rate model right off the bat, because with tweaking it looked just like the progressive tax model. So, rather than tearing down what we already had, we started with a progressive tax design, since we knew it worked and, better the enemy you know than the one you don't.

"Then, we started looking at ways to change it to make it

more of a tool for creative opportunity than an oppressive weapon. Look, if there's one thing the American people have always been known for, it's their willingness and drive to work hard toward some goal, as long as they understand what lies at the end of the rainbow. So, we stole some ideas from the fair tax playbook. Thanks to my newly reasonable legislature, we decided to give the consumption tax idea a try by setting the rate at 27 percent. And since the burden of tax collection now fell on businesses, we came up with a way to pay them a stipend for their trouble, based on the taxes they collected and reported.

"The last thing we had to do—besides make it work— was determine what should and shouldn't be taxed at the federal level. The list turned out to be fairly easy to compile, because most of it fell into a commonsense sort of formula. And most of the items that we ultimately ended up excluding from taxation were common across all segments of society, and pretty much necessary just to stay alive: food, water, healthcare, medications, childcare, education, that kind of stuff. Most other things were fair game, but there was a petition process for businesses to be considered for tax relief. For example, book publishers petitioned for relief on the grounds that they were educational in nature. They weren't granted tax-free status, but they did qualify for a lower rate at 20 percent. Meanwhile, tools, for example, did qualify, as long as they were purchased by someone who needed them for professional reasons—for example, a certified carpenter could buy their tools without being taxed. Same for plumbers, electricians, and so on.

"What ended up happening as an unintended consequence was that people's buying patterns began to change—slowly at first, but the more they realized how much control they had over the taxes they had to pay, the more creative they got. Conspicuous consumption gave way to thoughtful purchasing, as people began to realize that having friends over for a great meal was far more satisfying—and impressive—than putting more bling on their fingers and toes. And all those people injecting themselves with Botox just sort of drifted away. For God's sake: 'Hey, I have an idea—I'm going to inject myself with Botulism, one of the deadliest poisons on Earth, so that I can look like a Stepford Wife!'"

"And what happened?" I asked.

"Well, lo and behold, we discovered that we were collecting all the taxes we needed to pay for the things we needed to pay for. Take Defense, for example. It was a money machine. I'm as strong a defender of this country as anyone you'll ever meet. But take a look sometime at what China, India, Russia, Saudi Arabia, France, Germany, the UK, Japan, South Korea, and Brazil spent on defense. Add 'em all up: We spent more than all of them combined[lxiv]. In fact, we were spending 15 percent of our GDP, and about half of all discretionary government spending, on defense. Did you ever see that bumper sticker that said, 'It will be a great day indeed when our schools get all the money they need, and the Pentagon has to hold a bake sale to buy a new bomber'? Well, it was time for a bake sale. That's why I was able to steal a tiny piece of their action for the Africa project."

By now, the sun was hanging low enough in the sky that the shadows were getting long across the patio. I could see the farmworkers wrapping up for the day; Al excused himself for a few minutes to check in with them and see if they needed anything before their day ended. Birds flew overhead in great smoky swarms; I could smell the river. The long, lonely call of a riverboat horn broke the silence.

"Want to help me get dinner together?" Ahadi asked.

"Love to," I replied.

What a day this had been. When I arrived this morning— had it only been a day? —I was expecting the standard 'I'll ask a question and you answer it, except when you won't' kind of repartee. Instead, I was given incredible access to an incredible person whose story was far richer than I realized.

Ahadi's voice summoned me back to reality and the warm kitchen.

"Can you reach up there over the fridge and get down that big cast iron paella pan for me? It just feels like a paella kind of a night, if that's okay with you."

"Are you kidding?" I replied. "If it's anything like all the other food you've shoved into me today, it'll be amazing," I laughed.

"Don't eat too much, though, because we're having a special breakfast tomorrow and you're going to want to have room for it," she replied. "A friend of mine is dropping by to meet you and tell you a couple of stories of his own that tie in nicely to what we've talked about."

"Who's that?" I queried.

"Scott Pelley and his wife Jane are in town for a conference. He called to say hi, and I told him about you and your project. They have the morning free tomorrow, so they're going to drop by for a few minutes. I hope that's okay with you."

"Are you kidding?!?" I burbled. "OF COURSE, it's okay! He's one of my heroes! Thank you so much!"

"Oh, you're welcome, Michael. He wants to tell you the story about how he and I managed to con the television networks into turning the news agencies back into standalone, fully funded, independent entities so that they wouldn't have to be profit centers anymore. He's a little bit biased, but he thinks that *that* was the single most important thing that happened during my presidency. 'If it bleeds, it leads' —what a crock. And frankly, there are days I agree with him. Scott's favorite food is pancakes with Vermont maple syrup[lxv], so I'm going to take care of my boy.

"Can you grab me that bag of rice on the second shelf of the cupboard over there? And while you're at it, you can pour us some wine."

Epilogue

Epilogue

Hmmm…the courier must have left the box in the garage yesterday because the door was open, I thought. I picked up the package to carry it into the house. Placing it on the counter, I rummaged in the drawer for a knife to cut the tape that held the box closed. Finding one, I cut the ends, then ran it carefully across the top to split the seam that held the flaps together.

I placed the knife on the counter, and carefully bent back the flaps, first one set, then the other. I wanted this moment to last. Pulling away a sheet of protective paper, I uncovered what I had been waiting months to see: twenty books, *my books,* carefully stacked in the box. My baby had been born, and my dream had become real. After months of interviews, research, back-and-forth arguments with editors, and endless rewrites, I had a book.

I carefully extracted a copy from the box. The cover was glossy white, with dark blue lettering; a photo of Ahadi standing in the vineyard occupied a third of the space. It was beyond beautiful. It was also wet, the result of the unexpected tears that had begun to fall.

That's the moment I thought about as I cut open a box of books in a large meeting room at the St. Francis Hotel in San Francisco. I flew in late last night from Atlanta, fell into bed, and was now about to give another talk and book signing, my 21st in 19 exhausting, mind-numbing days. By now, I had the speech down; I could give it in my sleep, and, thinking back, probably had, on more than one occasion.

The book hit the shelves three months ago and had been unexpectedly successful. The publisher was awed as its popularity rose worldwide, driving sales through the roof and creating demand for translations in 11 languages.

Individuals were buying it; corporations were buying it as required reading for their employees. It wasn't the story, my agent told me; it was the hope it created. And the speech I gave at these events fed right into that hope.

As requested by the event organizers, I placed the books on a table in random piles, which they then arranged according to some arcane book display code. I still wasn't accustomed to the attention the book had brought. I stepped back, looked at the row of identical covers, and smiled.

There had been one unexpectedly sad moment six months ago. I received word that Al Gordon had decided to retire from the Secret Service, and that a new agent had been assigned to head Ahadi's protection detail. I was shocked and saddened by the news; Ahadi and Al had come to the very first signing, which took place in Memphis, and neither of them had mentioned Al's departure. We had spent a lot of time together, and I considered them friends—close friends, actually. However, last week, I received a personal letter from Al, explaining why he had left. To my utter delight, he and Ahadi were engaged, and their wedding was taking place a month after I returned from this trip. In the letter, Al asked if I would stand up for him at the wedding. Of course, I accepted. Turns out that the Secret Service isn't keen on its agents fraternizing with the people it's paid to protect. So, Al did it right. He joined the other side.

That first interview I did with Ahadi all those many months ago at Raccoon Holler had gone well and had led to others as the gears of information-gathering ground on. Over

the course of the book's development, the three of us—
Ahadi, Al and I— became unexpectedly close. I met Ahadi's
kids and grandkids; I met Al's older brother, the only
remaining family he had. They, in turn, got to know Sylvia.
She and I hit it off during my many weeks of research at
Ahadi's Library, and even though she accused me of having
the complexion of a mushroom because of all the time I spent
in the stacks of the Library, that wasn't enough to keep her
away. We'd been dating now for a year; I hadn't seen her
since the book tour started, but we would reunite in a few
days. More than anything, I looked forward to *that*.

Meanwhile, Van was making noises about me returning
to the Times. My responses to him were vague, but I had
already decided that I wouldn't be going back to New York. I
planned to move to Detroit to be with Sylvia; I had been
offered a position as a senior researcher at the Library, but I
hadn't yet accepted, preferring to keep my options open until
the flurry of activity associated with the book slowed down.
But deep down, I knew I wouldn't be returning to New York.

The other thing was that there were indications that the
effects of the Mulvihill-McCooey event were beginning to
wane. People were still more civil, more thoughtful, than
they had been before the Reversal, but some politicians were
beginning to go back to their old snarky ways. In one respect
it was something of a relief; polite politicians were walking
oxymorons, like a rattlesnake that wants its head patted. That
was probably the subject of another book; ideas were starting
to stack up.

The event coordinators caught my attention and ushered
me to my seat in the front row. I thought about the speech I
was about to give, and about how odd it was that I was giving
it.

Not long ago, an old friend, also an author, told me,

'Michael, there's something you have to be prepared for when this book comes out. As soon as it hits the shelves, if it has any success at all, you'll automatically be seen as the expert on the topic. Never mind that there are political scientists, sociologists, geophysicists and medical researchers out there who have forgotten more about your subject matter than you'll ever know. Because you wrote the book, you're the expert. Be prepared.' Boy, was he right. It was an intriguing but often mildly uncomfortable position to be in.

My attention snapped back from my navel-gazing as I heard my name being spoken over the PA system. My agent, sitting beside me, elbowed me in the bicep. As Sylvia liked to say, 'Send in the show pony!'

I stood to take my place behind the podium but chose instead to sit on the edge of the stage in front of it. The group, perhaps 50 people, was small enough that I could get away without the microphone. I shook hands with the woman who introduced me, faced the audience, smiled, and began the talk I had already delivered 20 times and would give several more over the next few days.

"Thank you for having me," I began.

"You know, when I started this project, all I really wanted to do was write a clear and compelling biography of Ahadi Fadhili-Mason and cover her time in office. She accomplished astonishing things over the six years of her term, although I'm quick to point out that she had help—of the electromagnetic variety (laughs).

"But something happened as I was doing my research. At first, I approached the project with the preconceived notion that Ahadi Fadhili-Mason accomplished everything she accomplished because of the Polar Reversal. After all, people were behaving in a more civilized manner than they had in decades; they looked at science and fact as the coin of the realm, instead of as one of many optional ways to view the world; they adopted the idea that 'to be wrong is to be strong,' instead of feeding on the echo chambers of antisocial media and depending on confirmation bias to keep them going in what they perceived to be the right direction. It was suddenly like the whole planet had become Stepford people.

"I admit, I assumed that the success of Ahadi's presidency was all about striking while the iron was hot. And you know what? There was definitely a lot of that. She certainly took decisive advantage of every opportunity that came her way, as all good leaders *should* do.

"But there was more to it than that—a lot more. The only reason Ahadi—and yes, I have permission to dispense with the presidential title—the only reason Ahadi was able to do the things she did was because of a collection of all-too-human qualities that she wielded, often subconsciously, but with enormous precision and impact. They're part of who she is as a person. The flux reversal, the ferroliths, the changes in human behavior that resulted from the poles flipping, that was all icing on the cake, as they say. The reasons for her success had far more to do with who she is and why she did the things she did, than with *what* she accomplished.

"A country—this country—is a big business to manage. It's geographically large, it's politically, ethnically, racially, and gender-diverse, and it's home to multiple generations who are very different in terms of how they view the world and what they want from it. It's a nation governed by the rule of law, as written by the founders, although many would argue that that particular fact had been largely set aside before Ahadi took office.

"When she became president, the country was licking its wounds after a long, ugly bout of extreme political polarization. Ideology was everything; my way or the highway; as Brenée Brown said, 'I'm right, you're wrong, shut up.' In other words, the country had gone into a dark place where what you did was more important than why you did it, or even more to the point, more important than who you were as a person. That's not who we are as a nation, and Ahadi saw it immediately as a force that was tearing the country apart.

"I want to take a moment to remind you what the country was like when she took office. Many of you will remember, but some of you may have been too young to really see what things were like. Both of the major political parties had retreated to their extremes, to the far edges of the political bell curve. They did so to the point that that they were no longer recognizable as the hard-working, honorable institutions that they once were. There was a time not that long ago when the Republican Party stood for a set of beliefs that made the country strong: a belief that the individual matters, that companies should be enabled by government policy to grow responsibly and be strong and provide the fundamental underpinnings of economic growth, and that government should be small and should serve the people and work closely with the States, and that hard work and perseverance will always open a door to a happy and successful career and life, and that new Americans, regardless of their origin, are the backbone of the nation. And Democrats were the people's party. They stood for the little guy, for Labor, for social policies that ensured a good life and a balance between people and the companies that employed them, and that ensured the availability of social programs, safety nets put in place to provide for those among us who were less fortunate. In other words, both parties wanted the same thing: to provide a mechanism, a pathway, for achieving the American Dream. And, even when they disagreed bitterly, the two parties always found a way to work together. They put nation before party, every time.

"But that remarkable model all but disappeared. Conservative Republican ideals yielded to the extreme right wing of the Party, while the more liberal Democrats did the same, but in the other direction. The right went far right; the left went far left. And the result? Hordes of tribal ideologues on either side of a gaping, smoking crater between them, hurling epithets at one another, a crater, a void, that represented the majority of people in the country who all wanted, regardless of their political inclinations, very much the same thing. They wanted to make a decent living; raise their families in safe neighborhoods; provide their kids and grandkids with a bright future; in essence, live that American Dream that we all hear about.

"Unfortunately, that chasm between the two ideological tribes was rapidly becoming too wide to reach across—or to heal. Both parties forgot what they truly stood for, and much more important, both parties forgot that they had more in common with the other side than they had differences. But they made a conscious decision to not see them.

"The result was a paralysis of the worst kind: one in which 'doing the right thing for the people of the nation' was equated with either pandering to the other side, consorting with the enemy, or straying from the party lines. In other words, to admit that the 'way we're doing things could be better' was tantamount to having failed, which is, of course, to any human being with a working mind, ludicrous.

"I'm reminded of a quote from Thomas Edison, who, after successfully inventing the light bulb, was asked why he stuck with it for so long.

'You had 999 failed attempts before you finally came up with a design that worked,' asked the journalist. 'After 500 or so failures, why did you keep going?'

"His response was great: 'Those 999 attempts weren't failures—they were incremental steps on the road to success.'

"In the early 2020s, people complained loudly about COVID fatigue, because of the necessarily slow development cycle of a safe vaccine, the slowdown of the economy, and the fact that people were essentially in a state of self-imposed or government-mandated lockdown for a couple of years. But more than that, they were suffering from polarization fatigue, and inane messaging fatigue, and zero progress fatigue. That's what was getting to them, even more than COVID. And why? Because of a glaring lack of plain old common sense. And that's where Ahadi comes in.

"Ahadi Fadhili-Mason didn't go to Washington to make a name for herself. She went to Washington to fix things—big things—that were clearly broken, but that had been broken for so long that nobody noticed anymore—people just shrugged their shoulders and said, 'That's just the way it is.'

Well, not on her watch. To her, 'How it is' should give way, every time, to 'How it could be.' And that's how she approached every challenge she undertook during her six years in office.

"What made her approach such a stroke of genius was this: She said to people, to every American, indeed, to every human on the planet, that the way things are is not the way they have to be, and that you have permission to not only dream about a better life for yourself, your family, your community, indeed, your country, perhaps even the planet, but the right and indeed the responsibility to make it happen. The Preamble to the Declaration of Independence, the document that founded this great experiment called America, stipulates that a set of self-evident truths grants us certain inalienable rights, including a right to life, liberty, and the pursuit of happiness—and that those rights are guaranteed by the presence of a government that works on behalf of the people, not the other way around. When she took office, government was at odds with the people. Again, not on her watch.

"And do you know where life, liberty, and happiness stem from? They stem from an abundance of the things that Ahadi worked her entire presidency to make available to all. We call them freedoms. Freedom from hunger. From discrimination. From want. From oppression. From ignorance. From poverty. She worked hard to put into place institutional frameworks that made it possible for people to live free of those limiting forces. She told the country, 'Good enough is not good enough.' And she did it all by applying common sense and getting others to do it as well. See what happens when common sense becomes—well, common? Great things happen. These weren't political arguments; they were human arguments. People shouldn't have to wait for their elected officials to negotiate a way for them to be free from poverty, or fear, or discrimination; according to the document that declared the country into existence, those freedoms are inalienable. They're inherently, undeniably, universally available to all. They're not up for discussion—they just are. But when Ahadi took office, they had become bargaining chips. Again, not—on—her—watch.

"Ahadi Fadhili-Mason wasn't a great president because of the things she did. She was a great president because of the reasons she did them, and the countless times that she turned people's dreams into reality. That's the Ahadi Fadhili-Mason that I came to know as I wrote this book; I hope that when you read it, you'll get a sense of the remarkable person she truly is.

"Thank you. I've got time to answer a few questions."

Appendix

Bibliography

Web Resources

An Exercise in Reconciliation and Understanding

Rockin' It in the DPRK! Screenplay

Author Biography

Endnotes

Bibliography

Barber, James David. The Presidential Character, 4th edition. Pearson; 2008.

Kriegel, Robert J. and David Brandt. Sacred Cows Make the Best Burgers: Developing Change-Ready People and Organizations. Grand Central Publishing, 2008.

MacKenzie, Gordon. Orbiting the Giant Hairball: A Corporate Fool's Guide to Surviving with Grace. Viking; 1998.

Peters, Tom and Robert H. Waterman, Jr. In Search of Excellence. Harper Business, 2006.

Shelley, Percy Bysshe. *Ozymandias.* Shepard, Dr. Steven.

Making the Call: How Brian Canfield Revolutionized Canada's Telecom Industry. Figure1 Publishing, 2016.

Shepard, Dr. Steven. Reverse-Engineering the Future: A Prescription for Change Leadership.

Shepard, Dr. Steven. The Deliberate Storyteller.

Terkel, Studs. *Working.* The New Press, 2011.

Twain, Mark. The Innocents Abroad.

Wang, C.X. et al., *Transduction of the geomagnetic field as evidenced from alpha-band activity in the human brain.* eNeuro, doi:10.1523/ENEURO.0483-18.2019, 2019.

Wilson, E.O. *Consilience: The Unity of Knowledge.* Viking, 2014.

Web Resources

African Rail Journeys:

https://www.telegraph.co.uk/travel/destinations/africa/articles/Africa-by-train-the-continents-best-rail-journeys/

Defense Spending:

https://www.pgpf.org/chart-archive/0053_defense-comparison

Human Sensitivity to Magnetic Fields:

https://www.eneuro.org/content/6/2/ENEURO.0483-18.2019

https://www.the-scientist.com/infographics/a-panoply-of-animal-senses-32915

Inspiration:

https://www.youtube.com/watch?v=wTjMqda19wk

Labor Law:

https://www.hcn.org/issues/52.1/interview-a-new-bill-in-congress-could-give-citizenship-to-undocumented-farmworkers

SpaceX's Starlink project:

https://www.starlink.com

Tax Code:

https://www.forbes.com/sites/kellyphillipserb/2015/08/07/our-current-tax-v-the-flat-tax-v-the-fair-tax-whats-the-difference/#2c5b13125561

Train Speeds:

https://slate.com/human-interest/2009/05/why-trains-run-slower-now-than-they-did-in-the-1920s.html

Water Use:

https://theconversation.com/farmers-are-depleting-the-ogallala-aquifer-because-the-government-pays-them-to-do-it-145501

An Exercise in Reconciliation and Understanding

Some months ago, I had a conversation with a well-educated man—I emphasize that, *well-educated*—in the deep south. He took exception to something I said about the polarized nature of American politics. So, I invited him to engage in a conversation.

"What do you believe?" I asked.

"I'm a Republican," he replied.

"That's not a belief—that's a club you belong to," I pushed back. He couldn't get past that. So, I tried to make it easier.

"Look," I told him, "I'm going to give you a series of questions; answer any one of them. Here we go: Tell me one thing that we could do in this country to fix the education system, or healthcare, or the economy, or infrastructure, or political gridlock, or the widening economic divide."

He was unable to answer. But he reiterated his position as a Republican three times.

This is our tribal problem as a nation. In the 60s and 70s, the chant that was often heard at rallies and campus gatherings or displayed on bumper stickers was, "My country, right or wrong." Today, it seems to be, "My party, or my candidate, right or wrong." And this is where I have a fundamental problem, and why we suffer from such a state of national polarization—and directional paralysis.

The quickest way to narrow the chasm of ideology is to show that there isn't one. Just a few days ago I called a friend of a friend who is an ardent, lifelong Republican. I've never actually met the man, but I know of him from the friend who introduced us. I knew him to be well-informed, reasonable, and passionate. I knew that he graduated from high school in a very small town in southern Ohio, never went to university, worked for a while as a high-end tractor technician, and was now a farmer. I knew that he was a voracious reader, and apparently didn't suffer fools well, of any stripe.

From our mutual friend, the man knew enough about me to be mildly interested in having a conversation. We were from opposite ends of the political rainbow; I lived in deep blue Vermont, he lived in the dark red center of the nation (although to be fair, we both leaned toward the center from a practical point-of-view). I had academic letters after my name; he had certificates from farm equipment manufacturers. Family was everything to both of us, and we both mourned the recent loss of a dog. We were roughly the same age. In my life and work, I had visited more than 90 countries; he knew everything about everyone in his town of 1,700 people, and other than a tour in the Army, had never been more than 200 miles from home.

He answered the phone when I called, and we chatted affably for a few minutes before I took us into the reason for the call. I explained my dismay over the ideological national divide and told him that I was on a one-person mission to understand and heal it, to the extent it could be healed. I couldn't do it alone, I told him, and if our call went the way I was hoping it would, we'd become allies on the same mission, working behind the lines of ideological distance.

I told him—his name is Alan—that for the next half-hour, we would both park our asses and elephants outside, and would have a conversation without political trappings—no party, no ideological speech-making, no tribal leanings, just two men, meeting for the first time, talking about life. He agreed; we agreed that we didn't know if it would work; and we laughed.

And, we listened.

I told Alan that I had a list of questions that I wanted to ask, and I encouraged him to direct questions my way, as well. I was very clear that this was not an attempt to trap him, or trip him up; this really was an exercise in understanding. Ultimately, Alan added a couple of questions to the list. We ended up asking each other all of the questions, we both learned a lot about ourselves, and our conversation lasted just over 90 minutes.

As it turned out, our answers were pretty much identical, other than a few areas that we couldn't get around.

Here are the questions, with summarized answers from both of us.

What are you interested in?

Alan: Crop science; technology that makes farming more efficient [we had a surprisingly technical conversation about IoT, Big Data, analytics, and geolocation]; how birds and other animals migrate; the futures market for corn, soybeans, and pork (what I raise).

Steve: Technologies that make life better for people, especially in places where the challenges of everyday life are crushingly difficult; the evolving world of publishing and media in general; how journalism actually works.

What do you believe?

Alan: I know we're not supposed to be talking politics, but I believe in the Constitution. I believe in fiscal conservatism. I believe that the Federal government should be small, and that the States have a major role in determining their future. I believe that America is a great country that is also imperfect. I believe that success is earned, not guaranteed. I believe that people have the right to become whatever they want to become, and that government should not get in the way.

Steve: I agree with everything Alan said, and I'll add a few things for clarity. I believe that the inalienable rights of life, liberty, and the pursuit of happiness are exactly that— they are rights. Government should do everything in its power to ensure that those rights are available to everyone. And, our political system is set up so that the government serves the people, not the other way around.

What do you read?

Alan: Our local newspaper and the Wall Street Journal; the Sunday New York Times; articles from Wired Magazine; history, mostly focusing on the Vietnam era [He just finished the Ken Burns video series]; anything by David Morrell and Carl Hiaasen.

Steve: Pretty much everything, but to be a bit focused, Seven Days [local Burlington independent newspaper]; The New York Times; the Economist; Wired; anything by David Attenborough; espionage thrillers; and surprisingly, anything by David Morrell and Carl Hiaasen.

What do you pay attention to?

Alan: Political decisions that lead to changes in demand for the crops I grow, especially as they affect China; shifting regulations around crop treatments, like Roundup; the Futures and commodity markets; jobs reports, especially in the Midwest; and technologies that affect job creation and destruction.

Steve: Trends in globalization, especially as they relate to changes in global power structures and market creation; the growing role of bleeding edge technologies like artificial intelligence, robotics, machine learning, natural language processing, IoT, and cloud; how the introduction of new technologies affects job creation and destruction; deliberate educational efforts to create jobs when new technologies cause legacy jobs to disappear; apolitical voices that make sense: Alan Alda, Greta Thunberg, David Attenborough, Fareed Zakaria.

Do you have any hobbies?

Alan: iPhone photography of patterns in my crops; hunting; fishing; I make terrible noises on a guitar, and worse noises when I sing; stargazing.

Steve: Nature and landscape photography; wildlife sound recording; SCUBA diving.

What do you want for your children and grandchildren?

Alan: A future that doesn't limit their ability to achieve their dreams. Affordable healthcare and education. Unlimited opportunities to grow and succeed. Safety and security. A country they can be proud to live in. Economic security. Peace.

Steve: I wouldn't change a single word.

What is one thing you would change in the world if you could?

Alan: I would ask that people be more respectful of each other and more willing to listen to opinions that are different from their own.

Steve: I would ask that people be willing to have their minds changed when a better idea comes along, and that they be more civil with one another when discussing ideas they disagree on. I'm going to cheat and add one more: I would make people more curious about pretty much everything.

What are you afraid of? What scares you?

Alan: I'm scared that we are teaching our kids to hate. I'm scared that people are learning to be afraid of each other because of their differences, instead of looking for things they have in common. I'm scared that so many people in this country turn to the government to help them be successful, instead of doing it themselves. I'm scared of creeping government overreach, trying to do things that I'm perfectly capable of doing myself.

Steve: I'm scared of leaving my kids and grandkids a world that won't offer them the things that you, Alan, described. I'm scared that we are allowing things like climate change and environmental protections to become politicized, instead of looking to the science to help us make the right decisions about them. I'm scared that corporations are becoming too powerful, and that government isn't being watchful enough. I'm scared that we aren't doing more as a nation to educate people and create jobs for the future.

How do you want people to remember you?

Alan: As a good husband, father, and grandfather. As someone who laughed a lot, and made other people laugh. As someone who always tried to do the right thing. As someone who made other people feel important. As someone who was a patriot and good citizen.

Steve: What he said.

I plan to have more conversations like the one I had with Alan, because what came from it was a clear realization that we are far more alike in our thinking than we are different. Of course, finding a path forward that works for everybody in its execution is much more difficult, but it begins with a conversation. As this book says, just imagine what could be, rather than what is.

Rockin' it in the DPRK!

A Reality Show Script

The 20-person SEAL team landed in North Korea without incident and made its way to the Port of Nampho under cover of darkness. From there they navigated 40 miles up the Taedong River on an unassuming fishing boat until they reached Pyongyang, the capital of North Korea.

This is a country of myth and legend, a place steeped in superstition and fear. There is no Internet; any knowledge of the world beyond the country's borders is provided by Kim Jong-un's government propaganda machine. Residents of North Korea believe that the beloved Supreme Leader has the innate ability to levitate above the city and fly effortlessly over it. They believe that he is a god placed on Earth with the ability to read people's minds. They believe that with a wave of his hand he can make people spontaneously disappear. They believe that he controls the weather, and that lack of rain means that the Supreme Leader is angry with his people. In other words, this place is wackadoo.

With that in mind, our team made its way into the capital city disguised as locals. There they set about to complete their mission. Splitting into four teams, they headed for their assigned destinations: Pyongyang University of Science and Technology, the Pyongyang Film Studio on the northwest side of the city, the Kaeson Youth Park, and a prosperous (by North Korean standards) neighborhood where many government officials lived.

By 6 AM the following morning, each of the four teams had accomplished its mission. From the University, team 1 had captured and subdued five professors and students. From the film studio, team 2 collected a scriptwriter, two directors and two actors. Team 3 captured ten teenagers from the Kaeson Youth Park, and team 4 captured the North Korean Ministers of Culture, Foreign Affairs, Finance, and two justices of the Central Court of North Korea.

Spiriting their unconscious captives through the streets of Pyongyang proved to be a non-issue; all were gagged and handcuffed after being rendered unconscious by a fast-acting, long duration aerosol anesthetic agent. Placed in laundry bags, they were carried into the back of a roving laundry truck that had been stolen the night before. From there, they were loaded on the fishing boat in the wee hours of the morning; the fishing boat sailed down the Taedong River and out into the East China Sea, where it rendezvoused with the escape vessel.

One week later, our thirteen-week show begins. Our contestants, now recovered from the trip to North America, have been examined by doctors, housed in luxury accommodations on the Big Brother set (the show is on temporary hiatus) and fed delicious food for a week. Until today, Episode One, they have been kept in isolation and told nothing about where they are. Today, however, the doors to their individual bedrooms swing open on national television, and for the first time they meet each other—and our program host.

And now, the fun begins. Our contestants are spirited off to a series of destinations where their hilarious reactions are captured by hidden cameras.

Week One: Las Vegas: Our contestants are taken to Las Vegas, where they have a rip-roaring good time! On the agenda are David Copperfield, Cirque de Soleil's Zumanity, Psy's Gangnam Style show, an evening at the Palomino Club, and dinner at Bubba Gump's.

Week Two: Costco: Each of our contestants is given

$1,000 and turned loose in Costco. Watch the fun as they struggle to spend it all!

Week Three: Disneyland: Our contestants are greeted by Mickey Mouse and Goofy and presented with the keys to the kingdom.

Week Four: Back at the Ranch: Meanwhile, back in North Korea, Kim Jong-un is having an apoplectic fit. Half of his government has disappeared!

Week Five: Best Buy: Throughout the series, our contestants have been granted full access to the Internet and have seen the remarkable availability of technology in the west that all have access to. In this hilarious episode, our contestants are taken to Best Buy, given $2,000 to spend, and released into the store. Watch as paralysis sets in!

Week Six: Miami Beach: Our episode begins on Friday evening in South Beach. Among the beautiful people, our contestants, with very little guidance, are asked to meet and interact with the locals. Watch as they meet beautiful blondes in thong bikinis, gay couples, body builders, and more. There's something for everyone in this episode!

Week Seven: Yellowstone National Park. Our participants experience a downshift in this episode as we take them from the frenzy of Miami Beach to the quiet majesty of Yellowstone. Watch as they gather at Old Faithful, interact with bison and grizzly bears and stay at the Old Faithful Inn.

Week Eight: Austin: In this episode, the Austin music scene overwhelms our contestants. Watch as they wander down Sixth Street, enjoying the music, street artists and Texas barbecue. At dusk, join them at the Congress Avenue Bridge to watch two million Mexican short-tailed bats fly into the sky, uncontrolled by the Supreme Leader!

Week Nine: Rodeo Drive and Beverly Hills: The ultimate

shopping extravaganza happens in this week's episode. And while our contestants don't actually get to buy anything, we have a few surprises in store for them. Along the way, they will "randomly" meet Kim Kardashian, Pamela Anderson, David Hasselhof and Lindsay Lohan.

Week Ten: Vancouver, BC: The majesty of the Pacific Northwest overwhelms our contestants in this episode. They will enjoy Stanley Park, tour a live movie set, sample the region's seafood, and spend a day on a cruise ship that departs from the Pan Pacific Hotel.

Week Eleven: UC Berkeley: Our program contestants are whisked away to northern California, where they spend the day touring the University of California's Berkeley campus and have an opportunity to take part in a protest. Watch as they stand, stupefied, when the police stand idly by and do nothing in response to the chanting masses!

Week Twelve: Manhattan: Our episode opens on the 106th floor of the Empire State Building as our contestants enjoy a 360-degree view of the New York area. From there they are escorted to the New York Public Library, the American Museum of Natural History, and Eataly, where they enjoy a fine Italian meal. This is also movie week: After the visit to the New York Public Library they attend a private screening of Ghostbusters, and after the visit to the museum they watch The Relic.

Week 13: A Tearful Farewell: Our contestants bid a fond farewell to their audience as they depart for home.

About the Author

Dr. Steven Shepard is the founder of the Shepard Communications Group in Williston, Vermont, co-founder of the Executive Crash Course Company, and founder of Shepard Images. A professional author, photographer, audio producer, and educator with more than 35 years of experience in the technology industry, he has written books and articles on a wide variety of topics.

Dr. Shepard specializes in international issues in technology strategy, with an emphasis on the social, geopolitical, economic, and competitive implications of technological change. He has written and directed more than 40 videos and films, and written and produced technical presentations, white papers, Podcasts, speeches, and articles on a broad range of topics for companies and organizations worldwide. He has written, recorded, and photographed in more than 90 countries, serving clients across many different industries including telecommunications, IT, media, advertising, healthcare, transportation, government, software development, education, professional services, NGOs, venture capital, and regulatory.

Thanks to a childhood spent in Spain, Steve is native fluent in Spanish and routinely publishes and delivers presentations in that language.

He lives in Vermont with his wife Sabine, who has put up with him for more than 40 years.

The Natural Curiosity Project

A few years ago, I decided to take on a somewhat Quixotic project. I started a Podcast. It's called the Natural Curiosity Project, and it's devoted to the idea that Curiosity leads to discovery, discover leads to knowledge, knowledge leads to insight, and insight leads to understanding.

I believe that curiosity is our sixth sense. I also believe that we don't use it anywhere near often enough. Curiosity is the destroyer of the status quo; it is also the catalyst for fresh, critical, motivational thinking, and ultimately, action.

The Podcast has no theme other than curiosity. I talk about business, technology, leadership, natural sounds, biology, education—pretty much anything I believe people should be curious about.

The Podcast is available on iTunes by the name shown above, or you can find it on SoundCloud by searching for my name or for https://soundcloud.com/user-80982638. The episodes are short, but they're interesting—please check them out. Thanks.

[i] https://en.wikipedia.org/wiki/View_of_the_World_from_9th_Avenue.
[ii] It's true. Check it out.
[iii] It's true. Check it out.
[iv] It's true. Check it out.
[v] It's true. Check it out.
[vi] It's true. Check it out.
[vii] It's true. Check it out.
[viii] It's true. Check it out.
[ix] It's true. Check it out.
[x] It's true. Check it out.
[xi] It's true. Check it out.
[xii] It's true. Check it out.
[xiii] It's true. Check it out.
[xiv] It's true. Check it out.
[xv] It's true. Check it out.
[xvi] http://realitycommons.media.mit.edu/pdfs/hcii_txteagle.pdf
[xvii] It's true. Check it out.
[xviii] It's true. Check it out.
[xix] It's true. Check it out.
[xx] It's true. Check it out.
[xxi] It's true. Check it out.
[xxii] It's true. Check it out.
[xxiii] It's true. Check it out.
[xxiv] It's true. Check it out.
[xxv] It's true. Check it out.
[xxvi] It's true. Check it out.
[xxvii] It's true. Check it out.
[xxviii] It's true. Check it out.
[xxix] It's true. Check it out.
[xxx] It's true. Check it out.
[xxxi] It's true. Check it out.
[xxxii] It's true. Check it out.
[xxxiii] It's all true. Check it out.
[xxxiv] It's true. Check it out.
[xxxv] It's true. Check it out.
[xxxvi] It's true. Check it out.
[xxxvii] SpaceX's Low Earth Orbit satellite-based Internet service.

[xxxviii] It's true. Check it out.
[xxxix] It's true. Check it out.
[xl] It's true. Check it out.
[xli] It's true. Check it out.
[xlii] It's true. Check it out.
[xliii] It's true. Check it out.
[xliv] It's true. Check it out.
[xlv] It's true. Check it out.
[xlvi] It's true. Check it out.
[xlvii] It's true. Check it out.
[xlviii] It's true. Check it out.
[xlix] It's true. Check it out.
[l] It's true. Check it out.
[li] It's true. Check it out.
[lii] It's true. Check it out.
[liii] It's true. Check it out.
[liv] It's true. Check it out.
[lv] It's true. Check it out.
[lvi] It's true. Check it out.
[lvii] It's true. Check it out.
[lviii] It's true. Check it out.
[lix] Check it out. It's true.
[lx] Check it out. It's true.
[lxi] Shepard, Steven. Reverse-Engineering the Future: A Prescription for Change Leadership.
[lxii] It's true. Check it out. And this is one of the great leadership books of all time. By the way, buy the physical book, not the eBook. Trust me on this—you'll be glad you did.
[lxiii] It's true. Check it out.
[lxiv] It's true. Check it out.
[lxv] It's true. Check it out.

Made in the USA
Coppell, TX
16 June 2021